ELTHEA'S NEMESIS

THE STORY OF ELTHEA'S REALM
BOOK FOUR

JOHN MURZYCKI

WARNER
TRAIL
PRESS

COPYRIGHT

ISBN | Paperback: 978-1-953815-09-5 | Hardcover: 978-1-953815-10-1

Editor: Marjorie Turner Hollman, https://marjorieturner.com/editing/
Cover Art and Design: Paul Silva Design, http://paulsilvadesign.com

1. Fantasy. 2. Science Fiction. 3. Techno-thriller. 4. Magical Realism. 5. Epic Fantasy. 6. Artificial Intelligence. 7. Thriller. 8. Metaphysical and Visionary. 9. New Adult & College. 10. Science Fantasy. 11. Quest.

WARNER
TRAIL
PRESS

CONTENTS

1. The Monsters I Loathe — 1
2. Secrets from the Past — 16
3. Never Think Less of Me — 27
4. Make It Right — 40
5. The Misery That Will Come — 54
6. Once in a Lifetime — 67
7. The Weave and Flow of Life — 80
8. The Offer — 93
9. Going Native — 106
10. The Sound of a Thousand Voices — 118
11. The Dark Pit — 131
12. Warrior and Champion — 142
13. Pledges Spoken — 154
14. They Took Everything From Us — 167
15. Our Only Hope — 181
16. Abducted — 195
17. You May Think Me a Monster — 207
18. Before Your Time Here Ends — 221
19. Cries of Passion — 235
20. The Secret Pocket — 247
21. They Will Be Born Again — 256
22. An Insatiable Passion to Rule — 271
23. This Ends Here and Now — 285
24. Live to Fight Another Day — 299
25. Never To Be Mortal Again — 314
26. If You Ever Loved Me — 326
27. The World Pauses — 330
28. Hope Dashed — 338

29. To Hell and Back   343
30. As For Tomorrow   352

Author's Note   361
About the Author   363
Acknowledgments   365
Also by John Murzycki   367

To my fun-loving dog Missy, and before her, Zoey. Trusted companions forever.

THE MONSTERS I LOATHE

How is it even possible to grasp what had taken place? Our enemy had turned my friends into monsters before my eyes, spiriting them away while I could do nothing but watch.

Our parting had been abrupt, not a moment for a heartfelt goodbye. Surely, we believed we would have laughter and lively conversations to come. Instead, I had been denied a final tender embrace.

Yet, isn't that the way of it? Who wouldn't want to have more time with those we love most?

For me, the ending was unspeakably cruel. I had tried to save them. God knows I had. Such an unthinkable transfer of energy had taken place during those decisive, painful moments. Yet, all my efforts had failed. And with it, my dreams of a happy life had ended, like a wisp of smoke blown away by an errant breeze.

So here I stood before the only person able to end this

nightmare. But did she have the answer I sought? And would she be willing to agree to my request?

Tess Armstrong's only reaction to my hurried description was a crease in her brow. Had she not understood the gravity of what had happened, of what I had done? Only her eyes belied her true feelings. But did I see pity, sorrow, or a hint of contempt as she looked at me?

She exhaled as though trying to understand. "You gave them a soul?" A sliver of the setting sun discovered us as we stood in the doorway of her house in the village of Haven. Her face was awash in the light, and for a second, she reminded me of another girl, Cassie McKenzie.

Cassie was younger than Tess, and her hair was darker. But on that day, when we strolled hand in hand through the Public Garden, the sun had also danced on her face, enhancing the natural radiance within her. Cassie and I had passed rows of tulips on the side of the walkway, harbingers of warmer days to come. I remember thinking how lovely she was, how much more vibrant than everyone else. Being with her was the most uplifting feeling in the world. Love has the power to transform a person, enabling them to see the allure that others might not.

Our life together was too brief, times like that so few. Little did we know the evil Bots would never leave us alone. We had no way of preparing for the terror they would bring to our lives. Was it even possible to foresee the unimaginable?

Tess's muted reaction made me cringe, knowing how preposterous it must seem. Even to my ears, my voice sounded too high-pitched. "Believe me, I had no choice. It was that, or I had to murder a race of innocent bystanders to save my friends." Instead, the Bots transformed my companions into monstrous versions of themselves. That thought overpowered all others, running through my head like a replay of a nightmare, over and over, never-ending.

"Phil!" someone called out from behind me. Tess's daughter, Rae, dashed toward us, boots pounding on the cobblestoned street. Only now did I realize my mistake in not searching for Rae as soon as I returned to Haven. We had been through great danger together, and I owed her that much. But in my haste, I went to Tess, knowing she might have the information to free my friends.

Neither had I sought my other closest companions here in Haven, those who had risked their lives to keep me alive. They had become as dear to me as my college friends, and I should not have ignored them, even for a brief time.

How did everything go so wrong? The past few months had been a blur, starting with the Bot attack on Haven. My enemy would have taken me captive right then, except for the unexpected appearance of a strange figure I later learned was Teivel, ruler of the Nizaem race. In the blink of an eye, he brought me to his mountain stronghold, along with Rae, Bevon, Ja'Krill, and Bryson. Had he saved us from certain imprisonment or death by the Bots, as he had claimed, or was there more to his scheming? In the end, all Teivel wanted was my obedience to help him become more powerful than the Bots. One of his own subjects, Silese, saved me, and dragons swooped out of the sky to fly us away to safety just as the Bots found me again.

The dragons brought us to a place far from the mountain home of the Nizaem race. There we found the Oakenrill, an odd creature who later became my trusted friend, as he tutored me on how to capture and use the magical powers in this land. He had asked my companions to leave us so I could focus all my attention on his training. It was a demanding time but also rewarding as he honed my skills and taught me about the Spirit of Elthea.

Eventually, the Bots found me, as they always would, and I sent the Oakenrill far away to spare his life. The Bots offered me an impossible choice: murder an innocent race to prove my allegiance to them, or they would kill Cassie, Matt, and Diane. A madness came over me. Or was it an epiphany? Only time will tell.

With no other option, I used the powers of Elthea to transform the Bots, a task that would have been inconceivable before my training by the Oakenrill. I gave the Bots a soul. But it wasn't something my enemy wanted, so they transformed my closest friends into the likeness of themselves. My companions had become Bots in their physical form, with their memories and thoughts remaining human, at least for now.

My life was over. How could I continue? But aid came from a strange source, a race the Bots wanted me to annihilate provided the inspiration I needed to continue. I now hoped to learn more about the Bots and find a way to defeat them. And the person who knew them better than anyone was the leader of a group of software engineers who inadvertently created them. I needed to speak with Tess Armstrong.

By summoning a dragon, intelligent creatures called the Skrill, I flew to Haven. It set me down in the open fields around the village. The once-mighty wall surrounding the city was still in ruins, although someone had already rebuilt sections of the wall. In my haste, I didn't waste a moment pondering how the villagers could have restored some of it so quickly. No warning bell had sounded as the raptor glided once over the village and landed before departing to its home. Like a man possessed, ignoring everything else around me, I skirted broken boulders, finding a cleared path into the town. My only thought was how to save Cassie, Matt, and Diane from the horror of living the rest of their lives as Bots.

Rae now bounded into my arms before I could offer an apology. Her eyes were bright, underscoring her glee. "We saw the Skrill. I knew it had to be you." She held me at arm's-length. "You're safe and alive. I can't believe you survived on your own."

I smirked, ignoring the knot in my stomach. "Yea, but just barely. The Oakenrill helped."

She took a moment to study my face. Could she see a difference in the man I had become from mere months ago when we departed? Glancing around, she frowned. Knowing what she was about to ask, I responded to her unspoken question, my shoulders sagging. "I couldn't rescue them, but they're alive."

Her frown deepened. "Still captive?"

How could I explain the impossible? My throat tightened as I saw in my mind what the Bots had turned them into. Tess saved me from voicing it. "Phil was about to tell me what happened, but it seems the story is more involved than a simple response."

Rae looked at her mom as if realizing where we stood. Before she could ask why I hadn't sought her first, I said, "Your mom knows those creatures better than anyone. If anyone can help save my friends, it's her."

"We already know them," she blurted. "They kill us, we kill them. I've told you that before."

I sighed, not wanting to explain once again that it was more complicated. Tess responded first. "They're not monsters, Rachel." Then glancing back at me, she added, "At least they weren't always so."

"That's what I need to understand," I cried out before Rae could say more. "Tess had expressed that opinion before when she talked about the Bots from long ago. Too bad I never paid much attention. It always seemed something more important was going on."

Looking into Rae's eyes, I added, "I can see why you feel that way about the Bots. Honestly, I do." A slight breeze ruffled the loose strands of her red hair. Did she appear more mature than when we were together? Had our journey these past months forced her to become an adult?

Something caught Tess's attention as she glanced at the other end of the street. "Phil, before you do anything else, don't you think you should greet your friends? They've been waiting months for you to return."

I looked in that direction to see a curious lot of individuals across the street a few buildings away. They held back, letting the three of us continue our conversation. A year ago, the sight of a group of otherworldly beings standing alongside humans would have scared the wits out of me. Now I smiled, the tension draining from me.

Setting aside my task for the moment, I stepped toward them. Before I crossed the street, Torermak, the giant Stonewraith, roared a greeting, "Ha, Master Philip! If truth be told, you are an unexpected sight."

I blinked, wondering what he was doing back in Haven. We parted ways when he returned to his home in Dal Tan while I continued to the Valnorian Forest. Before I could ask, Bevon moved forward and embraced me in a hug.

"I am fortunate you did not make a liar out of me, Earthfriend."

I furrowed my brow, unsure of his meaning.

"If you had not survived, I would have always regretted my decision to leave you alone with the Oakenrill. Did he guide you as he had promised?"

"You made the right choice." Scanning the others, I hoped to see my tutor, the Oakenrill, among them. He was not. "You have never failed me, my friend." Strange how this Astari, an entity from another race, had become one of my closest companions.

The two other Astari came forward, the pink-haired Quintia and the quiet, almost shy, purple-haired Riyaad. They both hugged me as tightly as Bevon had. "I missed you both," I said. "I'm glad we're together again. Never let me leave on an adventure again without you."

Quintia chuckled. "Hearing Rae and Bevon tell the story when they returned without you, it didn't sound like much of an adventure."

"No, I suppose it wasn't. Most of the time, we were inside a mountain."

"What are you talking about?" said Ja'Krill, stepping forward. "We had the joy of riding a dragon?"

Bryson, a human and member of The Guard of Haven, said, "Ugh, I wouldn't call that a joy. It was the worst experience of my life."

I smiled, noticing Bryson didn't look as boyish as when we parted. "So, riding the wire between two mountains wasn't that bad?"

His face blanched. He would prefer to forget about both events. Best that I not bring up the time he slipped off a ledge on the side of a mountain and nearly fell to his death.

Commander Russell Ingram extended his hand before turning it into a hug. "We were all concerned when the others returned to Haven without you. All of us are happy you are safe."

I nodded, knowing he meant it. Alan Sabrinsky, the

third software engineer from long ago, stood to the side. Normally, he looked out of place, regardless of the situation. But now, he wore a broad smile, as did everyone else. "You're a member of our family now, and you had us worried. You must tell us everything that happened."

I studied him for a moment, knowing there was more about him than his often comical demeanor. Wasn't it odd that both Alan and the Oakenrill had insisted I do no harm to the Bots? "What happened to me is less important," I said. "You, however, are the key to our future." Then, flicking my eyes toward Russell, I added, "As are you, and as is Tess. You three are the secret to defeating the Bots. Only I didn't realize it before."

Russell frowned, but Alan continued smiling. Did they have the answers I searched for, or was I fooling myself? Were they the only hope of salvation for Cassie, Matt, and Diane? Or would they provide more disappointment?

I STOOD ON A BALCONY, GAZING OUT AT THE PARTIALLY destroyed village of Haven. A line of rubble and boulders surrounded the town—the remnants of a once mighty wall that the Bots had shattered in seconds. The purpose of the attack had been to capture me; to claim me as one of their servants. But the Nizaem leader, Teivel, had saved me. With me by his side, he believed he could become a demigod, stronger than the Bots.

That was a role I wasn't willing to play. And still won't.

An army of giants now sifted through the wreckage of the fallen wall. They had already restored a few sections to their past grandeur. "The Stonewraiths are remarkable, are they not?" said Ja'Krill, who had approached so quietly I did not hear his footsteps.

I cocked an eye at him. "They're working with stone, my friend. Have you forgotten your roots as a woodland race? I seem to recall you disliking everything about this place with its cheerless rock."

He smirked. "Torermak has been showing me the astonishing skill his people have in fashioning stone, actually molding it in their hands. It is quite remarkable. You should—"

I held up my hand to forestall him. "Yes, I've seen." Gripping his shoulder, I added, "I admire how you are open-minded and curious about everything. You stood by me even when the rest of your race, even your Queen, considered me a threat to your Sacred Forest and wanted me executed. If there were more people like you, maybe we'd all be better off with races working together."

"Even the Bots?"

They were our one common enemy, reeking of hatred. "Even with them, maybe there's a way."

He raised an eyebrow as he studied me. "You've changed. I can see it in you since you returned."

I frowned. "How so?"

Ja'Krill shrugged. "It seems you are more contemplative, more aware of your thoughts and actions; the precision in your movements. And I can sense a new inner strength within you. There's more to you than we realize."

My attention dwelled on the Stonewraiths working to rebuild the fortress. At this rate, they would have the entire wall completed in a few months. Using my new powers, could I complete the task in a fraction of that time? Probably, but that was not my charge. Lives were depending upon me. "The Oakenrill taught me much. But all his training couldn't help me understand the Bots any better."

We turned away from the balcony and entered the adjacent room in the commander's residence. This space was one of his larger meeting chambers, with its colorful tapestries adorning the area. The rough stone walls and heavy wooden beams in the ceiling lent an air of permanence to the place, while an abundance of floor-to-ceiling open-air windows made it seem spacious. Even so, the room was small compared to a typical function hall on Earth. Governing Haven did not require the trappings of opulence. Russell was the commander, not the king, and his rule depended on administration as much as anything else.

The group who had greeted me on the street had already assembled here at Russell's urging. This wasn't something I had expected when I hatched my plan and summoned the Skrill to take me here. I had thought I would speak with only Tess, with possibly Russell and Alan—not this entire crew. "You seem nervous," said Ja'Krill, still at my side.

I eyed him again, noting that I should add him to the

list of those who seemed to know me better than I did myself. "Nervous?" I shrugged. "Perhaps, but not for the reason you might suspect." I took a deep breath. "What I find out here will decide the fate of Cassie, Matt, and Diane. I don't want to discover this is a dead end. Also, I'd rather not have everyone else in on it."

He also gazed at the assembled crowd inside. "You can send them away if you wish, but they are all on your side, Earthfriend. Everyone wants to help."

I nodded. "Of course you're right. Problem is, nobody else can. Whatever I discover, this is on my shoulders."

For better or worse, I somehow knew my battle against the Bots would come down to me alone. The Oakenrill had trained me well. But just as in life, some questions have no answers.

What would I do then?

RUSSELL HAD ARRANGED CHAIRS AND BENCHES IN A rough circle around the chamber, giving me the impression we were in an alcoholic recovery meeting. Maybe I needed the intervention of others. The guilt I felt often threatened to overwhelm me.

Looking at the expectant faces, I realized they were waiting for me to say something. My voice nearly faltered. "You deserve to know everything that happened once I was alone with the Oakenrill. The events I'm going to describe passed quickly in my mind, even though they took months. I'll stick to the most important parts."

I began with an explanation about practicing precise movements called the Arath by the Oakenrill, but words couldn't explain how it strengthened both body and mind. The more I described the link, the more it sounded like malarkey. Without living it, much of what I had experienced was difficult to grasp.

I gave up on it and stuck to specific incidents.

"My first experience with the powers of Elthea happened when I lit a tiny flame in my hand." I then recounted the increasingly challenging assignments, such as controlling the wind or dissolving a bolder and recreating it a mile away. I received puzzled frowns when I said, "Elthea's energies can achieve many results, but you have to choose the correct weave of energy to accomplish each task."

The explanation fascinated the Astari and Ja'Krill, while Torermak nodded with understanding.

Then came the heart of the story. I recounted the paradox inherent with Elthea's powers, and how the Oakenrill insisted I do no harm when using them. "To do so will diminish and ultimately destroy the Spirit of Elthea. And I trust him." I left out the Oakenrill's tale about Elthea naming someone to fight for her land. *A champion will she entrust to prevent her foe from inflicting suffering and destruction.* I still didn't want to believe I was that person.

I hated describing the time the Bots arrived, but I

pushed through it. "Our enemy finally found me." My words could never reflect the terror I felt at that moment. Even now, those minutes passed in confusion. "The Oakenrill tried to defend me, but he was no match for the Bots. I sent him far away in order to save his life."

My voice quivered. "They threatened to kill Cassie, Matt, and Diane if I didn't agree to serve them, to use my powers for their evil plans."

My gaze swept across the room, seeing the pain of my plight reflected in their eyes. They knew I faced an impossible choice. "That wasn't the worst of it. They brought me to a place where they ordered me to destroy an unarmed, innocent race. It was that or they would kill my companions."

Should I say how close I came to fulfilling their wish, how the destructive energy was at my fingertips as I searched for a way out? Better not to spell out the thin line between salvation and extermination. Just above a whisper, I continued. "At the last second, a thought came to me, and I acted on it. I gave the Bots a soul. All the Bots."

Silence greeted me. As with Tess, they needed time to process what I had done. After a deep breath, I pressed forward. "My solution was a way for them to move forward in peace rather than with hatred. Or so I had believed." What more should I say? Did I think they would become delightful, agreeable, and sympathetic? All I wanted was for them to return my friends unharmed. But they did not.

"I failed utterly. It would have been better if the Bots had killed them." Saying what took place next was more difficult than I expected. It was the worst experience of my life, and I hadn't even had the chance to explain it to Tess before we broke off our conversation.

"It turns out, the Bots didn't want a soul. They responded with hatred, as they always have. They turned Cassie, Matt, and Diane into one of them. My friends are now the same monsters I loathe."

2

SECRETS FROM THE PAST

Each one of those in the room would have marched with me to fight the Bots at that very moment if I had so asked. But I did not. That was not my purpose in returning to Haven.

The anger, puzzlement, the pity, all of it played across their faces as I explained the fate of my friends. Most of all, I saw the determination in their eyes and their unwillingness to allow this wrong to stand.

"They have gone too far this time," said Quintia through gritted teeth. She had always been the most compassionate of the Astari, and her words mirrored what others expressed in their faces.

I expected everyone to join her refrain, but Alan Sabrinsky forestalled them. "You cannot win this battle." He looked at me curiously, a spark of understanding passing between us. What Alan lacked in social graces, he made up by his intelligence, and by having a greater knowledge about the Bots than most anyone, except maybe the two other programmers, Tess and Russell.

I nodded. "You're right." Glancing around at the others, I added, "Blades won't win this, and neither will using the mystical forces of Elthea for death and annihilation. Our enemy hurls fire at us, intent on destroying this village and everyone in it. They don't care about the consequences of their atrocities. Or maybe they don't believe they are harming the very source of their power. If I responded in the same way, I would be as evil as them."

"You can't just give up!" Rae shouted. A fighter to the core, she wouldn't accept any other way. "What they did to your friends demands a response. Their attack against Haven requires action. Can't you see there's no other way?"

"Of course I need to act. It's the reason I'm here now." What did she think? That I was afraid of the Bots and wanted to hide from them while others protected me? "I will rescue my friends, but I can't use the forces of Elthea for destruction. All that is good in this land must survive. We cannot extinguish it." Her heart was in the right place, but she didn't yet understand the danger to the Spirit of Elthea by acting rashly.

"What is your plan?" asked Russell.

Now that the moment had come for me to explain my intention, I wondered how idiotic I would sound. Thinking something through in my head didn't always translate into the most coherent ideas. "The answer to the Bots' future remains in their past," I declared with all the confidence I could muster.

"What?" said Bryson as he scrunched his face. I almost laughed out loud at the young man.

"Ha!" Torermak blurted. "If I am not mistaken, our young lad has gained a speck of wisdom. This Oakenrill of yours has drummed some good sense into that head. I need to meet this individual." He grunted in satisfaction, but then added as he looked around the room, "Do not mistake me, young Philip has a heart of gold. It is his decisions that have been suspect."

Torermak's comment should have annoyed me. But it didn't. Such is the measure of unfeigned friendship; words are never said to hurt, only to support. And he was right. My choices in life have not been the wisest.

The others around the room smiled at his remark, each of them my closest companions. What would I do without them; how would I have ever survived? The Stonewraith, Torermak, had saved my life more than once. Even sitting, he towered over everyone else. The Astari among us, Bevon, Quintia, and Riyaad, would give their lives to save me. They had protected me from the moment I came to the land of Elthea. Ja'Krill, the Valnorian from the Sacred Forest, had lost his family because of a Bot attack and had followed me because he believed I could help this world. Rae and Bryson from Haven's Guard were so different from one another, she a skilled fighter and he trying to become one. I spent less time with the three original programmers, Tess, Alan, and Russell, but they have been no less supportive. And now, their knowledge would determine if I ever saw Cassie, Matt, and Diane again as human.

"I hope I've learned a little something," I chuckled in response to Torermak's barb. "I'm not the same person I was before." My expression turned serious. "I've come back to Haven because I need the support of everyone here. We have to defeat the Bots; it is them or us." Focusing my eyes on Tess, Alan, and Russell, I added, "I need you three most of all."

They gazed at me with a calm resolve. Everyone was ready to help, a reaction I knew well from this group. Rae spoke before I could continue. "We all know what we have to do. We must destroy them."

"No, I won't kill them. That's my dilemma. We need an alternative. That's why I'm here. Please, does anyone have another option?"

RAE FIDGETED, LOOKING LIKE SHE WANTED TO BERATE me again for being so stupid. To her credit, she bit her tongue this time, giving Russell the chance to speak first. "You're asking for an answer to an age-old question. If we knew what to do about the Bots, we would have rid ourselves of them long ago. A solution to this quandary might not exist." He glanced uneasily at Tess and Alan by his side. "I don't know if we have anything to say that will help."

It wasn't what I wanted to hear, but I expected as

much. "The three of you know more about the Bots than anyone else. Maybe this will be a waste of time—I don't know. But I have to try something, and you three give me the best chance of figuring out how to deal with them. You have a history with them from before they became the Bots. I've heard you tell stories of their lives during that time. But truthfully, I paid scant attention. It never seemed important; whatever they were before didn't matter. But I was wrong. I'm hoping you have some shred of information that I can use; something that will help me stop them and restore my friends."

The three glanced at each other. Tess finally spoke. "We can tell you all we know, but I don't understand how much it will help you."

I waved my hand to interrupt. "I have a better way. We can relive your experience. This will give me a true feeling of what took place, unfiltered by your telling of it."

"W—what?" Alan stammered.

I explained the Farseeing episodes from Cassie and how I then mastered the technique from the Oakenrill. "Your minds are a repository for every detail that took place, even if you've forgotten events. They're still within you, and this will bring them back with clarity more than you would have thought possible. I can take us back to that time when you lived among the race who became the Bots."

They remained stone-faced, and I had to wonder. Did they not understand? Were they afraid? Did they not want to share their most intimate beliefs and experiences?

When Cassie shared her thoughts with me, that was one thing. My relationship with Tess, Alan, and Russell was very different.

"How does this thing work?" Russell questioned. The suspicion came across in his voice.

"It's quite simple, at least for each of you. One of you—and you can decide who—merely thinks about that time in your life. I cast a Farseeing spell, which then takes over, turning events you had experienced into a visual in both of our minds. It's much like a movie that I can observe. Whoever we're using will also relive those events again, as if watching a projection." Glancing at the others in the room, I added, "I can also open it up to everyone here if you wish."

The three former engineers shifted in their seats but remained silent. Why were they hesitant? "You have nothing to worry about," I said, hoping to ease their apprehension. "If I can't destroy the Bots using Elthea's powers, I have to find another way, something to turn them around and end their destructive ways."

"You tried that by giving them a soul," the giant Torermak countered. "That did not go as planned. Is it possible you are searching for something that does not exist?"

"I have to find a way!" I shouted. Rubbing my fingers through my hair, taking a calming breath, I added, "There has to be something. Hope is the only thing that keeps me going. Don't you see?"

Tess, Alan, and Russell remained silent. "Each of you

once told me there was good within them because of what you had observed during a time before they became Bots. I have to see that for myself, find out how I can use it to turn them into a benevolent race once again. Will you help me?"

Tess's eyes were wide, as if the walls were closing in around her. She shook her head from side to side. I had never seen her appear so frantic. She was always the calmest person I've known. "N—no, I can't do it. I can't."

I looked at her in disbelief as she jumped out of her chair and made for the exit. Without realizing it, I also stood. "Wait, Tess. What's wrong?"

"Not now," she screeched without turning around.

"Mom?" Rae shouted, dashing after her.

Pandemonium broke out as everyone spoke at once, everyone except Russell and Alan, who remained silent. The cacophony of voices barely registered with me. With Tess gone, I cast a puzzled glance at Russell and Alan.

Ever the statesman, Russell was the first to speak, quieting the others. "Give her time. Maybe she'll come around."

Should I shout at him? Grab him by the shirt and scream that time was a luxury we didn't have? Instead, I looked at the hallway where Tess had departed as a sinking feeling came over me. This was the group I could always trust to help me when I most needed it. How was I going to restore my friends, make them human again, if I couldn't count on them for something as effortless as this? At least I thought it was simple enough.

I SPRINTED OUT OF THE ROOM, DOWN THE STAIRS, AND onto the street. Surely Tess Armstrong would wait for me after coming to her senses. There was no reason for her to behave as she did.

Only a few villagers walked the otherwise empty lane, homes huddled together shoulder to shoulder. Should I run to her residence as I did when I first arrived here earlier today? Was that only today? My confrontation with the Bots had happened this same day. It had taken long hours for the Skrill to fly me here to Haven after the Bots had transformed my companions. But we didn't fly through the night, which meant we were traveling with the sun as it made its way across the sky.

How long has it been since I last slept? Feeling light-headed from my rush down the stairs, I gripped the stone on the side of the building to stop myself from falling. Dark spots danced across my vision.

"You have not taken a moment to grieve, have you?" asked a voice behind me. Bevon studied me. He was alone.

I leaned against the wall, trying to clear my head. "I grieved plenty when I saw what they did. Besides, feeling sorry about it doesn't get them back."

"You should rest, take care of yourself. You have been on the go from the moment you arrived at Haven, probably since the Bots attacked. Tell me, how much strength did it take to give them a soul?" When I didn't answer, he responded for me. "I imagine it took a great deal."

"What's your point? That I should take a nap?"

He smiled. "Well, maybe begin with a deep breath. You discussed the meditation taught by the Oakenrill. Maybe you should pause and relax; refresh your body and mind so that you can deal with what will come."

Damn, why did he always have to be right? My temper cooled. "We will not solve this overnight, will we?"

Bevon didn't respond immediately. We both knew the answer. "Your plan is good if you can gain the cooperation of Tess, Alan, or Russell. Perhaps you will uncover something useful in the genetic makeup of the race that became the Bots. You must also realize you may find nothing. In the end, it may be a fool's errand, and you will have wasted time to no benefit. The Bots may be evil, plain and simple, and you might uncover nothing to turn them to the light. Once a heart turns evil, you might never succeed at restoring it to what it was before."

Why was he telling me this? Did he want me to give up, leave my companions to the fate of the Bots' machinations? From the moment I first stepped foot in the land of Elthea, all the Astari, but especially Bevon, have been unselfish in their support. Although not human, he had become as close as any friend and had never steered me wrong.

My shoulders sagged. "What will you have me do?" My voice quivered. "I'm in an impossible position, Bevon. The Oakenrill training me how to use this power of the land, yet I can't use it to stop the Bots, even after working so hard to secure it. If I lash out and destroy them, I will harm the Spirit of Elthea. And once her spirit is gone, all the goodness she provides for this land will be over. But even if I could kill every Bot, that would still mean that Cassie, Matt, and Diane would remain as they are. I don't know how to change them back to who they once were."

I exhaled, wanting to scream, but knowing it would do no good. "The Bots are devious, but this time they've outdone themselves."

He looked at me without expression, a trait that I once considered infuriating. Although the Astari often showed their emotions, they could also hide their feelings better than humans. His face softened. "In this matter, I am at a loss. Mayhap the path you seek is the only recourse, as slim as it is. You may find something in their past that you can use. As for Tess, I suspect she does not want to relive that part of her life. But you still have the memories and experiences of Russell and Alan."

"Tess is their leader, even though Russell holds the title. They will not want to do anything without her showing the way."

He smirked. "When did you become so perceptive? I may have to reconsider how hopelessly incapable you are of understanding the finer points in life."

This was the Bevon I loved the most with his quips about me. "If you think I understand little, wait until you see what powers the Oakenrill taught me. I'll finally put you to shame."

He clapped my shoulder and chuckled. "Ah, Earth-friend. You still have a lot to learn. In that regard, you will always be my understudy. But come now. I will ask Russell to assign you quarters so you can rest. Give Tess space to cool. Sounder minds may yet prevail."

I sighed, knowing how bone-tired I felt. Before he guided me back up the stairs, I took another long gaze at the narrow street, hoping Tess would have already changed her mind. But still no sight of her. What secrets did she hold so tightly that would cause her to behave like that?

3

NEVER THINK LESS OF ME

Ripples of sunlight and shadow played across the room as the white curtains stirred from a slight breeze. How long had I slept? It felt as if I had been here a considerable time, although I still felt fatigued.

Wielding the powers of Elthea has always weakened me—the greater the effort, the more exhausted I would become. And the force to accomplish the unthinkable was more than I had ever used before. But my failure was the real reason for this malaise. How had my life come to this... thirty years, and now the worst catastrophe I could ever imagine. Was it because of hubris? Did I believe I could remake evil into something good?

I groaned, throwing off the sheets and sat on the edge of the bed. This was not the time to fall into despondency again. Too many lives depended on me now.

After roughing it in the woods with the Oakenrill for the past months, this room felt resplendent, with its massive open-air windows and vaulted-ceiling. Along with the bed, several easy chairs and wall hangings decorated the room. One door led to a washroom, while another door opened to the stairs, which went out to the street. Either Russell felt sorry for me and provided this lavish space, or my reputation had moved up a few notches since the last time he assigned accommodations.

I slipped into my pants and buttoned my shirt before stepping out onto one of the two balconies. Regardless of where I stood in Haven, my eyes always searched for the wall. The immense structure signified permanence and safety. Whenever I sought solace or wanted to talk with Rae, I walk along the parapet. The massive barrier protected those in the village. And now, seeing only rubble where it once stood was a punch to my gut. Rather than safety, I saw defilement.

The Bots harmed everything they touched. There was no hope for them, even I could see that. Playing God was a disaster. No more would I try to help them improve their lot in life. That's not what they wanted. Was it even possible to rehabilitate them? All I had tried to help, my outpouring of compassion, had come to naught, worse than nothing. My only responsibility now was to restore Cassie, Matt, and Diane.

But the conundrum remained: do no harm. The only way to bring back my friends would be through peaceful means. I could not strike at them with violence. How could I persuade or force the Bots to agree to releasing my friends? My head ached from thinking about it.

I turned away from the balcony, laced my boots, and left the room, not even sure where I would go. Outside on the lane, I looked in one direction and then the other, trying to find my bearings. Last night, when Bevon brought me here, my attention was elsewhere, so I wasn't sure what part of the village this was.

"Master Philip," shouted a female voice.

My spirits lifted, believing it was Tess Armstrong, waiting to tell me she acted rashly by running out of the meeting yesterday. But it was not. A shock of pink hair identified Quintia. We walked toward each other as she smiled back at me. At this angle, the sun highlighted a thin scar along her cheek which remained after a Bot sliced her face, intending to carve the rest of her to pieces. It was yet another reminder about the inhumanity of those creatures.

"It is good to see you, Quintia, but you realize there's no longer a need to watch over me every moment." The Astari were fastidious about assigning someone to always guard me. "I've learned a few things these last months."

"That may be true," she responded. "But does that mean I cannot enjoy your company? We had little opportunity yesterday with everyone else clamoring for your attention."

We often engaged in heartfelt discussions in the past. "In that case, glad we can be together again. But speaking of yesterday, I didn't notice anyone clamoring for my attention. Although, now that you say it, maybe I could have been more cordial rather than only focus on what I wanted. I had hoped to find a quick solution."

She shrugged. "I understand the bond shared with the other Earthfriends. To see them transformed into those we hate must have been disturbing. We all saw how agitated you were when you returned, so it is not surprising that you were direct."

I winced. "Diplomacy isn't my strong suit, but I didn't expect any disagreement with what I proposed. Farseeing isn't dangerous. Do you think that's the problem, that Tess is afraid of what it might do to her?"

"Tess Armstrong is not someone who fears many things, so in my opinion, that is not the issue."

"Then what is? I need information, something to use against those bastards. She's one of the three who knew them better than anyone." Changing direction, I said, "Quintia, you're a female. Maybe you can help me."

She looked at me out of the corner of her eye. "Philip, where are you going with this?"

Her teasing was often a significant part of her personality. "Tell me, why did she react the way she did? Russell and Alan weren't that opposed. What is she afraid of?"

Quintia took a moment longer to answer. "We all have our demons, Earthfriend, events that we put away in the deep recesses of our minds. To expose them again, to relive them as a Farseeing, is more than remembering. It brings the experience front and center. From what you described, it's as if you were back in time once again. Maybe she is terrified of the experiences she had during that episode of her life. Or maybe incidents embarrass her as she recalls her decisions back then. She, and the other two, released the Bots into the world. That cannot be something they are proud of."

"But they also created the Astari."

The corners of her lips turned up. "Yes, at every opportunity we let her know how much all the Astari revere her. She still seems surprised when we tell her this. Yet, she has only met a few of us Astari. She has never viewed the glory of the Raised Isles of Loralee nor met the thousands of others, each with their unique personalities, ambitions, and accomplishments. It is still a remote concept to her, as it is with Russell and Alan. The Bots, however, are real to her. She has seen the pain and suffering they inflict."

"She should be proud of her accomplishment creating the Astari."

Quintia nodded. "We have made an offer to each of the creators, asking them to visit the Raised Isles one day so that they can see for themselves the wonders and beauty we have created." A moment later, she added, "Although Bevon, Riyaad and I have ulterior motives. By bringing them to our home, we hope that the ruling members of Loralee will let slip our infraction when we stole one of their prized sailing vessels."

I chuckled. My Astari friends had mentioned this transgression so often that it had become a standing joke. After what they've been through after leaving the Raised Isles, were they still fearful of a reprimand? I couldn't imagine the ruling Astari treating them harshly after what they accomplished. This was yet another example of their high moral standards and the guilt they felt. "Maybe someday I'll be able to return as well. That would be nice," I said wistfully.

We walked in silence for a time, heedless of our direction. The destination wasn't our purpose; we were content to renew our camaraderie. All around us the town was alive with villagers, some hurrying along the streets on one or another errand, others enjoying a leisurely stroll, and some going in and out of shops, their arms loaded with supplies. As we strolled, I tried not to ponder the fate of my dearest friends. But try as I might, it was all I could think about.

"Here is a place with so many people living under the shadow of the Bots," I said. "Yet, somehow they're not deterred from having a normal existence. If only I were one of them, content to live with the rhythm of everyday life, never needing to play the part of the hero trying to save my friends or save the world."

"Hmm, I believe I know you better, Earthfriend. Let me ask, when you lived on Earth, and you worked in your office place before we rescued you and brought you to Loralee, were you happy? Truly happy?"

A smile came to me as I recognized the wisdom of her words. "No, I suppose not."

"So, let me understand this, you were not content living an uneventful life, yet now when you have a chance to save your closest companions and eliminate the most dangerous force both in this and your world, you lament your fate?"

I was at a loss for words, knowing she had me there. I

had been dismal, experiencing an unremarkable way of life before coming to Elthea. Better to be truthful without excuses. "You have a sharp insight into other people, Quint. Here I am feeling sorry for myself when it's others who are worse off." Here was someone clearly not human, yet I had long ago stopped thinking about her as anyone but another person, a good friend.

"However you may feel about it, Earthfriend, the choices you have made put you on this path. For good or ill, how you respond is all that matters. Life is a journey that comes with both lows and highs. I believe that the difficult times in life allow you to better appreciate the pleasant days. The challenges you face will fortify you for what is yet to come. Welcome what now confronts you, for it will help you become a better person."

Quintia wasn't as timid as Riyaad, but neither was she prone to long discourses. "Well taken, my friend. I needed someone to tell me this, and I'm glad it was you who did the telling."

She beamed. "I thought it better than giving you a good kick in the pants."

That made me laugh. Taking stock of where we had wandered, I saw our way forward obstructed by a mass of jagged boulders. We had come to the base of the collapsed wall. "This was enjoyable, conversing with you, But I still have a lot to think about. Do you mind if I sit here alone for a while?"

"Of course not." She gazed at me before leaving. "You

realize that was the first time you called me Quint." She smiled. "I hope it expresses a fondness for me."

"We've gone through a lot, you, me, and the rest of the Astari. From now on, you three are Quint, Bev, and Ry." Thinking about it for a second, I added, "Well, maybe not Bev. Whatever I call you, no more formalities between us."

She dipped her head, signifying her acceptance. Without another word, she strolled away, leaving me to ponder my next move.

TESS ARMSTRONG APPROACHED ME AS I RESTED ON A waist-high boulder at the smashed wall. "Quintia said I would find you here."

I sat up straight. Would she hold the answer to restoring my friends or lead me to greater despondency? She hesitated before saying more, her expression calm. This was the Tess Armstrong I always knew.

"I'm sorry for putting you on the spot," I said. "Everyone wanted to hear what I had to say, and then Russell gathered us all together, and, well, I didn't think it through." Taking a breath to stop rushing my words, I paused. "We should have talked about it first, but there wasn't time. And then, I couldn't send everyone away."

Did I sound foolish, or did this help explain my reasoning? I rubbed the back of my neck, trying to relax my tense muscles.

She waved her hand to dismiss my concern. "No, it

wasn't your fault." She glanced at the stone next to me. "May I join you?"

"Please. I'm glad we can speak alone."

She sat on the rock, looking around at the wreckage. "It still seems strange not seeing the fortification in place. We've only known Haven with it, our barrier against danger."

She wanted to engage in idle talk before broaching events of yesterday. Better to take it slow rather than blurt out what I wanted to discuss. "You're fortunate that the Stonewraiths are here to rebuild it."

"We wouldn't be alive if not for them." She smiled sadly. "They are the fabric of our past. And now, they define our lives today. It is the same with the Bots." Her gaze turned inward. "How different our lives would have been if not for them."

Did she mean the Stonewraiths or the Bots? I guessed it was the Bots.

Her eyes sharpened as she fixed me with a stare. "Have you ever failed so miserably, Philip, that you wished you didn't exist?"

"Yea, right now. What I did to my friends was the biggest failure of my life. If only I had—"

"Don't think that way. The Bots were responsible, not you. Giving them a soul was brilliant. Only time will tell how your decision will play out. Until then, understand that the harm done to your friends was more of my fault than yours. If they never existed, none of this would have happened."

"Is that why you're so reluctant to take part in a Farseeing, because you feel guilty?"

She remained still, her face devoid of emotion. "Yes." She shook her head as if to clear it. "I mean no." A breath escaped her lips. "Both are true, yes and no. It's a guilt I carry with me all the time; so do Russell and Alan. But that's not the entire reason."

She remained silent as an internal struggle took place within her. "The worst of it is that I'm not very proud of what I had done back then. Creating the Bots was one, but we can explain that. They duped us into it. Other failures fall squarely on my shoulders." Her eyes took on an unfocused look again. "I was young and foolish—so foolish. I thought I could persevere by sheer willpower. I made decisions that weren't always the wisest. With the benefit of time, I realize the wrongs I had committed."

She fell silent, looking down at her hands in her lap. My heart went to her. "That doesn't seem so awful to me."

She smiled sadly. "That's because I haven't told you the entire story. It's a long tale, some of it even filled with happiness and joy. The events happened as if it were yesterday. But other aspects, well, I've blocked away, put them in a box and closed the lid. I prefer they remain that way. What happened would not make a difference in my life going forward. After that time, I met Evan and we were married. We had a son. Rachel was born later, here in Haven. She was a surprise, and a blessing. I never looked back at that earlier time in my life. I didn't want to."

Was telling me this as a prelude to accepting the

Farseeing, or the reason she didn't want to do it? "I understand how you feel. Many experiences in my past are best left forgotten." A vision came to me as my fingers tightened around Cassie's neck when I was under the control of the Bots. Did I really try to strangle her to death, or was it a bad dream? I dismissed the thought. "Tess, the lives of others are now at stake. I don't know what else to do now except find something in the Bots' past that will help me defeat them. If you can't help me, please tell Russell or Alan to agree to my request. Maybe they can..."

She held up her hands to stop me. "Phil, the reason I'm here is to say that I agree to take part in your Farseeing. You needed to know my reasons for my reaction yesterday. That's what this explanation was all about."

Relief, along with a feeling of foolishness, washed over me. "Oh, sorry for rushing to judgment. I thought—never mind."

Tess smiled in a pensive, genial sort of way, which only a person with worldly experience could. She grasped my hand. "Relax, Phil. I always believed you were wound too tight. Don't put the world's problems on your shoulders. The Spirit of Elthea may have granted you a great power to help this land, but you'll never solve the ills by yourself."

Her words felt like a soothing elixir, calming me to my core. "After yesterday, I was afraid you'd say no. You didn't want to go through with it."

"I can understand the reason you felt that way." She furrowed her brow. "I'm still not sure you'll discover anything relevant from this, but it's worth a try. Possibly you'll lend a different perspective to my experiences."

Her eyes swept across the village with its stone buildings, each one sturdy with precise angles. Nobody could ever accuse the Stonewraiths of shoddy construction. "I have one stipulation," she added. "We do this alone. I don't want you sharing the Farseeing, or discussing it, with the group assembled yesterday. Do not talk about it with anyone. Russell and Alan know what we experienced, and that's enough."

Before she could change her mind, I consented. "I agree. Can we begin right now?"

She held her hands up to rebuff me. "Whoa, not so fast. I only now agreed to do this; give me time to prepare myself." She could be both sagacious and childlike at the same time.

"That's the beauty of the Farseeing," I said. "You don't need to prepare anything." I touched her forehead with my index finger. "Everything we need is right there. All you have to do is sit back and relax. For you, the experience will be like a dream, only more real." A smile came to me. "Besides, I'm afraid you may change your mind."

She gazed appraisingly for a moment, a thoughtful expression, even for her.

"What?" I said as the seconds stretched out.

Tess shook her head as if awakening from a trance. "Oh, nothing. I was thinking about the first time I met you in the public gardens here in Haven. Rachel brought you to meet me. You were so lost and distressed, and I remembered how sorry I felt for you. When we go through this Farseeing, you'll see a younger me, maybe with the same bewildered expression on me as I once saw on you. Please don't think less of me."

"Regardless of what takes place, never will I belittle you. You've already earned a place of respect, and nothing will cause me to change my opinion. Take my word on it."

She seemed to accept my explanation. "We can begin later this afternoon at my house. I need to brief Evan about what we are about to do so he doesn't let anyone interrupt us. You should also take the time to inform the rest of your friends that we are doing this without them. Russell and Alan already know."

I would have preferred to begin sooner, but what other choice did I have? "Okay, it's a deal."

Tess left me, and as she walked away, I couldn't help but wonder if this was going to be a monumental waste of time or would lead to Bots' defeat.

4

MAKE IT RIGHT

Evan greeted me at the door of Tess's home. I had never met her husband before, and like most of the human villagers, he had a rugged, outdoorsy look about him. As with Tess, his smile came easily. We exchanged introductions as I tried not to let my sense of urgency prevent me from being cordial.

Her voice came from a room down the hall. "You're early. I expected as much." She turned a corner into the foyer, wiping her wet hands with a dishtowel. Looking at Evan, she said, "So, you finally get to meet the famous Philip Matherson. How is it you two were never in the same place at the same time?" She stepped close to him, bodies touching, an insignificant gesture that spoke volumes.

"I'm honored to meet you," I said as we shook hands. Shifting my gaze to Tess, I added, "But famous isn't the word I would use."

Both their smiles increased, as if sharing a private joke. "Fame is bestowed by others," he said. "Like it or not, it's part of who you are, at least here in Haven." He turned to her. "I'll let you two attend to your task. I should check on the herd, make sure they've been fed properly." He kissed her lightly on the lips before moving toward the door. I detected, as much as saw, the slightest hint of concern on his face before he left.

"Evan doesn't much care for this magical hocus-pocus, does he?" I said on a hunch after the door had closed.

Tess shrugged. "Most people in the village don't." She thought about it for a second. "Strange how some traditions from Earth still hold sway, even though we've all witnessed the mystical powers of this land."

She led me to the back of the dwelling, to a chamber furnished with plenty of comfortable chairs and brightly colored tapestries on the walls. The room looked out over a small flower garden, an oasis for chirping birds and a variety of insects flitting from one flower to another. The fragrance filled the area. "It seems you're not content with the communal gardens," I said as I stood near the open window.

"It's lovely, don't you think? Which reminds me, I must ask your Valnorian friend, Ja'Krill, for advice on a few of my lesser performing plants. With his knowledge of plant life, I bet he could do wonders here."

"I'm sure he would enjoy helping you. The Valnorians are to plants what the Stonewraiths are to rock."

"Hmm, I love Torermak and the others, but if only the

Valnorians had built Haven, well, I can only imagine." She thought about it for a moment, and even I had to wonder what such a place would look like. Her eyes came back into focus as she continued, "I'm sure you want to begin. Do the others know we're doing this Farseeing without them?"

"I told Bevon. He'll relay the information to everyone else."

"Okay then." She glanced around the room. "Is this location acceptable? How exactly do we do this?"

I had been through enough Farseeing episodes for them to feel like natural activities. But this was different. We would view memories from her mind, not mine. I pointed at two thick cushioned chairs facing each other. "We can sit there."

Once seated, I said, "Why don't we start from the beginning? Pick a time and place at the beginning of what happened."

"That's easy. I know the exact moment."

"Good. Simply keep that in your mind and I'll do the rest. Don't worry about overthinking it or focusing too hard. Before you realize it, you'll be watching events unfold as if they were taking place in front of you."

Tess closed her eyes. I pulled a small weave of energy, and a moment later, the familiar murky fog clouded my vision.

~

"Stop, you're killing me," yelled a young man as he stopped running, hands on his hips, face pink as he gulped deep breaths of air. A red-headed female, twenty paces ahead, pulled up and turned around, a mischievous grin spreading across her face as she took pleasure in his labored breathing.

Even though time had changed them into adults, I still recognized Tess Armstrong and Russell Ingram now in their youth. The oddity of seeing Tess at about the same age as her daughter Rae struck me. How strange to see them before they experienced the emotional rollercoaster we all go through in life. If they only knew then what they know now, would they make different choices? Would any of us?

The early morning sun reflected off the roofs of gray-shingled homes as a slight breeze carried a hint of salt and seaweed. Both wore tee shirts and shorts, and they stood on a dirt trail.

"I warned you about not being able to keep up with me, Rusty." She ambled back to him, her grin turning into a frown. "You're not going to puke, are you?"

He waved away the question.

"You do remember I had told you I ran the Boston Marathon two years ago?"

He lifted an eyebrow. "No, I didn't know that."

"Hmm, another example of selective hearing. That happens with you a lot."

He made a sour face. "You must have run it before you began at Kendil, so you can forgive me for the lapse." He stood straighter, taking a deep breath, his face still flushed. "Still, you could have run at a slower pace, Tess. This wasn't supposed to be a sprint."

Her eyes still sparkled with pleasure. "I'll take pity on you. We can take a shortcut up ahead and head back to the cottage. Let's walk for a while."

They continued walking at a fast pace as a set of parents and two children rode bicycles past them. Tess called a greeting to the riders, and the parents returned the acknowledgment. "We're lucky to come here off-season," she said. "Most tourists have packed and gone. Otherwise, this trail would be crowded by midday."

Russell's complexion had turned back to normal as he glanced at the homes they passed. "It is nice to get out of the city and to stop worrying about work all the time. I'm glad you invited Al and me."

She shrugged. "My parents are back home in Connecticut, so the place was open. What's the problem with work?"

He raised his eyebrows. "Didn't you pay attention during our department meeting the other day? They may reassign us to another project. The core technologies are where they make all their money, and ours is only a fringe program."

"Would that be so bad? I'd consider it a promotion." Her face lit up. "Hell, they might even give us a raise."

He scowled. "You know as well as I do—as does Al— that we're onto something big with our antivirus software. Nobody else has it yet. And when these personal computers and the World Wide Web become more popular, everyone will need our products. Otherwise, security holes will riddle their systems. I'm telling you, it'll sell like hotcakes, and then we'll be the top developers in the company."

"Rusty, the problem is, people don't care. People don't store vital information on PCs. Businesses will put their critical data on their mini or mainframes. That's one reason nobody's interested in antivirus for PCs."

"Look at it this way: if personal computers make the leap from intriguing gadgets used by mostly geeks like us, and they become business computers, then everyone will need our antivirus software. We're already way ahead of the curve with our development."

Tess chewed on her lower lip. They walked in silence for a time until she said, "Maybe you have a point, Rusty. I wouldn't mind being one of the top engineers, especially when everyone told me that this wasn't a profession for females. I'm gonna prove them wrong, and maybe this is a way."

He smiled. "That's the Tess I know."

She regarded him with interest. "Let's put our heads together when we're back in Cambridge next week. Maybe we can write a proposal to management on market trends in the field." His smile widened at her words, but Tess held up her hand to stop him from saying anything further. "Right now, we're on Cape Cod to have fun for a few days. Besides, we'd better get back to the cottage before Al devours the rest of the pizza from last night. I'll race you."

THE VIEW TRANSITIONED TO A VIEW OF TESS AND Russell stepping toward a quaint cottage with white trim and weathered wooden shingles. Alan Sabrinsky put down his book as they entered the screened porch. Tess looked at the cover: Advanced Fortran Coding. "What is it with the two of you?" Tess admonished. "This is supposed to be a mini vacation. No work stuff allowed."

Russell laughed at her outburst. "Don't be too rough on him, Tess. Without Al, we'd never be able to finish our project."

Alan smiled smugly, but she pointed a finger at both of them. "You both agreed that I would make the plans this weekend. This little girl's not getting pushed around by you two bullies."

Russell smirked. "Little girl? We've already learned that mistake."

Tess glared at them before her face softened. "Okay then, it's settled. We'll grab lunch at Ed's Diner in the town center. It's a landmark with the locals. We'll order it takeout so we can enjoy it with an ocean view. I know the exact spot. Then we'll visit the National Seashore and we'll end the day at Provincetown at the tip of the Cape."

A groan escaped Alan, but another sharp finger jab from Tess forestalled him from objecting.

"It's decided. We leave in one hour, and I call the shower first."

~

"Tess, where the hell are you leading us?" Alan grumbled. "Those benches next to the beach were perfectly fine."

"Hush, I told you, this is my special spot. I discovered it when I was a child." With stately waterfront homes and a sandy shore behind them, the three figures negotiated their way through a narrow dirt path bordered by a thorny tangle of impassable pink-flowered rugosa rose bushes on one side, and on the other by a three-foot high stone wall that ran parallel to a river which spilled into the ocean near the public beach. More than once, they had to push aside or duck under prickly branches on the way to their destination.

"We're almost there," she announced. Meanwhile, Alan already began taking more interest in his lunch bag than their journey. The path ended in a small and unremarkable clearing of grass. Sparse trees lent a fair amount of shade. A knot of brambles surrounded them on three sides while the view of the river opened on one side. By leaning forward along the knee-high stone wall, they could see the ocean beyond. "This is my secret spot," she declared.

Alan wore a befuddled expression while Russell smiled as if she had just told a joke.

Undeterred, Tess continued, "I found this spot when I was about nine or ten years old. I would often sit here and wave at the passing boats on the river. But here is the best part of all." She stepped toward the far side of the clearing and pulled some vines aside to reveal a stone statue about four-feet high. The cherub face was of indistinct age or sex. It appeared to be wearing a robe or cloak. Russell approached the statue to gain a better view while Alan peered inside his bag of food again.

"Look here," said Tess, pointing to the base. "It has a name: Elthea. Was that this person's name?"

Alan began munching on some fries from his lunch. "Tess, how in the world can something like this possibly fascinate you?"

Tess placed her hands on her hips. "Hey, admit it, this is out of the ordinary." She came in a rush. "Don't you have any imagination? Who put this here? Maybe it was pirates plying the shores of Cape Cod in olden times, and it marks a buried treasure; or a child who died in a terrible accident —maybe this is even the grave. Or was it placed by a wealthy landowner who had once lived here? What do you think?"

Alan shook his head in disbelief. "I believe that if you want to become a computer programmer, you should be more practical. Software engineers see things in black and white." Balancing his bagged lunch with his forearms, he imitated a set of scales. "It is this or that. You write code and it works the way you intended, or it doesn't."

"Welcome to the world of Al Sabrinsky," said Russell with a smile.

Tess rolled her eyes. "I hate to tell you, Al, but the principles of software code cannot explain everything."

He shrugged. "Whatever. Let's eat."

They sat on the stone wall facing the river. The sun shone with barely a cloud in the sky, holding the promise of a splendid day ahead to explore the waterside communities of the Cape. The statue was forgotten as the three chattered about their plans for the rest of the time, oblivious to the imperceptible shift about to occur in the future of worlds and countless lives.

You are the ones I seek. Will you join my cause?

The voice came from all around them and from nowhere at the same time. Everyone looked at each other for a second. Russell jumped to his feet, nearly falling off the wall. "What! Who was that? Did someone say something?" His eyes were wide.

Tess and Alan were on their feet a moment later, eyes darting left and right. "Who's there?" Tess demanded.

Alan nudged her. "Look at the statue." The surrounding air wavered, as if heated air mixed with cooler air. The statue itself had turned into an object that had become less substantial, almost translucent.

"What the hell is going on?" said Russell. "Is there a fire?"

But there were no flames, only the eddy of air surrounding the stone figure. The voice sounded again, words not spoken, but heard as clearly as if someone spoke out loud.

The world is changing—both yours and mine. Events that go unchecked spell doom for us all.

Alan and Russell bent low, searching the surrounding

brush for an intruder. "Someone's hiding here," said Russell with a hint of uncertainty.

Tess, however, remained still, riveted on the figure. "It's her."

The others stared at Tess, eyes wide. "Who? Who's her?" said Alan, his voice turning several octaves higher.

"This statue. Look how it's changed." What had been solid stone when they had arrived was now rippling in the breeze like a fine silk cloth. "And have you noticed: it's not speaking with a voice, yet we can hear it." Tess's face creased in fascination. "Isn't this odd?"

"Odd?" Alan squeaked. "I'm getting the hell out of here." Before he could move, the voice came again.

You three individuals have the mettle to confront wrongs and make them right. I lay upon you a heavy burden, yet such is my need.

Alan pulled Tess's arm. "We need to leave. Now." Russell stood still, as if frozen in place.

"Stop talking for a minute," she demanded. "We have to figure this out. In all the time I've spent here at this very spot, this has never happened. What's going on?"

Russell blinked, tearing his gaze from the figure. "Maybe Al's right. I don't like this."

She shook her head. "No, I'm staying. Don't be such scaredy-cats."

I am unlike you, Tessa. Yet we are the same.

Her mouth hung open. "That's what my dad called me when I was a child." She stole a glance at Alan and Russell. "This is not dangerous. You can hear it in the voice." She fixed them with a stare. "You hear her, don't you? It's as if she's speaking in my head."

The two others nodded. "I still don't like this," said Alan.

My realm needs you. What I ask is no small request. I cannot assure your safety, and success is far from certain. Yet, if ever there are three who can accomplish what I need, it is you, Tessa Armstrong, Alan Sabrinsky, and Russell Ingram.

The three companions stared at the statue and nobody spoke for a time as they absorbed what it had said. Tess glanced at her friends. "I realize this may sound weird, but I've known this figure and the face of that statue for most of my life. It's like an old friend, someone I came to visit with each new season. I trust what's being said." Looking again at the figure before them, she spoke forcefully. "Tell us what you need."

Russell and Alan both made a sound—a moan and a gasp. Tess glanced at them. "We can't just turn our backs on what this woman is asking."

"Why the hell not?" Alan shrieked.

Tess jerked her head toward the path. "Then go." She paused a moment, her mouth moving, but no words came out as she struggled with what to say. Her eyes darted between them and her voice cracked with emotion. "If I left now, I'll regret it for the rest of my life. I'm not like the two of you. The life of a computer programmer is only a small part of who I am."

Nobody moved. Heartbeats stretched to minutes as the

silence lengthened. Russell and Alan glanced at each other, uncertain about what to do next. The disembodied voice spoke again.

This is what I ask. Come to my land and remedy an ill taking place with a clan who lives here. If left unchecked, they will grow into a terrible force. The oppression and injustice happening here can last for only so long until a rot spreads throughout the land. Make it right.

Tess frowned. "I know nothing about..." She struggled to find the right words. "We might not be the people to solve this problem, whatever it is. Make it right? How do we..."

"Tess, I don't think we should get mixed up in this nonsense," Russell interrupted.

She frowned, her resolve wavering. She chewed on her lower lip, unable to speak. Looking back at the figure before them, she set her jaw and waited. It didn't take long for the voice to speak again.

If you assent to my plea, you need only place your hand on the sculpture. I will bring you here. And if you decide not, I wish you much happiness and joy on life's journey.

Tess looked at the statue, seeing all it meant to her. Some people expressed their feelings by writing in a journal. Tess would speak to this stone figure.

She once sat here and cried when Buster died, the dog she had known as a child; and she talked to the statue with excitement as the boy next door asked her out for a date, her very first crush; she was here the day before leaving for college, on her own for the first time in her life. This, and a dozen other life-defining moments she spent with the figure who listened to all she had to say. She recognized the shape of its face as if it were her own.

She brought her arm up and placed it onto the forehead of the statue named Elthea, her friend since childhood. A gasp escaped from either Alan or Russell; she was never sure. And then, between one heartbeat and the next, Tess Armstrong vanished, leaving the confines of Cape Cod far behind.

5

THE MISERY THAT WILL COME

Her vision was a blur of gray and white with shapeless forms floating about, as if adrift in a deep sea. Other sensations, such as touch, hearing, and smells, didn't exist. It was a wonder she remained calm as she did during this chaos, trusting in her belief that the statue of Elthea was not dangerous. Such was her affection for a piece of stone, strange as it may seem to another person.

And then, as if someone turned a page, reality erupted around her.

The redolence of freshly tilled soil permeated the air as the heat from the sun beat down from above. Tess Armstrong awoke from her disorientation, finding herself positioned on all fours with hands and knees mired in a half-foot of muddy water.

"What the hell," she grumbled, lifting one hand from the muck.

A nearby eruption caused her to cringe. It was as if a bomb had exploded, spewing water thirty feet into the air. Reacting on instinct, she covered her head, splattering her face with mud. Blinded by the grime, she attempted to clear her eyes by wiping them on her clean upper sleeve. Blinking rapidly, she jerked around.

What had sounded like an explosion was the sound of a geyser erupting nearby. She gaped at the sight as the water began falling gently back to the ground, soaking the rest of her previously dry clothes.

A young girl to her left giggled. Tess jerked her head in that direction. With the water still raining down on her, she tried to salvage some sense of dignity by getting to her feet. The rutted footing gave way, and she lost her balance, flopping into the muck again before gaining her footing. By now, in a matter of seconds, she had smeared mud on all her clothes, except for small spots that were drenched. Exhaling, she blew on a strand of hair that covered her eyes. When that didn't work, she brushed it aside, spreading more mud on her face.

Tess gave her full attention to the child. She wore a broad-brimmed hat, which kept the water off her face. The rest of her clothes consisted of a waterproof material. She appeared to be picking berries or small fruit from low bushes, filling a basket next to her. The bushes ran in rows as dozens of other people farther away bent over to harvest the produce. Everyone focused on the tasks in front of them, and nobody noticed her arrival. She could be thankful for that after making such a fool of herself.

"Where am I?" Tess asked. "What's your name?"

The child frowned and tilted her head. She placed a handful of berries she had picked into her basket and raised both hands in the air and moved them around as if conducting a symphony orchestra.

"Are you deaf? Is that sign language?"

Tess gasped as glowing squiggly lines and colored grids appeared in the air near the child. "What is that?" The girl nudged the images with her fingers as more meaningless glyphs took shape.

Frustrated, Tess looked at the field, trying to find anyone else who could help her. Maybe a grownup would understand her. They all remained hunched over, paying attention to their task of harvesting berries or some kind of fruit. The scene was reminiscent of the legions of migrant farm workers picking crops in southern California.

A squeal from someone behind Tess caused her to spin in that direction, the sudden movement causing her to lose her balance and almost fall back into the mud. Her arms flayed as she tried to remain upright.

Russell and Alan stood five paces away, their eyes wide as they surveyed the field. "Tess, where are we?" Russell said, rushing the words together with an edge to his tone as if he was blaming her. Alan stood as still as a cardboard cutout. Was he even breathing?

"Don't worry, I'll figure this out," she responded with a sad smile. "Thanks for following. I don't know if I could handle this alone. Whatever this is."

Another geyser roared in the distance. Russell and

Alan winced, two skittish figures trying to process what had just happened. Nobody else in the field reacted, except for a young man who began striding toward them. Tess eyed the man as he approached. "Good, maybe now I can get some answers."

He put his hands on his hips, eyes glaring as he came to a stop before them. He then shouted words that sounded like gibberish. The tone of his voice made it clear he wasn't happy.

Tess raised her hands. She enunciated each word. "I. Do not. Understand. You."

He scowled for a moment before bringing his hands up and performing the same motions as the child. Squiggly lines and grids materialized near him as well. Meanwhile, the girl's hands continued to move, and soon she was pushing some of her symbols into his as they both pushed them into a mingled tapestry.

"What the hell is that?" Alan murmured his first words since arriving. Everything was so unusual that it took Tess a moment to figure out what Alan was talking about. He was staring at the swirl of lights and symbols.

The stranger paid close attention when one of them spoke. Was he trying to communicate with those curious symbols? It seemed like he was playing some sort of computer game, like the ones that Tess had seen back home. Why was all this so confusing?

Now that Alan had found his voice, he continued. "Tess, how the hell are we gonna get out of here? And please don't tell me you don't know."

Tess looked at him, trying to frame a response. Before she could muster a reply, the stranger spoke in perfect English. "You should leave here right now. That is your best option before it is too late."

Tess spun around, splashing more mud on her jeans. "Who are you? Where are we?" She pointed to the transparent mass of colored lines and symbols still surrounding both him and the child. "And what the hell are those lights you keep playing with?"

He smiled. "Too many questions, lady, which I don't have the time or the desire to answer." He motioned toward where he had been picking fruit. "As you can see, we are busy working."

She flung her arms around as if gesturing to the field. "Wh... Are you kidding me!" she sputtered. She took a moment to catch her breath, and when she spoke again, her voice cracked as tears threatened to flow down her mud-splattered face. "We came here to help. At least that's what this lady asked us to do. And now I'm a mess, covered in mud, soaking wet, and you don't have the time to answer my questions? Why the hell did you take so long to speak in the first place?"

He smirked. "There is only one important thing about what you had just said. You are an outsider. That makes you a liability here in this place. Actually, you are less than nobody. As for providing us with help, it seems to me you are the ones who require it most." He cast a furtive glance around the muddy field. "If the Elite find you, they will kill you. That is all you need to know."

Alan groaned. "God, this is getting worse by the minute."

~

THE STRANGER PLACED HIS HAND PROTECTIVELY ON the little girl's shoulder. "Come on, Mara. Work closer to me from now on."

He turned to leave, but at that moment the child drew in a sharp breath and raised her arm, pointing in the distance. The man followed her gaze. "Damn."

Tess looked in that direction. At the other end of the field, a figure wearing a white and gold robe floated a dozen feet in the air. He looked left and right, as if searching for something on the ground. Before she could ask, the stranger hissed, "Everyone, down on your knees and begin harvesting." He and the girl began working again.

Still standing, Alan grumbled, "But we're going to get wet."

"Stupid idiots. Do you have a death wish?"

Tess gazed at the floating figure a moment longer. "We'd better do as he says." With her already sodden clothes, kneeling in the muck now made little difference. But Russell and Alan took a little longer, gingerly bending their knees. "Ugh," Alan muttered.

"Who is that?" Tess asked as she gave her attention to the bush in front of her.

The stranger didn't respond as he plucked multi-colored berries and tossed them into a basket. "Just my luck," he said, as much to himself as to Tess. "One of them has to come out today. If I'm caught with you..." He picked up his tempo as Tess, Alan, and Russell looked at each other.

Colorful symbols blossomed around the floating figure, who now came to a stop about thirty yards from them. Unlike the stranger next to them, this other figure projected a more intense, complex pattern of images.

"That must be one of those Elite this guy mentioned," said Russell.

"Hush now or he will kill you," the stranger muttered.

A booming voice forestalled further discussion. The floating figure spoke in a strange language, the voice amplified without a microphone or other device. A lone worker in the field stood, his shoulders sagged, head bowed. The two exchanged more words back and forth in their own dialect, the intensity increasing as if an argument were taking place.

During this entire time, spectral patterns floated around the laborer on the ground. His were much smaller and more subdued compared to the other floating above him. And then, with no weapons being drawn, the man in the field screamed with an agonizing, heart wrenching sound.

Shielding the girl from the episode, the stranger next to Tess put his arms over her and turned her head away. Out in the field, the lights circling the figure on the ground dimmed and floated into the air and dissolved like a wisp of smoke. He stood motionless for a second before he crumpled, splashing into the water, the mud and muck covering his prone body. Above him, the airborne figure sped away in the opposite direction.

"What just happened?" Alan gasped. "Is he dead? How did he die?"

The man near them wasn't listening; his gaze was far away, vision unfocused.

"Please," Tess implored, her anger spent. "We don't know what's going on here. At least explain it."

He looked at her without expression. Mara tugged at his arm. "She seems nice, Cal."

His expression softened as he gazed at the child. Taking a deep breath before speaking, he said, "I don't know what life is like where you came from, but this is how we live." He nodded toward the dead body. "And that is why I cannot help you. The Elite killed him for taking a tiny trinket from the fortress. He's a Reaper, like the rest of us workers, and his job was to clean inside the fortress. The ornament he stole was in the trash. His name was Gabe, and he said he took it as a birthday present for his daughter. He was stupid. Stealing anything from an Elite is a death sentence." He gazed at them another moment. "So is harboring outsiders."

"I still don't understand," Tess mumbled as if lost.

Cal turned to leave, still holding Mara's hand. "Can you help them just a little?" the girl implored.

He gritted his teeth, eyes scanning the distance. "I can show you the way to dry land, into the town. But you are on your own from there. You will need to scavenge to stay alive. Nobody will risk their life to help you. The rest of us Reapers will know about you because of my Directive."

Tess was about to say more, but Cal raised his hand. "Look, lady, you have already taken enough of my time. I have a quota to produce, and I cannot make my numbers by chatting with you."

"Fine," Tess snapped. "Just one question. Where can we find Elthea?"

He gaped at her before finding his voice. "You are an odd bunch; I will give you that much." He spread his arms wide. "You have found her; this is Elthea's Realm."

CAL STRODE ACROSS THE WET FIELD AS IF HE WERE walking on dry land. The slop and muck didn't slow him down. With the girl Mara in tow, a firm grip on her hand, he marched toward an area covered in trees. He cradled the half-full basket of picked fruit in his other arm, holding it as if it was a precious cargo. Mara carried her own smaller container, also careful not to spill any of its contents.

With a dazed look in their eyes, Tess, Russell, and Alan sloshed through the mud, splashing themselves with it as they did their best to keep up. Tess gestured toward Alan, who had fallen behind. "Please Al, hurry."

He picked his way through the furrowed mess, his face dour. "Damn stupid idea this was. I told you so." Alan picked up his pace, sending splatters of mud everywhere around him. The other workers in the field paid them scant attention.

Russell tapped Tess on the shoulder as they neared the line of trees. "Look at those homes."

From a distance, the covering of trees had obscured the small structures. Rickety huts and derelict shacks hugged the boundary between wet fields and solid ground. Tess frowned. "Do people live in those? It looks like the people who live here pieced them together with scraps of wood."

Once on dry land, Tess shook her pant legs and looked around. Other workers passed close to them, many carrying baskets of different crops. Nobody graced them with as much as a brief glance. The differences in appearance between the residents and the three newcomers were minuscule—those living here had a small difference in their complexion—their skin had a slight red hue. Minor facial variances included a somewhat elongated nose and bumps near their temples. Adults here were taller than the three from Earth. Although minor, the variations were enough to label those from Earth as people who didn't belong in this place.

They reached a small town square a short distance from the flooded fields. Most of the laborers brought their wares here to a row of tables, handing the contents over to other residents behind the tables who weighed or counted the items. Cal had not spoken since agreeing to take them to dry land, and he strode forward as if not acknowledging their presence, even though the three continued to tag along behind him. He went to an open table and handed his basket of berries to a man on the other side. Animals that looked like donkeys stood to the back, waiting to truck the various foods away to another destination.

Cal exchanged words in another language with those across from him, sharing a laugh. Was he going to ignore them forever, now that he had fulfilled his agreement to bring them to a dry spot? She tapped him on the shoulder. "What did you two just say?" she asked him, as much to capture his attention as wanting to know.

He focused on her for the first time since their discussion in the field. "He told me I'll need to work overtime to meet my quota, thanks to you."

"And that he's getting soft," the man behind the counter added without looking at her.

She lifted her eyebrows. "How—He understands us?"

Cal shook his head. "Didn't you listen? I told you, the Directive spread the language translation, at least among us Reapers. The Elite have their own Directive network."

She fumed. "I do listen. And no, you did not explain any of that. Although, I'm still not sure I understand any of it."

Alan moved closer. "What is a Directive?"

Cal threw up his hands in frustration. "Look, I said I would bring you to dry land." He stomped a foot on the ground as if to make his point. "The rest of the town is in that direction." He jerked his head to the side. "No Reaper is going to help you. There is food enough in the fields. But if you steal from anyone, you won't have to worry about the Elite." He tugged the girl, urging her to leave with him.

"Come along, Mara. Your parents will expect you home soon." As Cal led her away, the young girl turned back to look at them with puppy eyes. The only two people acknowledging their existence passed around the corner of a shack and were gone.

Alan and Russell, fear in their eyes, gazed at the cluster of strangers, nobody paying them any attention. "Now what?" Alan asked, his voice desperate.

Tess's lip quivered, betraying her dismay. "Maybe we should explore this village, find someone who can help us."

"Exploring is what got us into this mess in the first place," Russell shot back.

She took a breath. "Okay, I know this is crazy; it's not what I expected." She shook her head. "I don't know what I thought. When I heard that voice at the statue, it seemed the right thing to do. But now..." Her eyes welled up.

Russell relented as he exhaled. "I understand how you felt back there, and how you thought it had made sense, at least at that moment. Not everything works out the way we expect. We'll work through this and figure it out. Right Alan?"

The other programmer was bent over, busily trying to clear the mud off his pants. He looked up. "I think you're both crazy. What good can possibly come from us being here, and where the hell are we? If it was up to me, I'd leave this god-forsaken place this instant and go back home." He peered at Tess, gauging her reaction. When he saw her almost in tears, he softened his tone. "But since we're here, I don't see the harm in looking." He pointed in the other direction. "It seems these shacks go on for some distance. I think this place is larger than I thought." Another thought came to him, and his face brightened. "And those lights with symbols floating around these people. I want to find out what they're all about. They might be part of their thought process, which is fascinating."

A sad smile came to her. For all their differences, these two were always by her side. Even Alan, for all his focus on coding, was willing to go along with her now. "Thanks. I don't know what I would do without you both with me." She looked at a path between the huts. "Let's walk in that direction and we'll see what we find."

A journey had begun. For all their good intentions, none could anticipate the misery that one day would come from these first steps.

6

ONCE IN A LIFETIME

The day began as any other, except this was not a world known to most of humanity. Yet, for anyone viewing the morning scene, the view appeared almost identical to Earth. Fog hung in the air, just above the tallest branches of nearby fruit trees, birds flitting from one limb to another. The sun, a yellow blob low in the sky, would soon pierce the haze, promising a warm day. Mildew had formed on the grass, and all was tranquil. The land of Elthea's Realm was at peace.

Tess Armstrong always loved this time of day back on Earth, before the hustle of life gained purchase, forcing her to attend to one or another chore. This was when she could go for a run, or perform her yoga stretches, or meditate, or on the rare occasion, sleep in late. But today was different.

She stirred, here in this glen, hearing the song of birds, or maybe the movements of others who occupied this land.

And then, bang! A crack, loud as a cannon, split the air in the wooded meadow.

Tess, Alan, and Russell bolted upright at the same instant. Nearby, a small group of villagers were unloading ladders from a cart, sending the wooden frames crashing into each other on the ground, heedless of the racket they caused.

Alan moaned. "God, please tell me we're not still here." He looked around, one eye open, the other closed, before hanging his head between upraised knees. "Explain again, Tess, what is this place and what in God's name are we doing here? No—first inform me how we're gonna get home."

She looked at him with a knitted brow. "Al, we know how you feel. Must we have the same discussion every day?"

"Yes, when the logical world I had known my entire life suddenly turns upside down. I believe you owe me more of an explanation."

"Hey, we're trying to sleep here," Russell yelled at the intruders. "Can't you see?"

Like yesterday, none of the locals so much as glanced in their direction. The three outcasts might as well be invisible.

Russell moaned as he rose to his knees, rubbing his back. They had slept here in the open fields on their first night in this place, having no other choice. The clothes they wore were the same as those when they arrived here, except now they were mud-splattered and rumpled, bearing little resemblance to the crisp attire of yesterday when they enjoyed lunch on the shore of Cape Cod.

"Well, that wasn't the most comfortable sleep I ever had," said Russell as he glared at the workers who were now setting up their ladders around a tree near to them. The fruit in the trees had provided their only dinner last night. The only reason they had eaten it was because their hunger had overcome their fear of eating something unknown. Plus, seeing the local peasants pick the fruit yesterday gave them assurance it wasn't poisonous, although how could any of them be certain what was edible in this strange place?

Once the laborers had erected the ladders, children came over carrying baskets. Unlike the adults, who ignored the three, the youngsters stole covert glances at them.

Tess finished lacing her shoes and stood, stretching her limbs. "Let's get a better look at that fortress building we saw yesterday. It must be where the Elites live."

Alan grumbled as he pushed his foot back into one of his shoes. "Great, the exact people we're supposed to stay away from. Another good idea."

Tess turned on him. "I get it, you're unhappy. You've made that abundantly clear. I've already told you, this isn't what I expected. If I could do it again, I would have instructed you not to touch that statue. Then you wouldn't be in this mess with me." Her eyes watered. "But I can't take it back. I only did what I thought was right."

They were silent for a moment with only the playful cries of children and adults speaking to each other in another language filling the air. Russell cleared his throat. "You would have come here anyway, even after what we've seen so far?"

She nodded, running her sleeve across her face. "You still don't understand me, do you?"

He shook his head, his face a mix of emotions. "I know you trusted that stone sculpture friend of yours."

It took her a moment to respond. "Yes, that was part of it, but there's more. I don't like to play it safe or under-achieve. That's not me. The worst insult someone can tell me is that I failed to live up to expectations. I push myself, often harder than I should. And at times, that gets me into trouble."

"That doesn't explain why you would still choose to be here," said Alan.

Tess winced, an inner pain reflected in her face. "I answered a call for help as if she were a friend, because she was. The voice at the statue selected us—you heard her explanation—and I believe for a purpose. I'm convinced there are things in our life that we can't explain. This is one of those times. You may not understand this, but in my heart I know that the appeal was sincere. Someone here needs help and we are the only ones who can provide it."

"And you believed it wasn't some crazy person speaking?" Alan persisted.

She hesitated. "Let me point out something about me;

maybe that will help. As a child, I was often a loner, not that I didn't have friends—I did. And I enjoyed them. But I always needed my space, time away from everyone to think about whatever might trouble me. I guess it's how my brain is wired. Because I spent summers at the Cape with my parents, most of my school buddies, or neighborhood children, weren't around. That spot I showed you at the statue of Elthea was where I went for my alone time. Through the years, I would talk out loud to the figure as I would tell her about a crush I had on a boy, or about whether I should try out for the cheer team, or whatever else was on my mind, big or small. It was my safe place where I worked through many issues in my head by simply explaining stuff to her. She never answered me, but I never expected her to. The act itself was beneficial enough."

She gave an embarrassed shrug. "You probably think I'm a little unhinged, but ever since childhood, I bonded with that figure staring back at me. A spiritual connection took place whenever I went to that place, a feeling as strong as any religious person might feel at a place of worship. She absorbed everything I said to her, never passing judgment, always there. And then when it spoke, and it asked me to help her, I couldn't refuse. Through the good and the bad, we were a team. She was part of my life, and I loved her in a way that's difficult to explain." She studied both men, looking for some sign that either understood or empathized with her. "And that's why I didn't hesitate." She shifted her gaze to the nearby workers, now up on their ladders, reaching for the fruit on the upper branches. "Nothing here makes sense, but soon it will. It has to. We're here for a reason. We only have to discover what it is. The lady of Elthea wouldn't have brought us here otherwise."

Tess fell silent, her fervor spent. Russell spoke into the stillness. "All that may be true, but you haven't explained the correct reason for following the voice." She raised her eyebrows, about to object, but he didn't give her the chance. "I know you all too well, Tess. Maybe you believe all that claptrap about wanting to be alone. But let's face the truth. You're a hopeless romantic. You always have your head in the clouds, dreaming of what might be rather than the way things are." His voice turned softer. "It's one of your more endearing qualities, and why you're a good match with us boring, no-nonsense guys."

Alan spoke before she could say anything. "Hey, I'm not boring."

Tess and Russell burst out laughing. Alan reacted with a puzzled frown, which made them laugh all the more. She stepped closer and stretched her arms wide to hug them. "You're practical, Alan. Is that better?" His frown turned into a smile as they remained in a group embrace for a time. "I'm so glad you're both with me. If not for the two of you..." Her voice caught, unable to finish.

The three co-workers had reached an unspoken agreement. Tess, the junior of the three back in the office, would steer their course here in this unfamiliar land. They would band together to face whatever adversity would come.

If the laborers in the orchard thought of them at all, did they wonder about the embrace? Should someone explain to the strangers that affection alone would not overcome their misfortune? Hardships were still ahead, more than these foreigners realized. Or was it better that they not know? After all, knowing would only make it worse. They would need all their guile to remain alive, never mind fulfilling the wish of the voice at the statue.

THEY KEPT THEIR HEADS LOW AS THEY CREPT ON hands and knees along the embankment. Peering over the top, Russell whispered, "Are you sure this is a good idea?"

"I thought we agreed," Tess responded with a hint of annoyance.

"Yes, but I still don't enjoy being this close to them. What if they see us watching?"

"If you two don't shut up, they're going to hear us," Alan hissed.

Tess and Russell did as he demanded, staying flat on their stomachs as they hid behind some low bushes. Two hundred yards in front of them stood a bizarre, alien structure resembling a castle, but unlike anything they had seen before. Standing a dozen stories tall and many times as wide, the building appeared alive as it moved and swayed, much like a sapling in a slight breeze. The surface was smooth as stone, with no apparent windows or openings, although it contained many balconies and terraces. Flags whipped in the wind along the upper floors.

Two Elite guards in white robes stood at the only access. A raised roadbed cut across the wet fields, leading from the ramshackle village to this entrance. Peasants trudged in both directions along the wide path, some had carts loaded with food and goods. The carts heading toward the fortress were full, and mostly empty on their return.

Tess gestured at the workers going in and out of the fortress. "Those must be the Reapers who are delivering food or who work inside the building, like the one yesterday the Elite killed for stealing something inside."

Alan shuddered as if chilled. "It still gives me the shivers thinking that could happen to us."

They watched in silence for a time. "Look what happens when a laborer enters," Russell whispered. Floating symbols sprang to life around each Reaper as they approached the guards. The Elite sentries would inspect the image for a moment before allowing the Reaper access.

"Maybe those lights are some sort of identification mechanism for each person," said Alan.

"That would make sense," Russell answered. "Those lights came on when the Reapers brought their foods to the town to be counted."

Tess shook her head. "You might be right, but I bet it's much more than that. The little girl in the field used it when I first arrived, and then that man, Cal, did the same. They didn't have any reason to identify themselves."

"Then what was its purpose?" asked Alan.

Tess considered. "I think it gave the two of them the ability to understand me and use our language. He said as much, but that was the least of my concerns at the time."

"He called it the Directive," Alan added.

They remained silent for a while, watching the procession of Reapers entering and leaving the building.

"Well, there's no way we'll ever be able to sneak in without one of those Directives," Tess said.

"Why, in God's name, would we ever want to sneak in?" Russell asked.

"To find out more about these Elite people. The more we know about them, the better we can figure out what to do."

"I'll tell you what we should do," Alan shot back. "How about we get the hell out of here?"

"Don't you remember why we're here?"

Both Alan and Russell said nothing at first, until Russell responded, "Er... not really."

A huff of irritation escaped her lips. "The lady at the statue said something about repairing a rot before it spreads. She needed us to make things right."

"What I remember most was her saying that she couldn't guarantee our safety," said Alan. He spoke without ill-temper. Alan would always be this way, bemoaning his fate, yet be a team player when he they needed him.

"Who can guarantee anything in life?" said Tess. She turned her gaze away from the fortress to the wet fields on the other side of the embankment upon which they hid. This vista offered a good vantage to observe both the fields with the laborers and the Elite's fortress. Two geysers spouted water raining down upon Reapers bent over at their tasks. They were working in dreadful conditions with the Elites completely controlling them.

"Hey," Russell hissed. "Look at this." He focused his attention on the building. "Is that a body?"

Two Reapers were pulling a cart away from the entrance. A body lay sprawled upon the bed of the wagon. Long, dark hair flowed to the sides of her face, eyes closed, her body unmoving. Even from this distance, the red stains on her blue dress were visible. The parade of Reapers entering the building halted as they stood to the side as the wagon passed. Some put one hand over their chest. Sharp words from the two Elite guards prompted the Reapers to move again, as one after another they displayed their colorful insignias for the guards to inspect. But the stance of those going in the building had changed. Their shoulders sagged a bit more and their heads hung down, eyes to the ground.

"This is what she was telling us," Tess whispered, as if talking to herself. The two men looked at her, not understanding her meaning. "This is the wrong that she asked us to make right." Her eyes took on a clarity as she tore them away from the departing wagon. "Maybe once in a lifetime a person can sway the destiny of others, improve their lot in life. This is our chance." Her eyes lingered on Alan. "This is our moment, Alan. Forfeit it if you wish. But you might never have another opportunity such as this to help the lives of so many."

~

THE ELITE FORTRESS DIMMED AS AN OLDER TESS Armstrong gazed back at me. Her garden room had replaced the view of geysers and peasants. Here, the shadows now fell in long swaths across the room, signaling the end of another day. Hours had passed since we began the Farseeing.

Something was different in this lady seated across from me, an expression I had never noticed before. Even now, years after the events from her youth, the sadness in her eyes remained, made more pronounced as she relived the tragedy of those days. "This must be hard on you to look back on these experiences once again," I whispered.

She blinked, her thoughts still far away. "The greater pain is yet to come."

My respect for this remarkable woman increased. I never recognized how much inner strength she possessed. She was always calm and in control, a person at peace with herself. The one aberration in her unruffled composure had happened when the Bots shattered the walls around Haven and were about to take me away. She had risked death by standing before the attacking Bots with her hands raised, ordering them to stop.

What had she perceived in them during that violent

incident? They had ignored her, but they didn't kill her. Did a bond still exist between the two?

Not wanting to interfere with her introspection, I kept silent for a while. After a moment, I asked, "Did the Elite eventually become the Bots?"

She smiled wistfully. "Phil, if you had wanted me to explain events, I would have been willing. But you needed the full experience of the Farseeing. You'll just have to wait."

"Fair enough. Can we press ahead now?" Time was slipping away for Cassie, Matt, and Diane, my dearest friends.

She glanced at the garden on the other side of the open windows. "Dusk is nearly here. Let's continue again tomorrow." She rose without waiting for an answer, and I reluctantly followed, wishing we didn't have to stop.

She watched me as I stood. "When this is over, I hope you won't hate me."

Why such foreboding in someone so sure of themself? "Tess, you were in an impossible situation. How can anyone understand the emotional strain of what had happened to you? At least I had the Astari who cared for and protected us when we came here. You had nobody. I admire you even more because of what I've seen so far."

She knitted her brows, unfazed by my support. "Just know this; our intentions were always honorable."

She led me out of the house without saying more. Once outside, I took a deep breath, feeling the cool air of early evening radiate through the town. This Farseeing session had presented more questions than answers. Was I being foolish, thinking it would help?

The greater pain is yet to come. That might be true for Tess, but I felt it applied equally to me. I had painted myself into a corner, and now there would be no escaping the suffering I would soon have to endure, especially if this Farseeing was a dead end.

7

THE WEAVE AND FLOW OF LIFE

Rae slipped into step next to me as I strolled away from Tess's home. She was quiet, and I was so lost in my own thoughts about the Farseeing, that I only noticed her after we had gone a half-dozen paces.

"Well?" she asked after she had my attention.

"Well, what?"

"Come on, don't be dense. Give me some dirt."

I looked at her, seeing once again the similarities in her features to the younger Tess. With both of them at the same age, they appeared like sisters. They were each playful occasionally and deadly serious at other times. I wasn't sure which role she was playing right now. "What're you talking about? What dirt?"

She let out a breath. "Mom has always been tight-lipped about her time on Elthea when she was young. She never wanted to say much about it, and now, well, I figured this was my chance to learn more about her." Rae pouted. "Don't you want me to be closer to my mom?"

I had to smile. "I have no intention of getting into the middle of anything between you and Tess. If she wanted to explain what happened, she would have—maybe she's waiting for the right time. Besides, if she wanted everyone to see what took place, she would have agreed to my idea of allowing others to view the Farseeing."

Her lips tightened. "I figured you'd say something like that. It's just that she's always been open about everything else in her life."

"Tess is a remarkable person, Rae. In so many ways, she's a lot like you. Give her some space on this. Whatever her reasons, she wants to keep this past to herself. I wouldn't have intruded myself, except the lives of my friends are at stake."

"Speaking of which, did you learn anything that will help?"

I shook my head gently. "No, but we've only just begun. The Bots have a history, a past life, which I never considered before. I was too busy being angry at them for all the destruction and pain they caused. Maybe if I find out more about what motivates them, I can free my friends and stop them from doing more harm."

"I think you're wasting your time." Her voice softened. "You want your friends back, and I understand your feelings. But whoever the Bots were in the past doesn't change what they are today. They're killers. It's all they know, and we have no choice but to respond the same way."

She stopped walking and put her hand on my shoulder. "Your loyalty to your companions is admirable, but it's clouding your thinking. I hate to be the one to tell you, but nobody may be able to restore your friends. And if it comes to that, you'll fall into a depression that will make your previous ones seem mild."

Did she have a valid point? My past mood swings often rendered me incapable of taking action. I couldn't risk falling into another cycle of despondency.

The light of the setting sun played across Rae's face, giving the impression that she was older and wiser than someone who was only now coming of age. "I'll admit I haven't always handled myself all that well in the past." Tears threatened to come as I considered the good times with Cassie, Matt, and Diane—like the time we finished the final presentation of our Utopia Project at Woodbery College. We were so young, so full of vitality. The world was ours for the taking, and we could accomplish whatever life threw at us.

"They're still alive, Rae. And I'll not accept that they're gone. I just can't. With my last ounce of strength, I'll do whatever is necessary to bring them back. Right now, that means understanding our enemy and finding a solution."

A brief nod of her head told me she wouldn't say more about it, even though she wanted to. She believed I had no chance of success; I could see it in her eyes. "Whatever you decide, you know I'll always support you," she said. "I realize how you must feel." I had no response for Rae, knowing she was only trying to help.

How could anyone possibly understand? My closest companions would live a life of torment as monsters. Would it have been better if I had killed them? Either way, the pain over what I had done would always be with me.

We resumed walking as the shadows in the town continued to lengthen. Celeus, the larger of the two moons, hung low on the horizon, shedding enough light to illuminate the village. On those occasions when neither moon lent some light to the night, townspeople would hang a lantern on the fronts of their homes. The elixir used to light the flame in those devices was of a mystery to me. A thimbleful of the liquid was enough to keep the lanterns burning for the night. When I had once asked Russell about it, he responded with a twinkle in his eyes that it was yet another gift provided by the Stonewraiths.

My thoughts drifted as we continued our aimless stroll. I glimpsed one of the Astari following me at a distance. The purple hair identified him as Riyaad. With the protective barrier of the wall destroyed, the others had now tightened their watch over me, even within the town of Haven. How I longed for a time when I was a nobody walking the streets of Boston without bodyguards or anyone else caring about me. Back then, I had felt like such a failure. Yet now I felt little satisfaction knowing I might be the most powerful person in this world. Was fame and glory something to only desire, never to possess? What about happiness?

Rae lapsed into silence, sensing I needed a chance to think. She had that knack of understanding when to prod and when to allow time for me to remain lost in thought. We had traveled only a short distance when the clapping sound of running footsteps came closer. Rae put her hand to her waist, resting it on the hilt of a blade, a reflexive motion more than a conscious response. Before the runner came near, Riyaad was already by my side.

I didn't recognize the man who approached, but he wore the black garments marking him as a member of The Guard. He stopped before us, nodding his head toward me first before turning his attention to Rae. "Sorry to interrupt. The captain wants all members to report to their defensive positions. We have a sighting."

"Sighting?" I asked. "What does that mean? Who's been sighted?"

Before the destruction of the wall, The Guard would announce friends, strangers, or danger with rings of a bell resounding through the town. The Guard had yet to put another one in place after the collapse of the wall. Rae answered my question. "Bots."

My heart raced. Could it be my companions? My voice caught in my throat. "How many?"

He shrugged. "Not sure, sir. As much as I know, only one so far. It's staying near the tree line beyond the fields."

I took off at a run without waiting to hear more. It wasn't long before I realized I might be racing toward the opposite side of the town from the sighting. No matter. I would find out soon enough as I angled in the direction of the collapsed wall.

This street, however, ended in a tangle of boulders, a jumble of rocks pressed up against the houses. Unable to find an open path to the other side, my only option was to scale the demolished wall.

As I searched for a way forward, I realized Riyaad had come up beside me. "Where are you going, Earthfriend? This way is blocked."

My impulse was to shout that I knew it now, but Rae called from a block behind us. "Over here." She gestured to a street perpendicular to the one I had taken.

I uttered a cuss and dashed toward her, with Riyaad following. Rae and the other Guard member were already a half-dozen buildings down that road by the time I reached them. "Just stay with us," said Rae. "You'll get there faster."

Swallowing my pride, I did as she suggested and moved with her at a brisk walk rather than a sprint. We took two other streets before we reached the edge of the town and passed along an open lane through the remains of the wall. More members of The Guard had already assembled there. I searched the line of the woods. Dusk had settled and the trees in the distance had turned murky. "I don't see anything," I mumbled after a second.

One of the other guardsmen pointed. "There, near that tall broadleaf."

I squinted, trying to discern the figure in the dying light of day. To hell with it. "I'm going out to talk with it."

Rae blocked my way, arms outstretched, before I could move. "No, you're not. You hope it's one of your friends; I get that. But it may be another Bot, and they are still our enemy. I can't risk it."

"You don't have to risk anything. I'm going alone."

She didn't withdraw. I considered pushing her aside, but I knew her skill in hand-to-hand combat had far surpassed mine. Unless I used a charm to freeze her in place, my chance of getting around her was slim. "She is right," Riyaad said. He glanced at the others. "We are not large enough of a force to protect you, and you put them in danger," he nodded to the other sentries. "They will defend you, regardless of what you say. It is their obligation as members of The Guard.

"I don't need protecting," I said, louder than I intended. "I can take care of myself now."

Nobody moved. Everyone knew my capacity to call upon the power of Elthea. They also understood I wouldn't use it to harm others, even a Bot.

I tightened my lips, wanting to shout at them. But Riyaad was right, and the bluster left me once I realized it. "Okay, you win. I won't go charging off on my own."

Rae dropped her arms, a wry smile forming. "At least you can still listen to reason now and then." She concentrated her gaze out beyond the darkening fields, her smile fading. "This has become more difficult, hasn't it?"

I raised my eyebrows, not understanding her meaning. "How's that?"

"We no longer know who's a friend, and who's not.

More than once I've said, 'The only good Bot is a dead Bot.' Now, well, I'm not so sure."

And there was the crux of the matter, at least for her. When to kill, when not to. Without the Do No Harm restriction, I would want them all dead, except for Cassie, Matt, and Diane. Yet, was death better than living as a monster? A day might soon come when I would have to make that decision.

I STOOD ALONE ON THE BALCONY NEXT TO MY ROOM, looking at the slender view afforded of the fields beyond the town. Darkness had fallen long ago, and I should have been asleep by now, restoring my strength for tomorrow's Farseeing with Tess. But knowing that a Bot stalked the woods so close, possibly one of my beloved friends, made sleep impossible.

"Where are you, Cass? Is that you?"

Hope was failing me; I could feel it in my gut. Only a few days had passed since the Bots changed my three friends into their own likeness, but already it felt like forever. Restoring them seemed like an impossibility when it first happened, and less likely with each passing hour. For all my training by the Oakenrill, and all the power granted to me, I felt more impotent than ever. Not only did I lack the ability to make them human again, but I couldn't even lash out against the Bots and make them pay for the harm they inflicted. The Oakenrill's mantra came to me. *Do no harm least you destroy the Spirit of Elthea.*

My only hope, the Farseeing with Tess, had so far yielded nothing of value. Would the entire exercise be a waste of time as Rae suggested? What would I do then?

Phil, can you hear me?

I froze and held my breath, hoping my imagination wasn't getting the better of me. The voice I heard in my head was soft, almost musical, unlike the harsh pounding of the Bots. Could it be?

A moment passed before I dared to speak. "Who is it?"

Nothing. Only the stirrings of a gentle breeze rippling across the stone structures of the town broke the silence. Was I finally going crazy? After all the bizarre events of the last year, would it end like this?

I steeled myself, not allowing what little hope I still had to slip away, not now. With everything lost to me, it was all that remained. Cassie had appeared to me as a spirit before, using a Farseeing episode to show me how the Bots had interfered in our lives before we ever realized it. Could she take shape again?

I waited for her on the balcony, searching for a sign, anything that would tell me it was Cassie. The quarter moon, Halcyone, a fingernail on the horizon, moved through the sky as I lingered. My eyes were drooping by the time the smaller of the two moons had reached its zenith. I could wait no longer as exhaustion came over me.

Stumbling into my room, I collapsed onto the bed,

feeling an emptiness inside me unlike anything I had known before.

DAWN ARRIVED WAY TOO SOON. NORMALLY, THE LIGHT of a new day buoyed my spirits, regardless of how dismal my attitude had been during the darkness of the night. The promise of events yet to come would fill me with hope. But not this morning.

After sleeping for only a brief time, I left my room after waking to seek Tess. My need to continue our Farseeing session outweighed everything else. Maybe it would yet reveal the answers I sought.

Nobody answered my knock at Tess's door, so I pounded harder with my fist, belatedly realizing that both she and Evan might still be asleep. No matter. How could they sleep with something so important waiting for us? Nevertheless, the door remained unanswered.

I stepped back onto the street to view the second-floor windows. Should I shout her name?

"She's likely at the public gardens this time of day," said a raspy voice behind me. A lady with white hair tied in a bun was sweeping the entranceway to her home. I hadn't noticed her when I first arrived. "That's where she normally spends her mornings, Master Philip."

Had I met this person before? So many villagers knew me, probably everything about me, yet I hadn't attempted to become familiar with anyone besides those within my small circle of friends. I nodded my head. "Thank you, Miss..."

She broke into a smile. "Anna. Pleased to meet you." She extended her hand and I shook it. "You'll get them back. We're all with you, hoping you find a way."

I wasn't sure how to respond, so I mumbled my appreciation and walked away, knowing I should say more. I did nothing to deserve the loyalty of these villagers. They should hate me for nearly destroying their village. It was me the Bots sought as they tore down the protection offered by the wall. Yet, the people here continued to show one act of kindness after another. How did they become so resolute?

I knew the location of Tess's plot in the gardens, so I had no trouble finding her. As I approached, her back was to me, so she didn't notice me at first. She pushed and tugged a hoe around the rich loam between a row of lettuce plants. A slight smile was on her lips, reflecting the pleasure she took from the simple task. Tess was at home here in the garden, just as her daughter, Rae, handled a blade as if she were born to it. Before speaking, I cleared my throat to announce my arrival. "I still can't understand your obsession with gardening."

She slowly angled her head toward me, as if knowing I would find her here. Her smile broadened. "No? I thought you would have figured it out by now."

So much about this woman was still a mystery. "In case you haven't noticed, my attention has been elsewhere."

"Hmm, maybe that's the problem."

The muscles in my neck tensed, but I knew she was only trying to help. "My problems are way too many for us to discuss right now. Besides, that's not why I'm here."

She smiled. "You misunderstand me. What I mean is that the answers you seek may not always be apparent. Don't expect them to come hitting you over the head." Her smile diminished. "It's a mistake I've made before. And I've paid for it dearly."

Did she mean events that occurred long ago in the Farseeing, or something more recent? I could never be sure with her, and I didn't know if I should try to elicit an answer. Tess could often be difficult to puzzle out, but it was part of her charm. It was her way of teaching. When she wanted to be clear, she could. She resumed tilling the soil, happy to continue her avocation.

She realized why I was here, didn't she? Should I ask if she was ready to resume the Farseeing? Instead, I said, "Did you know The Guard sighted a Bot last night?"

She raised an eyebrow. "Yes, you seem to attract them."

For someone who wasn't responsible for overseeing the village, she knew a lot about what happened here. "Do you think it was..." I couldn't bring myself to ask if it was Cassie.

Her gazed hardened. "Do I think it was one of your friends?" She shrugged. "I don't know. Only time will answer that. The Bots are different now—they must be because of how you changed them. We still can't fathom the implications of what you did to them. Maybe they don't grasp it either and are here to figure it out. Or maybe your friends don't yet understand what the Bots have done to them and are here for the same reason."

A spasm of grief came over me. How could my good intentions go so horribly wrong?

Tess set the hoe aside. "We should continue with this examination of the past, shouldn't we?"

I unclenched my fists. "Yes, please, if you're ready. This is my only hope of understanding them."

She led the way back to her home, and once inside, we settled into the same easy chairs in her garden suite. "Think about what I told you," she said before we began. "Pay attention to the ebb and flow of everyday life. I still don't know what you expect to find, but I feel that's where you'll understand our enemy's mind."

I considered this as I reached for a strand of energy. The room and our surroundings fell away.

8

THE OFFER

The fetid and murky air hung over the squalid marketplace, steam rising in waves from the hard-packed ground as puddles of muck and water dried in the morning sun. The stench from the sweating, unwashed Reapers was overwhelming as they crowded the square, waiting in long lines to hand over their harvest.

Tess wrinkled her nose as she perspired, knowing she was overdue for a bath herself. The air would cool with nightfall, as it did every evening for the past week. But that was still many hours away.

Alan and Russell were by her side as they sat at the edge of the town market; at least that's what they called this place. It hadn't taken them long to discover that this was the best spot to find scraps of food left behind by the wagons that carted most of it to the Elite. At this time of day, an unending stream of adults and children lugged baskets or sacks of fresh foods picked from the fields, or they brought meats from the butchers. Those behind the tables counted or weighed every item before transport. Whatever method they used to keep a record of the count was still a mystery. Nobody recorded any totals.

Russell pointed. "There he is." They fixed their eyes on one of the tables to watch Cal hefting a large sack and exchange a joke with the person on the other side as they both laughed. Even from this distance, Tess could hear them speak in their own language.

Tess stood. "Let's go." They moved through the square without worrying about being seen. Everyone ignored the strangers as if they didn't exist, a practice followed by the residents since their first day here. After seeing how the Elite treated the workers, the three avoided them, but they rarely visited the town or fields. As she reached the low tables, Tess put her hands on her hips as she stood a few paces from the crush of Reapers as they handed over their wares.

Cal turned from the table, a flicker of recognition reaching his eyes. He moved past Tess without reacting as he stopped a dozen paces away. He continued to look in the opposite direction from the three. A display of colored symbols bloomed to life around him. He pitched his voice loud enough for them to hear. "I see you haven't starved to death yet." His face widened into a grin.

Tess balled her hands into fists. "That son of a bitch," she muttered.

Russell blocked her way before she could pounce on him. "Anger won't help, Tess."

She exhaled a breath, inching closer to Cal. "All your friends received your message. Everyone here has ignored us. Not a single person has offered the slightest bit of aid. Thanks for that."

He fiddled with a thread on his sleeve, still facing away from her. "Nobody's obeying any orders from me. They already understand what to do to stay alive. We can ill-afford to stick our necks out. You know nothing about our life, yet you judge us so easily."

"Damn right we know nothing, and you're not making it any easier for us to learn more."

He scanned the area, confirming no Elite were present. Satisfied it was safe, he turned his head to gaze at her, regarding her up and down. "If you want some advice, I suggest you try to fit in better. You stand out like you don't belong here. Find some other clothes, such as the kind we wear. And you need a place to hole up rather than sleeping in the fields every night."

"How do you know where we slept? That's none of your business. Besides, nobody has invited us into their homes. And you should talk about clothes. Yours are one step away from the ragbag."

He smiled. "Exactly what I mean."

She huffed before speaking again. "I'll tell you another thing, Mister. We don't fit in because we don't belong here. Of all our problems, that tops the list."

His smile broadened. "I like the fire in your belly, but

you have to learn when to turn it off. Nobody receives handouts here. We have to be smart and careful. That stunt the other day, hiding near the gate of the fortress, was not smart. You were lucky."

She lifted her eyebrows. "How did you—"

"Everyone could see you; that's how I knew. And if one of the Elite had seen, well, it would have been the end of you. But, stupid as it was, that told me one thing. At least I know you're not one of their spies. That, and Mara's opinion about you, are the only reasons I'm still talking to you."

He glanced at them, his smile now gone. "I have a quota to make." He might have wanted to say more, but he set his jaw and walked away. Three forlorn figures watched his back.

Alan kicked up a small plume of dust with the toe of his shoe. "Well, that didn't work out as we planned."

"Plan? We had a plan?" said Rusty. "We're lurching from one idea to another. Nothing here makes any sense. That's the problem."

"It was worth a try," said Tess. "He's the only one who cares about us, even a little." She glanced at the throng of Reapers streaming around them as if they were invisible. "Come on, let's head back to the orchards. I don't know how long we can live on only fruit, but at least it's something."

Alan groaned as they shuffled away with heads bent low.

Tess sat with her back against a tree while Russell and Alan sat cross-legged, facing her. Each of them munched on an orange-sized piece of fruit. Alan made a face as he bit into his. "Should we be eating the skin of this thing? Don't you think it's too chewy to be edible?"

"It won't kill you," Russell responded.

"Yea, well, one of these times it might. How do we know when something is poisonous without a native to warn us? They'd just as soon let us die than lift a finger." His tone dripped with bitterness.

Tess frowned. "This is no time to lose it, Alan. We're here for a purpose. Remember? There's a wrong happening here that we're supposed to make right. That's what the voice at the statue told us."

He glowered at her. "If you mention that again, I'm going to throw this—whatever it is—at you."

The ringing notes from a musical instrument sounded from the other end of the orchard, where a rutted path crossed the field. They looked at each other, uncertain what to make of it. A crew of Reapers laboring at that end of the green stopped working and moved closer to the path and stood facing it.

"This is odd," Russell muttered. "Should we go see?"

Tess chewed her lower lip, giving a shake of her head. "No, not until we know what's going on. Remember what Cal said about us not fitting in?" She squinted in that direction. "That footpath runs near this part of the orchard. If someone is on it, they'll come by here. Let's find a spot to hide."

Rows of shacks lined the other side of the road from the orchard. A throng of Reapers had already gathered there, standing with hands at their sides or crossed in front of them. Tess grabbed both Russell and Alan, pulling them to the ground as a figure in white strode forward on the path. An Elite. He blew into a small instrument not much larger than his hand, producing powerful musical notes. Those along the roadside stood straighter as he neared.

"What's going on," Russell whispered.

"Shh. Keep your head low," Tess hissed. Knee-high grass and a small berm along the edge of the path hid them from whoever walked along the road. Not much of a hiding place, but running away now would mean certain discovery.

The Elite playing the music passed. Behind him came the sound of laughter from someone else coming this way. Whoever it was, a bend in the road still obscured them. Tess exchanged a confused glance with Alan and Russell, motioning for them to keep down. Did these Elite monsters even laugh out loud? It didn't seem likely. Tess, Alan, and Russell kept their faces against the rich earth as they listened to a male and female Elite speaking in their own language as they passed right in front of them. The tone was playful, almost animated.

Tess risked a peek once the sound faded. She lifted her head a fraction of an inch, just enough to see above the grass. The Reapers on the other side of the road remained in place, now with their heads bowed low. The two Elite receded from her. They were both young adults, radiant skin the color of sand on the shores of Cape Cod, white robes flowing around them—a stunning contrast to the backdrop of grimy, defeated Reapers lining the path.

The two Elite took no notice of the others, enjoying themselves as if they were out for a Sunday stroll in the park. They each flaunted a dazzling display of lights and symbols, radiating a spectral glow around them. At this moment, they looked like gods come down from heaven. Could they be the same ones who committed the atrocities?

Only after the two Elite had long passed did the Reapers along the side of the road dare to lift their heads. Most shuffled away to return to whatever task they had been doing. Some would first sigh or grimace. Their subjugation came across with every movement in their bodies.

Tess sat up to view the two Elites as they walked away. They continued to talk in their language and occasionally chuckle over something. The man came to a stop and turned. Tess froze as he looked at her. His slate-gray eyes studied her, his face showing no expression. "Get down," Russell whispered. But she had lost all capacity to move. His stare bore into her, taking control of her awareness.

Time stopped. She heard nothing, only saw his face. Would death come next? Cal had been clear: the Elite kill all outsiders.

The figure in white frowned, his eyebrows scrunching

together. His self-assurance of a moment ago vanished, replaced with confusion.

The Elite female had continued walking forward, unaware that he had stopped. She turned and said something in their language. Even though the speech was unintelligible, it sounded playful, almost chiding. He blinked, as if coming out of a trance of his own. A smile spread across his face and he answered the girl, turning again to stroll beside her. They renewed their march through the squalid sections of the Reaper town and soon were out of sight.

Tess sucked in air with a gulp, realizing she had not taken a breath since he had spotted her. "What the hell, Tess?" said Russell. "What just happened to you?"

She blinked. "I—I don't know. He looked at me and I froze." She shook her head. "No—something more happened. I felt as if he had put a spell on me."

"What were they doing here?" Alan muttered. "The music, the Reapers lining the path, it was almost like a parade."

Russell shrugged. "I suspect it was another way to exact obedience from the workers. Maybe a few of those Elite prance through the town from time to time, while they force the others to pay their respects by standing along the road and bowing their heads as a sign of their submission."

Alan sat up a little straighter, still reluctant to stand. "The real question is why he did nothing once he saw you. Your Reaper friend said they kill outsiders."

Tess furrowed her eyebrows. "He's not my friend. And don't say that again." Both Alan and Russell grinned. "What?" she demanded. "Just because he's the only one who has talked to us, he's no better off than the rest. If he were our friend, he would help us right now." She fixed her eyes on them, daring them to disagree.

Alan replied sheepishly. "You're right. It's only that we've noticed the way you look at him."

Tess opened her mouth and then closed it again. "I'm not even going to respond to that."

She stood and looked around, expecting the Reapers to have returned to their tasks. Many did, but a handful of them still stood along the side of the road, looking at her with interest. This was the first time they didn't pretend the three of them were invisible. Tess frowned. "Will you look at that."

Alan whistled a breath. "Odd. I wish I knew whether this was a good sign, or a warning of something unpleasant to happen."

"Yea, that would be nice to know," Russell agreed.

More warning signs would take place. Yet, Tess's dogged determination to help the peasant Reapers would color every choice she would make.

THE WORK GANG IN THE ORCHARD BEGAN PUTTING away their ladders and tools as the sun lowered on the horizon. Tess, Alan, and Russell watched from the other end of the field as they sat under one of the fruit trees. Russell elbowed Tess. "Look there," he pointed. "Isn't that—"

"Mara," Tess finished for him, the girl from their first day in the muddy fields.

The young girl waved to the work crew as she strolled toward the three of them. She was alone, smiling as she approached. Her grin widened and the unreadable symbols came to life around her when she reached a few feet from them. "Cal said I would find you here."

Tess huffed, holding back a retort. Her voice was gentle as she responded. "It's good to see you again, Mara." In an icy tone, she added, "Does he have a problem with us being here?"

The girl looked confused. "Why would he? He wants me to bring you somewhere."

Tess frowned. "Where? Why?"

She giggled. "He also said you would ask too many questions." She looked at Tess sideways. "He sure knows a lot about you, seeing as how you just came here." The girl shrugged. "Anyway, he said to tell you that the three of you should follow me before you start—hmm, how did he put it?" Her face creased as she tried to remember. "Oh, yeah, before you begin an interrogation."

Tess set her hands on her hips. "Well, you can tell him I don't enjoy being ordered around. I'm not doing anything he says until I know more."

Mara frowned, but didn't respond. Russell stepped closer to Tess and placed his hand on her shoulder. "Let's be rational about this. Cal is the only one who has offered some advice, as little as it's been. Maybe we should at least find out what he wants. It's not like we have something pressing to do."

Tess pursed her lips, looking at Russell and then the girl. "Why didn't he come here himself to ask? Besides, how do we know this isn't a trap and you're not planning to deliver us to the Elite?"

Her eyes grew wide. "Because I wouldn't do that. I like you. And he works now; he has double quota because he provides for mom."

Tess's face softened. "Oh. All right, Mara. I suppose I should be more trusting of you, maybe even of him. You lead the way."

Mara beamed. "Oh, good. I think this will make you happy."

Tess stepped alongside Mara as they crossed the field and moved through the streets of the Reaper town. "Cal is not your father, is he?" she asked.

"No, silly. He is my uncle. My mom, Astra, is his sister."

"Oh, I was wondering," said Tess.

They traveled through an unfamiliar area of the town, a section they hadn't explored yet. Tess had avoided investigating most of the Reaper village, fearful of being assaulted in the narrow, crowded pathways. Even accompanied by the young girl, the three newcomers paid attention to the dark recesses between the shanties lining the dirt-covered streets. Mara moved without hesitancy, someone born to the village, taking one turn after another.

As they walked, Tess asked, "Mara, can you tell me more about those lights and symbols around your people?"

"It's the Directive," she answered, as if that explained everything.

"What purpose does it serve?" Alan asked, suddenly interested in the conversation.

She shrugged. "It's just a part of me." She looked at him. "Like your face is a part of you."

The three exchanged puzzled glances. Russell asked, "But what do you use it for?"

She tilted her head as if trying to understand the question. "The Directive is something in each one of us. Everyone has a different one. It is how we communicate to the rest of the Reapers. It tells us how to speak in your language. Even that is a small part. It is our life, and without it, we cannot exist."

"Is it a thing you are born with, or do you learn it?" Tess asked.

"It is part of us from birth. We all have it, both Reapers and Elite. I can see you do not have one. Other outsiders have come here in the past, and they lack it as well."

The three remained quiet for a time, thinking about her explanation. Other villagers streamed by them, some acknowledging Mara with a smile or greeting. But Tess, Alan, and Russell might as well be invisible.

"Here we are," Mara announced, coming to a stop before a shack that was indistinguishable from the others in the town.

"Here, where?" asked Russell.

She pointed to the dwelling. Like all the rest, it looked as if it might blow away in a strong wind. "Cal said you can have it." She frowned. "It's not much, but it is vacant. The prior residents, well, they were not careful. Or maybe they were stupid. Either way, they don't need it any longer." Her smile returned. "And it will give you a place to stay rather than the orchards during cool nights or when it rains."

Alan stepped forward to look inside an opening that served as a window. He wrinkled his nose. "No, thanks. I'd sooner sleep in the fields."

Mara giggled. "Cal thought one of you might also say that. He told me to explain that if you turn down this offer, it will be the last gift you will receive from him." She raised her eyebrows, waiting for their reply.

The three exchanged nervous glances. Tess finally spoke. "In that case, tell your uncle Cal that we accept with gratitude."

She clapped her hands. "Yea!" She cupped her hand on one side of her mouth as if to convey a secret. "I didn't want to mention that as a reward, I get cake for desert tonight."

Alan groaned. "Tricked by a child. Has it come to this?"

9

GOING NATIVE

A mixture of muck, grease, and other assortments of grime covered most of their clothes and much of their faces by the time they had finished. Before they had started, the shelter was barely livable, no doubt because the prior residents had—by the look of the place—abandoned it a while ago. Dirt was everywhere, bugs had taken refuge inside, and it had no running water, although probably most Reaper hovels didn't either. On the plus side, it contained a small stove, a few chipped plates, silverware, and two tiny rooms. The furniture included a wooden box, which served as a kitchen table, and two rickety chairs.

They did much of the cleaning on their hands and knees, washing the mud-caked wooden floors and walls with hand brushes they had found in a cabinet. They had already discovered the communal wells located through the town, and now they took turns carrying one bucket after another of clean water for their task.

Considering the filthy condition of the shack when Mara first showed it to them, it would have been easy for the three to fall into a malaise, bemoaning their fate. Strangely, the opposite had happened. Once they had scoured the two rooms, smiles replaced sullen expressions, even with Alan, who had pitched in to help as much as Tess and Russell. They finally had something to do. Here was an accomplishment they could point to and say, "We did this." And after sleeping in the fields, it was a place they could call their own: here was a dwelling with a roof over their heads.

"It may be a ramshackle of a home, but it's something, a beginning of sorts," Tess said, admiring their work once they had finished. She gazed at the others. "We're going to get through this. Nothing has made sense, so far, but I feel it will get better. It has to."

Once done, the river that passed on the other side of the village afforded a place to wash the sweat and grime off their bodies and clothes. It wasn't private, but they had little choice. They left their garments to dry on rocks in a sunny spot, and then returned to the new home refreshed, clean, and invigorated for the first time since their arrival.

As the day's light was dimming, Cal arrived. Tapping once on the flimsy door, he opened it without waiting for an answer. Casting an appraising look around the room, his face broke into a smile. "I have to admit, I didn't think you had it in you."

"What's that supposed to mean?" Tess shot back.

He held up his hands in mock defense. "Hold on, you can't blame me. This is the first work I've seen from you three." He furrowed his brow. "You cleaned this yourself? Right?"

"Yes, we did," Tess responded, her hands balled into fists. "This place was a mess, and we—"

"Tess, be nice," Russell interrupted. "He didn't have to provide this to us."

She glared at Russell for a moment and let out a breath. "You're right, Rusty." Gazing back at Cal, she said, "Thank you for this house." Adding in a whisper, "Although it made no difference to him."

He smirked, pleased with her comment. "I assume Mara told you that the former residents departed in a hurry. They didn't have time to tidy up, and it's been vacant since."

"Well, thank you anyway," said Tess. "We don't intend to stay for long, but it will be nice not sleeping in the fields."

He tilted his head. "Oh? I had assumed you wanted to be here because you were fleeing from somewhere worse."

She barked a laugh. "Worse than this hellhole? I don't think that's possible. No, we came here voluntarily because someone... err, something asked our help to make things right. A stone statue spoke to us. It had the name of Elthea on it, and the voice told us the people here needed our aid. Seeing what's happening here, I believe we're supposed to assist you Reapers from the oppression you're under."

He stared at her, his brow furrowed in thought. "Is that so? Well, tell me now, just how do you plan to accomplish this good deed?"

She blinked, hesitating a long second before answering. "We'll know when the time comes."

"So, you don't have a plan, do you?" He stared at Tess, daring her to disagree. Before she could frame an answer, he continued. "I'll tell you what, if you manage to stay alive for a time, then we can talk about you freeing us from this oppression, as you call it. Maybe by then, you can come up with an idea on how to accomplish it."

Tess looked like she was about to smack him in the face, but Russell said, "Cal, you've been very kind to us so far. Maybe you can help us with this bit about staying alive."

His smile broadened. "In case you haven't noticed, that's what I've been doing." His eyes swept around the room. "What you needed most was a place to hole up, and now you have it. Listen to my advice and possibly you will stay alive for a while longer. Do something stupid like stick your head up when an Elite walks by, and you will find it detached from the rest of your body. And by the way, that Elite happened to be the Prime Elite, our supreme ruler."

Tess squirmed. "Oh, you know about that?"

"Lady, my business is to know what is going on here. That is how I stay alive."

Alan cleared his throat. "Getting back to that issue of staying alive, will you agree to help us while we figure out how to save you from the Elite?"

He thought about it for a moment. "I will if you do as I say. But understand this: I'm not willing to risk my life for you. Neither will I put any of my kin in harm's way."

"We'll listen to you within reason," Tess responded.

He stepped closer, invading her personal space. Tess refused to back away, not giving him the satisfaction of knowing he intimidated her. Cal was a half-foot taller than Tess as he stared her down. His breath held a trace of peppermint, and his dark eyes locked onto hers. The small physical differences between Reapers and humans had already faded from her thoughts. He spoke without rancor. "Just so we are clear, you do anything to harm us, and you will not have to worry about the Elite. I will kill you myself."

Tess swallowed, unable to hurl a retort. He moved toward the door, glancing back before he left. "Here is my first instruction. Stay inside for now. I will be back later with something warm to eat." Looking Tess up and down, he added, "You don't look the type to put together much of a meal. Plus, I don't want you burning down this place trying to figure out how to use that stove. Wait until I return before you try to light it."

He stepped away, muttering loud enough for them to hear, "The trouble I get myself into."

DARKNESS OVERTOOK THE VILLAGE, LEAVING THE three of them to sit alone in an unlit room. A ray of moonlight from the half-full larger moon was their only illumination. They were sitting on the floor, backs against the wall, when Cal burst into the room with the radiance from an oil lantern he carried. "Glad you haven't wandered off," he said with a half grin.

They tensed as another person followed Cal into the cabin. He held a steaming kettle and something wrapped in cloth. The aroma of cinnamon from the kettle filled the air before he stepped across the threshold.

Cal set the lantern on the stove as he introduced the guest. "This is my uncle, Brent." Strands of gray hair creased his temples, identified him as older than Cal, even though he maintained a youthful appearance. He took stock of them for a moment as the squiggly symbols and grids sprang to life. "Mara spoke well of you. I was curious and wanted to find out for myself." He glanced around the room. "Mind if I?"

"Please," Tess replied, offering him one of the two chairs. He placed the kettle and bundle on the knee-high box table before sitting.

"Hmm, smells good," Alan said as he eyed the pot. "Who's the cook?"

"My wife, Des," Brent replied. "You haven't had a warm meal since you arrived here, and I guess it might be about time."

Tess regarded him warily. "Why the change of heart? Everyone has avoided us like the plague."

He chuckled. "We are not fond of strangers. Part of our learning experience, you could say."

"So I've been told," she replied.

He motioned to the kettle. "We can talk while we eat."

Cal produced bowls and spoons from his pockets while Brent opened the cover. Chunks of beef and a mix of colored vegetables and potatoes floated in a thick brown sauce. Brent ladled the stew into each bowl, while Cal uncovered the cloth bundle to reveal a crusty dark bread, which he began cutting into slices. Conversation took a pause while Tess, Alan, and Russell concentrated on their first warm meal in weeks, all other thoughts forgotten for the moment.

After giving them time to enjoy the meal, Brent asked, "Strangers rarely show up in our village, but your arrival was especially unusual. According to Mara, and other Reapers, you simply appeared. One second she saw only empty space, and the next, you took shape. If you don't mind me asking, how were you able to accomplish it?" Tess was about to answer, but he raised a finger. "And also, can you move at will through space by appearing anywhere you wish?"

Tess wiped her lips with the back of her hand. "It was as much of a shock to me as it was to Mara. Another, I guess you would say another entity brought us here."

He nodded. "That would be a helpful little trick if you could do it at will. But this other entity, from your discussion with Cal, you had said it was called Elthea. And it was some sort of sculpture?"

"Yes, that was the name on its base. I've since found out from Cal that Elthea is the name of this world."

"Cal also tells me you believe you are here to help us Reapers."

She shot a glance at the unusually silent Cal as he allowed Brent to take the lead in this discussion, which was feeling more like an interview. She pursed her lips. "I only know what we were told before coming here. This statue told us to right a wrong. I see an injustice being committed against the Reapers."

Brent nodded, looking at Russell and Alan. "And you are prone to doing what an entity tells you, even if it brought you to another place to help those you never heard about before?"

Russell barked a laugh. "You have to understand, Tess can be impulsive. But to her credit, that particular statue and place held a certain significance for her. And once Tess disappeared, Al and I felt obligated to follow to be sure she was safe."

Brent smiled at Russell's response. He cast a sideway glance at Cal. "Yes, my friend here knows what it is like to be impulsive."

Alan maintained his full attention to the bowl of stew, showing no sign he was listening to the conversation. Before Brent could continue, Tess said, "Can I ask you a question?" When he nodded, she continued, "How are the Elite able to control you Reapers? Except for clothing, it seems you are the same race."

"We are the same clan," Brent answered. "Through the generations, we've become two distinct classes, a matter of selective breeding. You must have noticed the difference between us?"

After receiving blank stares from the others, he explained. "The Directive is more robust in the Elite. You can see the distinction without needing to know the power within it. We cannot exist without our Directive, and because the Elite are much more powerful, they can extract it from any Reaper. I believe you have already seen an example of how this works."

Alan perked up at this. "Can you please explain this Directive? I still don't get it."

"It is everything to us, bound to our core, and possibly unique to our race." He rubbed his hand across his beard. "Where to start? Think of it as an extension of our mind, a sort of shared repository with information. Since each Directive is exclusive for each one of us, others can examine its makeup and understand family relations, events in one's life, feelings, many things about that individual. We use it to predict the weather, and it provides glimpses into our destiny, at least generally."

"Are you saying it predicts the future?" Alan asked.

"Broad sweeps, not specific incidents that might happen. Fate has a way of messing it up. When I walk out of here tonight, an Elite may end my life for no other reason than he is in a bad mood. I cannot predict that."

Alan placed his now empty bowl on the floor next to him. He often became animated when speaking about a subject that excited him. This was one of those times, as his hands moved with his voice. "How is that possible? What makes it work? Tell us about the things you can see in the future. What about us? How do we get out of here and back home?"

Brent smiled as the glowing symbols continued to float around both him and Cal. "Don't ask me how the Directive works, it just does. But when considering the future, we risk placing too much stock in its predictions. Events it foretells may not come to pass in the way we have expected. You or I may interpret it differently, and neither of us may be correct."

Alan's voice took on a higher pitch. "Still, this is quite amazing. What can you tell us about what lies ahead?"

Brent didn't answer right away. He exchanged a glance with Cal as he considered what to say. Finally, he spoke, his voice taking a hushed tone. "I can tell you this. From the time of my father and his father before him, the Directive has shown us a convergence of events that will change life as we know it. For us Reapers, this has become a legend, something that gives us hope. Most of us believe we are approaching a juncture of great significance. Some interpret it as a sign of our liberation from the Elite."

He paused again, his eyes raking over them. What did he see in them? "Not every Reaper believes our redemption is at hand. There are some who claim we will face even greater hardships. Which brings me to the three of you."

"What do you mean?" asked Tess.

"You will play a part in the pivotal events that will

change our lives. That is clear. What remains murky is whether you will aid us, or if your actions lead us to ruin."

His words hung in the air long after he had departed.

LONG AFTER THEIR VISITORS DEPARTED, THE THREE remained quiet, content to listen to the crackle of wood in the stove and take pleasure in its warmth. Before they left, Brent and Cal had lit a fire and provided instructions on its use. At last, they would not have to spend another damp, chilly night in the fields.

Alan broke the silence. "Tess, you realize we have no hope of improving the lives of these peasants. No matter what Brent said he sees in the Directive, the Elite are in total control."

"I feel the same," Russell added. "I don't understand how the Elite control the Reapers, beyond being able to take away their Directive, but their rule appears to be absolute. Al is right. What can we possibly accomplish?"

Tess chewed her fingernails as she listened. She looked at one and then the other before speaking. "The problem is that we haven't figured them out yet."

Russell threw his hands in the air. "We've been observing them for weeks. How much more can we expect to discover?"

She shook her head. "No, we're outsiders. We're not one of them, living their lives with their hopes and dreams. We've caught glimpses into their emotions, but that's not enough. Until we are part of this community, we can't hope to fully understand or to change it."

Alan sat up straighter. "We will always be an outsider, Tess. We can never have a Directive, and without it, we will never be one of them."

"True," she replied. "But we can do a better job of understanding their feelings if we were one of them. We need to understand this hold the Elite have over them."

Russell and Alan looked at her blankly.

"We have to go native," she blurted.

Alan groaned. "I'm liking this idea less with each passing minute. Never mind going native, for the millionth time, Tess, how are we ever going to get back home?"

Her face softened. "I'm sorry, Alan—and to you, Rusty. I never thought this would happen. And once here, well, now we have no choice. We need to play it out in a way that fulfills the wish of that voice at the statue. We must right what is wrong. Maybe then we'll find a way back. That's all I can offer."

Alan hung his head, but Russell smiled sadly. "Don't worry, Al, we'll get through this. After all, we're still a team, and we have to stick together now more than ever. Right?"

Alan raised his head, and his eyes brightened as he nodded. Seeing this, Tess moved over and embraced them both.

Their intentions were noble, these three lost souls in an unfamiliar world. Yet, they still had no idea of the storm they would one day unleash on an unsuspecting universe.

10

THE SOUND OF A THOUSAND VOICES

The elation of spending the night in their new home soon subsided. They discovered the fields might be cool during the evenings, but the grass offered a soft cushion, unlike this hard, unforgiving wooden floor. How had the prior occupants slept without beds?

Tess rose as the first light brightened the chamber. She stepped softly as she stretched aching limbs. Russell and Alan sat up soon after, neither of them looking rested. She put on a cheerful face. "I hope you're ready. We have a big work day ahead of us."

"You're not still serious about going through with this idea, are you?" Alan moaned.

Her smile widened at his surly mood. "I'll tell you what, Al. You can pick the work crew we'll join. Does that make you feel better?"

"No."

"Okay then, how about we help out the workers in the flooded fields by picking berries?"

Alan raised his hands. "Definitely not. We wouldn't last an hour there."

"We agreed to do this, Alan."

He exhaled a puff of breath. "I didn't agree with anything. But if we have to pick one, I say we join that crew working in the orchard where we slept most nights. At least it's dry and shady there."

"Okay, done."

Several orchards surrounded the town, and by the time they found one with a crew working it, the Reapers were already in full swing, with a dozen adults on top of ladders and a greater number of children already hard at work.

"Seems simple enough," said Tess after observing them for a moment. She pointed. "Each of us can grab a basket from that pile there and bring it back full." Russell and Alan followed her, walking a little less enthusiastically. They selected a tree that wasn't being worked and began picking the red and yellow fruits.

The other Reapers ignored them, a practice the three expected. After filling each container, they carried them back to the spot where the Reapers were collecting their quota. The companions earned a few surreptitious glances from the work crew after they had left their full baskets with the others.

By midday, the work crew had stopped for a rest. A few ladies, presumably wives of some crew members, brought containers of food for them. Tess suggested they pause as well.

"Seven years of college and here I am picking fruit from trees," Alan grumbled. "My mom would be so proud of me."

Tess smirked. "Tell me the truth, Al. Doesn't it feel a little good digging in and helping rather than feeling sorry for ourselves? Just like yesterday when we cleaned the house, we were doing something productive."

"No, I'd be happier sitting around moping and bemoaning my fate," he said with a smile. "And I'll tell you what else would feel good, I'd enjoy another tasty meal, like the one from Brent and Cal last night. I'm so sick of eating only fruit or greens we find in the fields. Would decent food be too much to ask?"

"You have food on your brain," she responded. "Ever since I've known you, that's been your chief priority in life. We have more important things to deal with now."

"Hey, check this out," Russell interrupted. He gazed at the work crew. Three young children approached, each carrying a small bundle. More significantly, the youngsters had fixed their attention upon the three. They advanced cautiously, as if any sudden movement would send them scurrying for safety.

Tess, Alan, and Russell tensed. "You don't think it's a bomb or something, do you?" Russell mumbled.

"Why would they..." Tess said to herself.

Russell stood, looking as if he was about to flee in the

opposite direction. "Maybe we violated one of their customs. We still know nothing about them."

At twenty feet away, the oldest girl among the children held her arm out to block the others from walking closer. They bent their knees to place the packages on the ground. Once accomplished, they turned and ran back to their families.

"This doesn't feel right," said Alan. They were all standing now, ready for anything. "Let's run. Quick. Those things might explode." He began backing away, and Russell followed his example.

Tess shot a glance at them before staring at the bundles covered in some sort of paper. The children were still scurrying back toward the others. An older man in the work crew caught her attention. He was the only one looking directly at her. Tess had already singled him out as the leader of this crew because he was the one always directing the workers.

A slight smile came to him, accentuating the wrinkles on his face. The man had a grandfatherly look about him. He touched the rim of his broad-rimmed hat, as if tipping it to her, before turning his attention back to his companions. The man's gesture might have gone unnoticed during normal situations, but here it carried the weight of a momentous change. These workers still risked death by associating with outsiders, but their attitudes had softened.

"They wouldn't harm us," said Tess. "They've ignored us, but they're not hurtful."

Alan grunted as if to disagree. She paid no attention to

him as she crept toward the packages. Russell and Alan stayed where they were. She bent over to uncover a bundle and smiled, holding it up for them to see. "They provided lunch."

The offering might have been minor, but the Reapers had taken the initial step. More aid would follow, but like a first love, this would be the one they would always remember.

Their meal contained a mixture of greens and pieces of meat with a savory sauce wrapped within pliant bread. Tess gazed at the workers at the other end of the field, for the first time seeing them differently. What she had taken for an unsympathetic attitude was their way of staying alive. She understood what Cal had been telling her: harboring outsiders put all Reapers in danger, and they didn't want to risk it.

Yet now, after weeks without a decent meal, the Reapers provided them with food, both last evening and now today. It was a simple act of kindness that meant so much.

The emotional gap between humans and Reapers had narrowed. More than ever, she believed they were benevolent, a conviction that would cloud all her decisions going forward.

THE SUN-DRENCHED ORCHARD GREW DIM. A SPATIAL shift took place, as if sitting within an auto or train that was gathering speed. When the sensation ended, we were back in Tess's garden room. She opened her eyes, serene as ever, with only the slightest tightening of her brow indicating her unease. Her focus was still far away, thinking about the events we had just witnessed.

Of all the people I knew, Tess was the most even-tempered. Rarely did she act recklessly or erratically. She carried herself with confidence and an inner calmness, yet the Farseeing revealed a new aspect of her temperament. Her fervor and zeal came across more clearly when she was younger. Her daughter Rae has many of those same qualities from Tess's youth.

My thoughts were also far away. Much like remembering a dream upon waking, I wanted to cement the vision in my memory. "I'm still puzzled," I said. "What does this race have to do with the Bots? Did the Elite become the monsters out there? Did they exterminate the Reapers?"

A sad smile came to her. "Evolution doesn't happen with a snap of a finger, does it? You have more to see."

She wouldn't explain further. The Farseeing was my idea, and I needed to play it out. She would not spoil it by describing what had happened.

She stood. "I'm tired of sitting. Why don't we continue this again later today?"

She walked me to the door, and I paused, gripping the handle. Once again, my doubts about the Farseeing rose to the surface. "Tess, tell me now. Do you believe this is a gigantic waste of time? So far, everything you've shown me hasn't helped."

She let out a soft breath. "I don't know, but without hope, you surely will not save your friends. Cling to it, and maybe you will find the solution you seek. It's all I can offer you right now. You might yet see something beneficial in the past."

I nodded, not convinced. Time was running short for my friends, and soon the Bots would subsume what still remained of their humanity. How long could they remain with their human memories and emotions?

Once outside, an irresistible urge came over me to see Cassie as she was when life seemed so much simpler. With the power of Farseeing, I could be with her, and with Matt and Diane, reliving a day when we were together at Woodbery College. What did they think of me now? Did they hate me for what I had caused?

The pull to live in the past was tempting, but the Oakenrill's warning was stronger. "If you live your life in bygone times, the attraction of today's world will pale," he had said. That road would lead to my ruin, as if I needed another way to mess up my life.

Before I realized it, Bevon and Quintia fell in line on each side of me as I strode forward, still unsure where I was going. "You realize I don't need an honor guard within the town," I quipped.

Quintia smirked. "You misuse the phrase, Earthfriend. Honor guard implies a ceremonial role. We have saved your life before, and we will do so again if necessary."

Bevon chuckled. "Perhaps he believes he has become all-powerful and no longer has a need for us. Maybe he forgets we enjoy his company, as flawed as he is."

Quintia narrowed her eyes as she regarded me. "I suppose his behavior has been quirky at times."

I smiled and placed my hands on each of their shoulders as we continued walking. "If my head ever becomes too big, I know I can count on you to kick some sense into me."

Bevon leaned forward so he could catch Quintia's eye. "You may not have understood that because of the human colloquialisms he often uses. He is rife with them."

I smiled more broadly, realizing what they were doing. With my attention fixated on saving my friends, I had paused the rest of my life, including time with my other companions. Bevon, Quintia, and Riyaad knew when to lighten the mood.

Several blocks ahead of us, someone shouted my name, putting an end to our banter. "Master Philip. Come quickly." Torermak stood a dozen buildings away, waving at us. The giant Stonewraith—another friend I had ignored—was two feet taller than most humans. His race knew more about this land than almost everyone else. Why hadn't I sought his advice about bringing back my friends? What quirk of personality always made me believe I had to do this all on my own? Was it because I had botched things up in the first place by giving the Bots a soul?

We quickened our pace as we trotted forward. He regarded me with a thoughtful expression as we approached. He always gave me the impression he was looking inside me, observing my core, seeing the substance that made me who I was.

Perhaps he could. After all, he was the one who first explained that the Bots had tainted me. It was a time before I realized how to control Elthea's energies. He studied me now, even as we stood before him.

"Well?" Bevon demanded. "What is it?"

Torermak blinked, breaking his stare. When he spoke, his tone was more somber than normal. "They gather."

A chill passed through me. Before I could say anything, Quintia asked, "Who gathers?" But I already knew.

Torermak never took his eyes off me. "An army gathers. A swarm of Bots have congregated in the woods beyond the fields."

Bevon instinctively grabbed his retractable blade, pulling it out of the holster at his waist. "Are they massing for an attack?"

The Stonewraith glanced at the Astari. He shook his head. "I don't believe so, although the village Guard thinks differently. The soldiers are preparing a defense against an assault. With the wall only partially restored, they have an arduous task."

My body tensed, hearing the conversation as if from far away.

"What do they want?" Quintia blurted.

Torermak didn't answer. They knew the reason, even Quintia. The only time the Bots had ever approached Haven was because of me. I was the antithesis of their hopes and desires. They would never leave me alone. And now, with my ability to draw upon Elthea's power, I had become a tool for them to conquer worlds. "They're here for me," I said without realizing I had spoken out loud.

Nobody responded, confirming my belief.

The road ahead ended in a jumble of rubble, the place where the wall had once stood. An apparition of the future came to me in my mind's eye: Bots clawing their way over the top of the wreckage—hundreds of them—intent on taking me alive, killing any human attempting to stop them. "It's no use opposing them. My friends are beyond saving—I have to accept it. Unless I capitulate, they'll overrun Haven, killing innocent villagers. The Bots will stop at nothing."

Forcing my legs to move, I took a step toward the mangled wall, but Bevon stepped in front of me. "You give in now and your friends are surely dead. You are their only hope. Do not take that away from them."

Damn him. Why was he always right? Once again, I faced the same quandary: submit to the Bots or suffer the loss of my companions. Bevon didn't move, waiting for a response. "How do you expect me to stop them? Killing them would weaken the Spirit of Elthea. I had tried giving them something—a soul—hoping they would believe in the goodness of life. That only made things worse as they turned my friends into monsters." I raised my voice. "What else can I do? I have nothing left."

Bevon's expression remained impassive as he considered my plea. Several heartbeats passed before he spoke.

"This is a decision only you can make. As the most powerful individual in this world, only you can decide. But realize this: many others now depend upon you. If you surrender to the Bots, one day they will kill us all, or worse, enslave us. Maybe not today or tomorrow, but they will never leave us alone. And then nobody will stand a chance against them. These villagers, all the other races, your friends, none of us will survive when the Bots decide to move against us. You will not be here to prevent it."

He held my gaze for another moment before stepping aside to let me pass. Taking a shaky breath, I noticed that both Torermak and Quintia watched me with what seemed like a mix of pity and respect. "Let's go see what our enemy is doing," I said. "Maybe we can discern their intentions."

We walked toward the outskirts of the town, past the rubble of the collapsed wall, to join The Guard and the reserve volunteers who vowed to give their lives to protect the village. Rae stood a few dozen paces away, and we exchanged a grim nod. I looked out across the wide field, baffled to see it was empty without a sign of the Bots. It took me a while until I discerned them from the backdrop of trees at the edge of the fields.

There they were, hundreds of them, waiting for what was to come. Did they even know why they were here? Were Cassie, Matt, and Diane among them, and if so, did they remember their past lives?

Torermak broke my trance. "You have given them a

soul, yet I fear they want more. I sense the gift of a soul does not satisfy them."

I lifted my eyes toward him. "What else can I possibly give them? I'm the only thing they want."

He shook his head. "If that were true, they would come for you now. Yet, they linger in the woods, waiting. But for what?"

I took a calming breath as the Oakenrill had taught me, focusing my attention on the horde across the field. Ever so slowly, their voices penetrated my awareness. But this was unlike the pounding, throbbing sound of the Bots speaking in my head. A collective murmuring came to me, as if I was listening to their raw, unfiltered thoughts.

None of the verbalizations made sense. They did not string together their garbled words into cohesive sentences. The voices soon grew urgent. They knew I was observing them, and it was as if each Bot was trying to be heard above the others.

The clamor became overwhelming. Putting my hands to my ears, I tried to block the noise. The sound only intensified further while my friends looked at me with alarm. Bevon grasped my shoulders. "What is wrong, Earthfriend? Tell me."

He didn't understand that the Bots and I were bound together. Torermak knew. He reached down, yanked me off the ground until I was eye level with him, and shook me. "Use your mind and your power to unhook yourself from them. You began the contact, you can end it." He shook me again. "Concentrate."

My world was spinning, partially because of him jiggling me like a rag doll, but his words broke through the racket in my head. I tried to focus, even as I felt reality slip away. Pulling on a weave of power, all I needed was a trickle, I grasped a strand to break the link. Nothing happened. The blaring was consuming me, blotting out my awareness.

This would take more than a fragment of energy. Reaching deeper, I drew upon an inner strength, dampening the voices until they grew silent. The hush washed over me as my senses became numb. The feeling was pleasant, and I didn't want to resist. Better to be deprived of feelings than overcome with emotions.

I gave in and felt no more.

11

THE DARK PIT

A horde of figures pursued me. These were no ordinary beings, not born of this world. They were apparitions of my worst fears come to dispatch me.

No matter what direction I turned, they followed. I tried to run faster, but my legs were leaden and those pursuing me were nimble. Unable to flee, the swarm surrounded me, a mass of faceless, murky, swirling shapes.

My heart pounded, knowing death is what they craved. Or was it something worse? Would I become one of them, a hideous monster for the rest of my existence?

They had already taken everyone else, each person I had ever known and loved had turned into one of them. And I was the only one left. They would never let me go.

I took a ragged breath as I swung a blade to keep them at bay. How long could I last? The alternative was to become a savage, gruesome beast, which is what they were.

Never would I let that happen. Their hatred emanated in waves, nearly overwhelming me with a foul stench.

What began as a buzz in my head now became louder. I realized they were screaming, their words lost in the cacophony of voices. Although I couldn't understand what they were saying, their tone left no doubt they were furious. All their loathing was directed at me.

Cornered, I turned to face them. Maybe I could blast them out of existence. Hadn't I done that once? I felt my pulse quicken with excitement as I reached for the unearthly strength to annihilate them forever.

At the last moment, something held me back. No, I shouldn't kill them, but I wasn't sure why. All I knew was that a terrible outcome would result if I ever unleashed my force to destroy them.

Slimy hands began tugging at me. The creatures were trying to pull me into a black pit which had appeared at my feet. No light escaped from that darkness. I kicked at the demons, still unable to see their faces. They remained hidden in shadows.

"Who are you? What do you want?"

They became more vehement, their cries more intense. Slowly, my feet slid closer to the pit. There would be no escape from that chasm once I entered. My arms flailed, legs thrashing against the hands clawing at my ankles.

Then I sensed, more than saw, another presence. It was that of Cassie, Matt, and Diane. The three dark shapes stood out from the rest. They were bigger, stronger, more powerful than the others. Did they come to save me?

My spirits brightened. They would never allow me to be taken by this mob.

Yet, now they clawed at my legs like the rest, intent on pulling me into the abyss. How could they be in league with my attackers?

"What are you doing?" I screamed. "It's me, Phil. Can't you see?"

My friends didn't answer or react to my plea. Did they know it was me, or did they even care? I stumbled and fell onto my backside, still trying to dislodge the grip my friends had on my ankles.

They were too strong, unnaturally strong, as they pulled me closer to the inky blackness of the open pit. What did they want from me? These were people I loved.

I looked into the pit again and felt a terror emanating from it that was worse than death. They were about to toss me in, and I could do nothing to stop them.

I screamed like never before.

A CRY DIED ON MY LIPS AS I OPENED MY EYES TO A curtain of light streaming into my room. I was sitting up in bed, covered in sweat, my muscles still twitching from the nightmare.

What was I doing here? The last thing I remembered, I was observing the army of Bots surrounding the town. That had been midday, but now the sun cast long shadows across the floor. Was it early morning or late afternoon?

The door to my room burst open as the Astari, Riyaad, charged in with his sword drawn. His eyes wild, he swung the blade in a defensive position, expecting an attack from any corner. I pressed myself flat against the bed, hoping he wouldn't swing the thing near me.

Once he realized nobody else was in the area, he lowered the weapon, but did not sheath it. He looked at me and frowned. "I heard you shout a warning and thought someone had assaulted you."

He must have been standing guard outside the room. Still troubled by the bad dream, I took a breath before responding. "Sorry, Riyaad. I guess I was dreaming." I glanced at the low-hanging sun, realizing from the position that it was early morning. "What happened? I was on the outskirts of the town observing the Bots, and now I'm here. Did I sleep through the night?"

"You have slept since yesterday afternoon, after losing consciousness. Bevon thought it was an intentional act by the Bots, but Torermak convinced him otherwise."

"What about our enemy? Are they still out there?"

He nodded. "They remain as before. More have arrived, swelling their force to thousands. None of them have made a move to assail the town, and the Stonewraith, Torermak, does not believe they are here for that reason. At least not yet."

I shuddered. "Torermak believes they want something more from me than the gift of a soul. That's what he said before I passed out."

Riyaad retracted his blade and hung it at his waist. He gave no sign if he agreed.

"What do you believe? Why do you think they're here?"

He looked at me for a long time without speaking, and I wondered if he had heard my question. Finally, he said, "I sense no hostility from them, which is remarkable considering their past. But something troubles them, and I fear their emotions could boil over. If that happens, who knows how they will react?"

"So, it's as I thought. They want me, although now for a different purpose. What could I give them that's more valuable than a soul?

I didn't expect Riyaad to respond, and he didn't offer a solution. More than ever, it appeared the explanation rested in Tess's Farseeing. Regardless of my misgivings, the answer had to be in their past. "Where's Tess? We need to begin our next session right now." Jumping out of bed, I reached for my shirt, but the movement was too sudden and my vision clouded as the room spun. Riyaad caught me before I fell to the floor.

"You try to do too much, Earthfriend. After your ordeal, you should take it easy. When was the last time you had a meal?" He sniffed. "And you need a bath."

I sat back on the edge of the bed. My vision cleared and the room stopped swirling. Letting out a breath, I gazed outside. The world out there was changing, and somehow I was at the center of it all. Riyaad looked at me, wondering if I would listen to him as I remained seated.

"Okay, my friend. As usual, you're right. I can't do any good if I'm not able to even stand on my two feet."

He smiled. "A wise choice. I will draw the water for a bath and wait outside to accompany you to the mess hall."

The warm water did more than soothe my strained nerves. It gave me time to recover from the voices of the Bots in my head. They had somehow tripped a circuit breaker in my brain, at least that was my explanation about what had happened. Like a sensory overload, my human mind had reacted the only way it could by shutting down. Thank the stars it wasn't permanent.

As promised, Riyaad was waiting in the hallway after I had bathed and changed into clean clothes. "We can still make it in time for the morning meal, but even if we do not, I suspect they would provide something for you."

I smirked. The residents had been treating me like visiting royalty, even though I had done nothing to justify their veneration. "Anything small will be fine," I mumbled, distracted by the lack of activity around the town. "Where is everyone?" It was not early, and by this time, the village would be in full swing, with people coming and going with their daily business.

My question did not surprise him, which told me he knew more than he wanted to reveal. "With the wall not repaired, and with Bots at our perimeter, they have taken precautions. The villagers who are not volunteering to work with The Guard have been asked to remain indoors or stay in protected shelters."

I groaned. Here was yet another reason these people should hate me more than ever.

Riyaad steered me away from the outer edges of the town as he led the way to the dining hall. He wants me to avoid seeing the Bots again. After my failed attempt to reach out to them, he fears I would pursue it again.

Like the other Astari, he was concerned about me. But what other choice did I have if I could learn something, anything, about my friends? I thought about marching out to the broken wall this minute, but a hollow feeling in my stomach told me to take his advice and eat first.

As he surmised, the hall contained a smattering of townsfolk and members of The Guard. The soldiers were bent over in their chairs, many with elbows on tables and talking little after a long shift of duty. A worker noticed our entrance and directed us to one of the vacant round tables. "I'll be right over with a plate, Master Philip."

Eying him and waving politely, I wondered if we had met before. So many lives here now rested on what I would do, yet I hardly knew most of them.

"Have you seen Tess this morning?" I asked Riyaad. "Has she been looking for me? We need to move faster with this Farseeing."

He shook his head. "She has likely heard about your collapse. I am sure she wants to give you space to recover."

"We don't have time," I blurted before thinking about it. Taking a breath, I continued in an even tone, "Events are moving too quickly. We don't know why they're out there. Hell, I don't even know if Tess's Farseeing will do any good." I furrowed my brow. "What if it's a waste of time? Maybe I'm giving the Bots an opportunity to kill everyone here."

He placed his hand on my forearm, an unusual gesture for an Astari. "Calm down, Earthfriend. Your self-doubts threaten to overwhelm you. That has always been your downfall."

He wasn't the first person to tell me that. I took another deep breath as the Oakenrill had taught me. That's when I felt someone approach from behind. "Hello, Philip."

Turning around, I saw Bryson and felt a stab of remorse. I had barely spoken with him since my return to Haven. I jumped up and embraced my traveling companion. After clapping him on the back, I held him at arm's length, noting how much he had changed since our experience in the mountain stronghold of the Nizaem. He now wore the black garments of The Guard. "You look older," I said.

My greeting brought a grin to his lips, even though it seemed a sad smile. Or maybe it was because he was weary. He had the look of someone who hadn't slept well. "You forced me to grow up during that episode in those damn mountains."

"Yea, but I bet the girls around here are giving you more attention after they saw you return on the back of a dragon. Now tell me the truth. Am I right or not?"

His smile broadened, and he shrugged. "Well, maybe a bit. There is one girl..."

I playfully threw a punch at his shoulder. "I'm sorry

we haven't had time to talk much since I returned. Are you a full member of The Guard now?"

He stood a little straighter. "Received my commission soon after we returned." He looked around and lowered his voice. "I suspect Rae had something to do with it. She said if I could survive what we went through, I deserved to be promoted. By the way, did you know she's a captain now?"

I lifted my eyebrows, wondering why she hadn't told me herself. The reason was obvious once I thought about it. Our recent discussions were always about me or getting my friends back. I never took the time to understand her life. It was yet one more entry to add to my increasing list of self-improvement goals. "I'm happy for her. She has the skill for it."

Bryson chuckled, but didn't say more. Here was another way this young lad had matured. I recalled a time when he would babble endlessly about the least important topics.

"Is everyone on guard duty at the perimeter of the town now?" I asked, forcing myself to avoid saying the wall.

He nodded. "We spend most of our time just watching. Nobody knows why the Bots are out there, or what they intend to do. But they've never been friendly in the past, so we're guessing they're not here to help rebuild the wall." He looked at me expectantly, as if asking me to tell him more.

"I don't have any answers either, Bry. Their purpose is

as much of a mystery to me as it is to everyone else. But I'm trying to find an explanation."

The cook returned with a tray full of fruits, cheeses, and breads, along with a small bowl of what looked like oatmeal. He also placed another tray on the table for Riyaad. Bryson put his hand on my shoulder and leaned forward to whisper in my ear. "We're all with you, Phil. Every last member of The Guard. We all know what happened, who they took from you. They know the Bots could do that to any of them. If you need us to help, just give the word."

My throat tightened. Bryson had never been overly sensitive about others' feelings. "Thanks. That means the world to me." I studied him, trying to picture the awkward young man I had known. "You're a good person, Bry. You've come a long way since that scrappy kid I first met. I'm proud of you."

His eyes brightened, and he clapped me again on the shoulder. "I'll let you eat. We'll talk again." He turned to leave, then stopped. "Oh, if you don't mind, can I give you a bit of advice?"

I raised my eyebrows, seeing another example of how he had matured. Providing guidance had never been one of his strengths. "Of course."

He looked a little uneasy. "Well, sir, it's just that the troops, they look up to you. But they don't know you like I do. Maybe if you could say a few words to them in passing, it would go a long way to lifting their spirits. I think they can use it right now."

And there it was. Without realizing it, or understanding how it happened, I had somehow become their messiah. It was yet another cord pulling me in a direction I neither wanted nor asked for.

Bryson waited for a reply, shifting from one foot to the other. During that moment, he looked more like the kid I first met. "It's an honor I don't deserve, but I'm happy to do whatever is possible for these villagers. I owe them a great deal. We'll be going out there, and I'll express my gratitude to as many of the troops as I can."

He smiled as if he were a child who had received a birthday gift. "Thank you."

I watched him leave, wondering if I had played any role in how he had matured beyond his years.

12

WARRIOR AND CHAMPION

Russell Ingram skidded to a stop. In his haste, he had nearly passed the table where Riyaad and I sat as we finished our breakfast. He had just entered the dining hall, and as usual, moved at a brisk pace. As the commander of Haven, he always had some task to administer or attend to, and today was likely busier than most.

"Master Philip. I am so happy to see you awake. You gave everyone a scare." He gestured to an open chair. "May I?"

I nodded, and he took the seat, giving us his complete attention. The gleam in his eyes was so similar to Matt's expression. They were so alike, something I never realized before now. Both were full of positive vigor, invariably making me feel that whenever we talked, I was the most important thing on their mind. Today, I spoke up before

Russell had the chance. "You have some explaining to do, commander."

He raised his eyebrows. "Oh?"

A smug smile came to my lips, proud of putting him on the spot. He was always in control of any situation, so it was nice to see that he was like everyone else, with our insecurities and uncertainties. "You never told me you go by Rusty."

He chuckled. "Nobody's used that nickname in many years." He furrowed his eyebrows. "So, the Farseeing with Tess is already revealing quite a bit. Are you uncovering useful information beyond my long-lost secrets?"

My smile faded. "Nothing that I can put my finger on, at least not yet. I wish I had a way of knowing whether to spend time on this, especially now when the Bots are on our doorstep." I furrowed my forehead. "You were a part of that past. What do you think?"

He shifted in his seat. "Your powers are beyond my understanding, Phil, so that's difficult for me to answer. You might discover something that will help you defeat the Bots. Knowing their past is to know who they are now. I could miss the clue completely." He thought about it for a moment. "So much in this land still surprises me." He glanced down at our empty plates on the table. "If you're finished with your meal, let's walk. I want to show you a thing that could inspire you. Riyaad, please join us."

With hurried steps, he led us out of the dining hall and toward the edge of town, frequently exchanging a greeting with the townsfolk as we passed. He had a slight smile on his face, knowing he had piqued my curiosity. "I realize how you must feel right now," he said as he glanced at me. "You don't know where to begin as you observe the past lives of the Reapers and Elite. I can't give you an answer, but here's what I do these days when I'm looking for inspiration."

I could already see where he was going—it was difficult not to. The new wall under construction by the Stonewraiths loomed ahead. He walked right up to its base and placed his palm against the dark stone, looking up at the top, which soared over thirty feet above us. He took a deep breath as he gazed at me, his eyes beaming. "You might not know this, but when the wall collapsed during the Bot attack, I lapsed into despair. The pressure of ruling this, the only human village in this land, can be daunting. It was the only time I had ever considered giving up the job, passing the baton to someone more capable."

"It was my fault. You should have been angry at me."

He made a sour face and shook his head. "You weren't to blame, and you should never put that on your shoulders. The Bots were going to do whatever they could to amass more power. They saw you as their salvation, but you blocked their plans. If not for you, they might eventually enslave us."

"That may be, but I still don't understand why you brought me here."

He chuckled. "Yes, I digress." He motioned to the hundred yards of the newly constructed wall. "This here is a tribute to all that is good in this land. For all the damage and hurt that the Bots inflict, the living beings here are a counterbalance. We humans, the Stonewraiths, all the other races, we all serve as a barrier to the Bots. They may have their victories now and again, but the forces of good will always oppose them. In the end, I believe we will triumph over them. And this here," he slapped the wall with his palm, "demonstrates how we rebuild after whatever damage they cause."

I looked at the length of the wall before us. The engineering feat to construct such a massive fortification was astonishing, and the Stonewraiths were doing it by hand, albeit with a bit of their own special magic. But what did this have to do with me or freeing my friends? "Is this a pep talk? Like everyone else, you're afraid I'll abandon hope and give up."

He fixed me with a steely gaze. "I'm trying to help you see beyond the pain you feel. None of us can know what will happen to your companions or how you will succeed. But understand this: many others besides myself will do all we can to help you. And the most significant strength of all is the Spirit of Elthea." He softened his expression. "Take comfort. You are not alone in this struggle."

The nightmare from last night came to me, and my resolve faltered. "I accept what you're saying, but it's difficult to imagine how this will end when I'm at the bottom of a deep pit. And right now, I don't care about winning any battle. All I want is my friends back."

He nodded. "Rightly so. That's the way we fight battles, one step at a time. You're taking the first step by doing the Farseeing with Tess. It will help you learn about the Bots before they became Bots. And as you go through it, you must believe, and hope, that you will find something useful."

Looking away from him, my shoulders sagged. He frowned at my reaction. "Phil, I count you among the most remarkable people I have ever met. What you've already accomplished is amazing, and don't tell me it wasn't. Regardless of the hardships you've faced, you overcame them." He blew out a breath. "I never asked for this responsibility as commander, just as you never wanted the burdens placed upon you. Somehow, whether by divine intervention or plain dumb luck, we had these roles thrust upon us. And in the end, we do what we must."

I nodded. "That doesn't make it any easier, does it?"

He smiled, but there was sorrow in his eyes. "No, it's never easy. I wish otherwise, but if anyone can struggle through this and succeed, it's you."

"It's time we see the Bots again," I said to Riyaad after the commander had departed. Riyaad didn't object, but I knew what he was thinking. "Don't worry," I said with a forced smile. "I'll be more cautious about trying to get inside their heads."

We skirted the newly constructed wall for a short distance, but had to turn away from the perimeter once we reached a dead-end of boulders. Bevon, Quintia, and

Ja'Krill joined us, positioning themselves near me. Somehow, they knew I was going within sight of the Bots, as if that mattered to our enemy. The Bots knew I was here, even if they couldn't see me.

We followed a well-worn path through the collapsed wall. Beyond the broad field, the tall oaks and pines swayed in a gentle breeze as if nothing was amiss. How could the view appear so serene at first glance? As before, it took me a few seconds for my eyes to adjust to the army assembled under their canopy.

"My God," I muttered. Thousands of them, many more than before, now stood shoulder to shoulder, oscillating as if keeping a tune to some silent music. I looked to the left and then the right. A solid mass of them ringed the village, extending back into the woods.

Nobody knew how far into the trees they stretched. Those visible could be the tip of the iceberg. The sight took my breath away and now I understood why Riyaad wanted me to avoid seeing this until I had gained my strength.

Bevon edged close to me. "They have been like this since daybreak. Most of them must have arrived during the night." The view was spellbinding and horrific at the same time.

My voice was tense. "What are they planning?" Tess Armstrong wasn't out at the permitter, and I needed her. Without thinking about it, I moved back toward the town to find her. "Have to find Tess," I blurted to the startled guards around me. Before going a few steps, I glimpsed a soldier watching me. His expression was impassive, but he tightly gripped his spear.

Bryson's conversation replayed in my mind. "They don't know you like I do."

Hesitating for a moment, I strode toward the man. "What is your name, soldier?"

His stance became more rigid, as if he should come to attention for me. "Samuel, Sir." He couldn't be any older than eighteen.

"I bet everyone calls you Sam, don't they?" He nodded slowly, confused about why I was talking to him.

"Well, Sam, I want to thank you for protecting the village. It must be difficult standing here with no wall to stand behind."

"We do our best, Sir."

"I know you do, and that's why I want to tell you how much I appreciate your work. You're a good man, Sam."

Ten paces away, another member of The Guard glanced curiously at us, wondering what we had said. She was not much older than Sam, so I strode over to her. "Have you been in The Guard for long, soldier?" I asked.

Maybe fearing a reprimand, her face blanched. "S-six months," she stammered.

"Well, I imagine you know how to handle that weapon by the way you are holding it. You must have taken your training seriously. Have you always wanted to be in The Guard?"

She brightened. "Since I was a child, Sir."

"Please, my name is Phil." She nodded, but didn't say

it. "I know someone just like you who's in The Guard. Her name is Rae. Do you know her?"

She smiled. "Of course, Sir—I mean Phil. Everyone knows Rae of the Blades."

I chuckled. "I didn't know she was called that. It fits her well."

And so, my conversations continued, from one soldier to another. My greetings soon attracted a throng as I made my way around the outer edge of the town. Nobody wanted to be left out. As I spoke a few words to each person, I caught sight of Rae standing on the boulders of the demolished wall, where she could survey the defensive positions of the troops. She watched me, her arms folder across her midsection. An incline of her head and a faint smile told me she was pleased.

Soon I reached the place where the Stonewraiths were constructing the new wall. Regardless how many times I viewed it, the hundreds of yards of rebuilt wall was an impressive sight to behold. Some of them stood at the top of an uncompleted section, pulling up enormous boulders by ropes, while others were fitting the stones at the top by magically softening them to take a suitable shape and fit precisely.

They paused in their task as I neared, and Torermak strode forward. His expression was unreadable. Was he upset my stunt had interfered with their work?

As he approached, I took a step back, his imposing bulk looming over me. Hands on his hips, he glared down at me. "Humph. About time you finally embraced your mantle,

Master Philip. I had wondered if you would ever understand your capacity to lead."

He reached toward me with both hands, and I froze. Before I could scream an objection, he lifted me like a bag of hay and sat me down on one of his massive shoulders, deftly keeping a grip on me with one hand. "If you are going to greet the Stonewraiths, you must do it properly."

Before I could object, he bellowed, "Hail to Philip, our warrior and champion!"

The other Stonewraiths took up the chant, "Warrior and champion," as he paraded me around to them. I wasn't sure if I was mortified or pleased. Soon everyone was cheering, many members of The Guard banging swords against shields. I had no choice but to accept it, waving and smiling at the crowd as if I were a newly ordained king.

For the first time, I wondered: was I their champion? It was not a responsibility I had wanted to put on my shoulders, but someone had to assume the role.

Like it or not, I had no other option. Saving my friends and saving the village had converged. One would not happen without the other.

THE CHEERS OF THE IMPROMPTU CELEBRATION BROKE off, replaced with orders shouted by the officers of The Guard to their troops. Had I gone too far and breached their protocols? With the Bots gathered a short distance away, this was potentially a life-and-death situation, and here I was, causing a commotion.

Torermak stopped parading me around and gazed out toward the Bots. That's when I saw what had caught everyone's attention. A single Bot strode forward. The Stonewraith placed me back on the ground. His face was grim as he gazed at the figure. "Maybe now, Master Philip, you will discover what they seek."

I squinted as I watched the Bot approach, hoping for some sign that it differed from the others. Could this be one of my companions? All other thoughts fell away as I studied the Bot coming closer, still seeing nothing that would identify it as anything other than a foe. My stomach clenched, knowing I could no longer distinguish my friends from my enemies.

At one hundred yards, it came to a stop. Only then did I realize that a dozen or more guardsmen had notched their arrows with strings drawn. "Wait! Don't shoot." I shouted before one of them might release an arrow. Only moments ago, I had tried to bolster their confidence, but I knew many of them were raw recruits. Scores of ordinary villagers had also volunteered to defend their town, and they would give their lives if needed. But at this moment, the risk of someone making a mistake was too great. I moved toward the Bot, counting on the soldiers not launching an arrow while I was near it.

The three Astari and Ja'Krill formed a defensive ring around me, their weapons drawn. I stopped several paces away from the massive figure, still hoping I could discern anything different about it that would identify it as one of my friends. That wish ended as the thundering voice in my head signaled otherwise.

—You delay the inevitable, Philip Matherson. Join our cause and together we will rule the universe.

I balled my hands into fists at my side. If I could lash out and kill this thing this second, I would. "You will never control me. Return my friends and go back to your hole in the ground."

The faceless monstrosity loomed over me. Would they ever leave me alone? I didn't wait for a response before asking, "What are you doing here? You know I will never help you."

—Give us what we want and we will leave. You supplied us with a soul, but that is not something we desire. Your power increases, making you both dangerous and more useful. Restore what is rightfully ours and you will have your friends.

Rightfully ours? What was it talking about? "I gave you a soul to make you better, improve your life." Bile rose in my throat. "And for that act of kindness, you repay me by taking my closest companions, making them into one of you? And now you want something else? What can you possibly expect from me?"

—You must grasp our need on your own, or it becomes tainted, a fragment of what we desire. You spend your days watching us as we once existed. Figure it out.

How did they know I was using the Farseeing with Tess? My shoulders dropped. They knew so much while I understood so little of what was happening. "Who you are now bears no resemblance to what I've seen in the past. I don't yet understand the connection. You can't expect me to read your mind."

—*The lives of your companions depend upon you understanding us. The human portion of your friends will diminish until they become entirely Bots. And then, they will be one of us forever. Do not delay. Time is not on your side.*

Without saying more, it turned and walked back to the others at the edge of the forest. I watched it recede in the distance as an icy fear came over me. This would not end well.

13

PLEDGES SPOKEN

"I understand you created quite a stir today," said Tess. She spoke kindly, but almost everything she said came out that way.

I cleared my throat, unsure whether she was happy or displeased. "Which stir do you mean, the incident with the troops or speaking with a Bot?"

She held onto her smile. "Both actually. But I was thinking about your pep talk to The Guard. It spread through the town like wildfire."

"Well, I didn't mean it to be disruptive or anything. I started talking with a few villagers on guard duty and it just sorta got out of control from there."

She chuckled, motioning me to take my seat in her garden room. "No need to be defensive, Phil. You're well-liked by people. The talk with the troops was a brilliant move. The townsfolk still have vivid memories of the last time the Bots arrived and tore down the wall. Everyone has been on edge with them massing out there. You gave them a chance to cheer, at least for the moment. But I take it your conversation with the Bot was not as productive."

I shook my head. "They want something, but won't tell me what. How do I respond to that?"

She took her seat, measuring me with that calculating look of hers. "I guess that depends on what you discover here, doesn't it?" She sat facing me. Gone was her reticence at reliving her life in the past. She still hadn't shown me anything that she should be ashamed of.

"Before we begin, thank you again," I said. "This is my only hope of ever understanding them." When she didn't respond, I pushed forward. "Ready?"

She nodded once and closed her eyes. I pulled a weave of energy and my view of her fell away, replaced with a version of Tess from her youth. Once again, she was in the orchards picking fruit along with Russell and Alan. Russell now stood on a three-legged ladder used by the other Reapers to reach the upper branches. He lowered a full basket to Alan, who reached up to take it, groaning as he did so. Looking at Tess, he said, "We've been at this for four days now, and I still don't understand what we hope to accomplish."

She made a face. "You're a smart guy, Alan. We talked about how we need to be part of their community if we're going to learn anything."

"The only thing I'm learning is how to pick fruit."

Russell looked down at them. "Hey Al, think of it this

way. We get a free lunch every day. Would you prefer to give that up?"

Tess smiled at Alan's silence. But after he had time to think about it, Alan said, "At least we should be able to knock off early. I mean, we've been at this since early morning."

She glanced over to observe the work crew, who hadn't slowed their pace. "We need to be committed to this as much as they are. Otherwise, we're not like them and they may resent our meager efforts."

Alan groaned a little louder this time, but continued working.

Only when the sun was low on the horizon did the work crew at the other end of the field pack their equipment to leave. Tess and Alan carried the borrowed ladder over to them and left it with the others. The white-haired gentleman who led the crew responded with a courteous nod. As the two returned to Russell, the man continued to regard them with a slight smile on his lips.

Russell sat rubbing his calves as they came back. "Let's go home," he said. "I didn't realize standing on a ladder all day would be so taxing on my legs."

"Don't start calling that little shack home," said Alan. "Home is Earth."

Tess nudged him. "Come on Al, we can call it home for now. Can't we?"

The walk back along the unpaved path wasn't long. They were learning their way around the village by now, even though they had yet to explore sizable sections of the

Reaper town. Tess pushed open the flimsy door to the hut and stopped short. Alan and Russell froze, not able to see around her. "W-what," Russell stammered.

She stepped inside so they had a better view. All three gaped at the sight. A porcelain tub filled with steaming water now occupied one section of the smaller second room at the back of the dwelling. Someone had also placed a brush on the floor next to the tub, along with what looked like a bar of soap on top of several threadbare towels. They had also put three piles of giant eight-foot long, spongy green leaves on the floor, presumably to serve as bedding. And most telling of all, a flavorful aroma filled the room from a simmering pot sitting on the blazing stove.

Alan ignored everything else in the room and went over to the pot, lifting the top with a cloth mitt. He bent closer and took a deep breath. "God in heaven, this smells amazing. Let's eat."

Tess put her hands on her hips. "Not so fast, mister. As I recall, you were the one who complained the most about our work detail. Before we do any eating, I'm taking advantage of this tub. I call first dibs."

Russell eyed her. "You think this was from the work crew in the orchard? Not Cal or Brent?"

She shrugged. "Just a hunch. We'll find out later, but first things first." She twirled her index finger at them. "You two, outside. I'm not bathing in front of you. And while you're out there, you had better draw fresh water from the well for your turn in the tub." She glared at Alan.

"If there's one thing we all need more than a meal, it's a bath. So get to it."

After soaking and drying herself, Tess decided that her clothes also needed a wash, so she dumped them into the tub and began scrubbing. After ringing them out, she positioned them over the stove to dry.

With only a thin towel around her, she opened the door a crack. "I'm waiting for my clothes to dry. Can you wait a little longer?"

"Oh, for cripes' sake," said Russell. "I'm going to take my turn now and you can look the other way." He smiled and added, "Unless you don't trust yourself." She rolled her eyes, but let him in.

Once everyone had washed, they sat around the small table and spooned the stew into three bowls. Outside, twilight had fallen. A light mist lent a ghostly reflection to the other huts, a place so unlike anywhere they had lived before. Earth had already become a distant memory, over-shadowed with survival and adapting to life among the Reapers. They were no longer the three innocent software engineers concerned only about their careers. They had a new mission: saving an entire population from tyranny.

"I'll give you this," said Russell. "Your plan of fitting in has worked out well. I had my doubts about it at first."

Tess motioned with her spoon. "Now, we figure out who we can trust."

"Why?" asked Alan with a frown.

"We haven't accomplished anything yet. If we're going

to free the Reapers, we'll need their help. It's not something we can accomplish on our own."

"Oh," he sighed. "I thought you were angling at getting us promoted to chief fruit picker."

They laughed, but before anyone could respond, someone knocked at the door. They looked at each other, eyes wide. Tess whispered, "If that's an Elite, they wouldn't knock."

She stepped over and cracked open the door enough to see who was there. Her mouth formed a frown before she swung it open. A Reaper female stood outside, a slender woman with a timid smile on her face. "I am so sorry to disturb you. My name is Astra. I am Cal's sister, and Mara's mom."

Tess blinked, still not understanding. The Reaper's gaze darted to the street, before she added, "May I come in?"

Motioning her inside, Tess cast a furtive glance along the deserted roadway before shuttering the entrance. "Did something happen to Cal? We haven't seen him in days."

Sparklingly symbols came to life. Even after all these weeks, moments like this, with the lights springing into view, were still a disconcerting aspect of this race. The person appeared human until the images swirled about her. "No, he has been working double shifts to make up for his deficit." Her eyes swept the room, taking in the tub, the bedding, and the unfinished meal. "It appears you have found supporters amongst our ranks. I am glad for you."

"We wondered if this was another gift from Cal," said Russell.

The woman shook her head. "No, he has spent all his time these past days working. I don't know who provided this to you, but it must have been someone you impressed. Our community can be an inhospitable place for outsiders, and I cannot remember an occasion when we have accepted strangers." She looked at each of them curiously. "But I suspect you three are different."

The lady didn't wait for a response, if she ever expected one. She was carrying a small bundle and extended it out to Tess. "I've made three fruit tarts. They are still warm."

"This just keeps getting better," said Alan, as he hurried another spoonful of the stew into his mouth.

Tess held a chair out for Astra to use. "Please join us. You are welcome to a bowl of our surprise meal."

The Reaper smiled weakly. "Oh, no. Thank you. I ate with the children and saved leftovers for Cal when he's finished. I keep telling him he needs to find a proper woman to help him." She shrugged. "But you know Cal, he can be thickheaded."

Tess sat on the floor. "So, he doesn't have a partner? Cal doesn't say much about his personal life."

She laughed. "No, he's not the most talkative person. I suppose that's a reason he is still unattached."

Tess and Russell exchanged glances, waiting for the stranger to explain the purpose of her visit. It wasn't every day that other Reapers dropped by. Sensing their anticipation, she blurted, "I'm sorry. I shouldn't bother you like this, but both Mara and Cal have taken a liking to you."

"That's nice of you to say," Tess responded. "But I feel we barely know them."

"What you have accomplished in a short time is remarkable. Before you, Reapers have never accepted outsiders. The Elite forbid us, yet some of us, myself included, skirt that rule as long as we are careful." Her eyes swept across the three of them. "You have survived longer than any other strangers. Quite astonishing."

"It's because of the hospitality and advice of other Reapers," Russell replied.

Astra shook her head to disagree. "No, Mara understands you are different. She has that ability, you know."

Finished with his second helping of stew, Alan chose that moment to ask, "Are we going to eat the tarts while they're still warm?"

Tess shot him an irritated look and spoke without inflection. "Yes, Alan. Go ahead." She returned her attention to Astra. "What do you mean, she understands we're different?"

Astra bunched her eyebrows together. "She senses it because of the Directive, of course."

Alan leaned forward, now interested in the conversation. He gestured with the tart, crumbs on his chin. "Explain please. I'm still confused about this Directive of yours."

"Yes, it is still somewhat of a mystery to us," added Tess. "Mara doesn't know us that well. She's a sweet girl, but we've only spoken to her a few times. How can the Directive help her judge us?"

"How much of it do you understand?"

Alan responded. "Cal and Brent explained the basic concept. But I still find it puzzling."

Astra clenched her hands. "I am not the person to explain the workings of it. Others have a better understanding. But you probably know the essence. It is more powerful in the Elite and they breed only with other Elite, producing offspring that also have strong Directives. The Reapers have variations in its intensity, and once in a generation, someone is born with unusual strength." She lowered her voice as if someone else might hear. "Mara has one that is potent, possibly as formidable as that of the Elite."

Alan had placed his half-eaten tart back on the table. "And because hers is more vibrant, she can understand or do things that other Reapers cannot?"

Astra nodded, a mournful expression on her face.

"But that's good, isn't it?" Tess blurted.

Her eyes were downcast. "No," she murmured. "If the Elite discover she is powerful, they will take her to the fortress and raise her as one of their own. It has happened before. They may also kill the parents to prevent another offspring with a similar strength."

The discussion paused for moments as they considered this news. The cracking of the wood burning in the stove was the only sound for several heartbeats. Tess cleared her throat. "The Elite would abduct an innocent child because of that?"

Astra looked as if she had tasted something bitter. "Innocence or guilt has nothing to do with it. They care only about maintaining power." Her voice shook and she took a breath. "We do our best to prevent her from standing out from the rest and to shield her from the Elite. That was one reason Cal was so angry when he first met you in the wet fields. He did not want her to be seen talking with outsiders. When an Elite arrived... Well, let's just say things got off on the wrong foot between the two of you."

Russell spoke for the first time. "But what did Mara mean when she said that we're unlike other outsiders?"

"Yes, sorry, I digress. It's the reason I came here to talk with you tonight." She rubbed the palms of her hands on her legs. "You recall discussing with Cal and Brent about the convergence that we believe is approaching?"

"Yes," said Tess. "But that discussion raised as many questions as it answered."

"Life without a Directive must make it difficult to understand how much we rely upon it. We use it for most of the functions in our daily existence. But the piece of it that gives us a hint of the future shows us we will soon experience significant changes in our lives."

Alan shook his head, now excited to be talking about something that interested him. "Brent told us that this convergence will change the lives of the Reapers."

Astra smiled sadly. "Whether the change is for good or

for ill, we cannot be sure." She studied them a moment before continuing. "He explained how you three are central to whatever will occur."

"But he couldn't say how we were involved," said Tess.

"No, future events are not always that precise or clear. Again, the Reapers are not as strong as the Elite. But Mara's Directive is more powerful than other Reapers, and she is certain your presence here will spark a massive upheaval. Whatever will happen, she believes the convergence will remake our lives."

Tess exchanged a glance with Alan and Russell. Astra didn't give them a chance to interrupt. "Here's the important thing you must understand, and the reason for my visit."

"That wasn't important enough?" Russell mused.

She didn't smile. "If Mara understands you have a part to play in this impending upheaval, so must the Elite."

Astra let that sink in. Tess reacted by saying, "But an Elite had already seen me when we were out in the orchards. He looked at me for a moment and turned away." She didn't describe how the Elites' gaze had paralyzed her for several seconds.

The woman shrugged. "I cannot explain the choices they make. But know this: they will never allow you to disrupt the control they have over us. Mara has identified you as the spark for what is coming. The Elites' power is stronger, so they are surely aware of the threat you pose."

"What should we do?" Russell asked, his voice cracking.

Was it pity in Astra's eyes as she returned his gaze? "If you have a way to return to your home, now would be a good time to do so."

"And if not?" Alan asked.

She hesitated. "I fear you will become a tool of the Elite. They will use you to do their bidding as they enhance their power and diminish ours. From time immemorial, it is all we have known from them. We have suffered enough already and I beg you, do not make it worse for us." She stood to leave, a haunted look in her eyes. "Cal would never say this to you, at least not now. But I will tell you. Better that you should run away than to become the pawns of the Elite. It will only result in more misery for us."

She stepped toward the door as the others stood. With one hand on the handle, she stopped. "Know that I hold no ill will against you. But you should understand the nature of the storm that approaches."

Tess placed her hand on Astra's shoulder. "We came here to help. That's what we intend to do."

Astra frowned. "Pledges spoken in a moment of calm are honorable. Deeds are what will matter. Your actions will spell the difference between life and death for many Reapers." She opened the door to peer outside, looking one way and then the other before hurrying away.

Once she left, Tess faced Alan and Russell, her lips taut. "Well, what did you make of that?"

"Not much," Alan grumbled. "Everything she said was

based on speculation. Show me the facts, and I can give an opinion."

She shook her head. "Astra told us what she knew. She made it clear we have a purpose here. We may have wondered about it before, but now we know." Her face hardened. "More than before, I'm certain that our reason for being here is to free the Reapers."

Russell rubbed his cheek. "I understand how you feel, but Alan's right. Your emotions are clouding your thinking. Supposedly, some cataclysmic act is about to happen, yet nobody seems to know what the event will be and whether we can change its outcome."

He stared at Tess with an intensity he rarely displayed. "I'll be truthful, Tess. Whatever's going to happen, I believe we should let it take place. It's not up to us to determine the future of a race we barely know."

Alan raised his hand. "I second that."

Her eyes darted back and forth from one to the other. "And I will tell you this: I didn't come here to watch things happen. That statue of Elthea asked us to help right a wrong. If you want to sit on the sidelines, that's your decision. But it isn't mine."

Tess spun around and dashed out the door, letting it slam behind her.

14

THEY TOOK EVERYTHING FROM US

The sun had barely risen as the three companions left their home the next day. Nobody had spoken about Astra's warning or their argument after she had left. As always, they would find common ground. Besides, the early morning was a time to feel good about their lives. Despite the troubles they encountered since arriving in this place, life had improved.

So this morning they walked with a spring in their steps, heads up, eyes wide. Even Alan beamed. "For the first time since coming to this godforsaken place, I had a good night's sleep."

Tess returned the smile. "Those leafy bed cushions were comfortable, weren't they?"

"And the food," Russell added. "We both know that Al responds best when he's well fed."

Another Reaper fell into step next to Tess. She

groaned, trying to ignore him. Cal flashed her a smile. "I see you've been busy making friends."

She kept her eyes forward. "Which is more than I can say about you."

He put his hands to his chest, feigning a blow. "Ow, that hurts, especially after all I've done for you."

She glared at him. "Tell me the truth. Did you put the tub and those cushions in our room? How about the warm meal last night?"

His smile turned into a grimace. "Well, maybe not those things. Those were from Sol."

She furrowed her eyebrows. "Who?"

He chuckled. "Sol's the crew leader you've been working for. Don't you know his name yet? By the way, that was a clever idea. I wouldn't have expected it from you three."

She stopped walking, putting her hands on her hips as she glared at him. "It's a good thing we did. If we had to wait for you, we'd be dead by now. I seem to recall from our last conversation that you said you would help us. But then you disappear for what, weeks?"

He shrugged his shoulders. "I fell behind in my quota. It's not something that's looked upon kindly by the Elite. So I needed to make it up fast."

Alan and Russell watched the exchange without speaking. Tess's expression softened. "I heard you were pulling double shifts."

"How did you know that?" His eyes narrowed. "Have you been spying on me?"

She laughed, avoiding saying anything about the visit from his sister, Astra. "How do you like the tables being turned? You seemed to have spied on us more than I care to know about."

She began walking again, and Cal kept pace. "Anyway, I came to tell you that Sol's crew isn't in the usual orchard today. His boss assigned them to harvest a field on the north side of town today. The Elite want more berries."

Alan's head whipped around upon hearing it. "I hope not in the wet fields with those geysers."

Cal smiled wickedly. "Don't worry, fella, although it would do you good. The north fields are dry."

Tess looked to her left and then right, trying to determine their location. She pointed. "North is that way, correct?"

He adjusted her arm. "Just head in that direction. Ask anyone if you get lost."

She grunted. "Yea, everyone's so willing to help."

"I've told you before, we have a reason for shunning outsiders. But your work with Sol's crew hasn't gone unnoticed, and not only with Sol and his workers. Others have become more accepting of you. Believe me, the change in attitude by other Reapers will surprise you. If only you could read our Directive, you would realize the difference."

Tess chewed her lower lip as she considered this news. "So everyone's willing to help us now?"

"Whoa. I didn't say you're a full-fledged Reaper. It's

more like the residents feel sympathetic toward you. Like a lost puppy."

"Yea, until one of the Elite comes to get us," said Russell.

Cal hesitated, looking around. "The Elite have the advantage, but that doesn't mean we're ready to roll over. Some of us talk about a different life without them as rulers. They've taken so much from us already." He kept his face forward, his eyes unfocused. It was a contemplative side of him she had not seen before. The others looked at him, waiting him out. "This is very unusual, but Brent has authorized me to include you in on our discussions."

"About what?" Tess blurted.

He studied them for a moment, the lights of his Directive blooming around him. "About our plans for a rebellion."

"How? When?" Russell asked.

Cal held up his hand. "We'll not discuss it now or out in the open. I'll find you." He walked in another direction, then stopped to look at Tess. "Oh, and please try to avoid Rowan Sarroff."

She furrowed her eyebrows. "Who?"

"The Elite who spotted you the other day. Why he didn't take you on the spot, I'm still not sure. Just don't give him another chance. He's the Prime Elite, head of all others. The whole Sarroff family and all other Elites fall over each other to gain his good graces. If he takes you, there's little we can do to save you."

He continued walking as Tess chewed on her lower lip,

a habit that was becoming more common with her. "Don't worry, he's only trying to scare us," she said weakly as they went on their way.

Alan and Russell exchanged a look with each other. Neither, however, voiced an objection.

TESS NODDED TO THE CREW LEADER, SOL—HIS TEAM already at work—once they found the field. He returned the gesture with a slight smile. Rows of shoulder-high bushes filled this area rather than the typical fruit trees from the orchard of the past days. Multicolored berries grew on the shrubs, which the other Reapers harvested by raking a pronged tool along the branches, causing the fruit to fall into a pouch attached to the bottom of the tool.

"No problem; this should be easy," said Russell. "As long as I don't have to climb ladders today, I'm happy." Despite his confidence, they were soon sweating in the unrelenting sun. At least the orchards provided some measure of shade. The motion of raking the berries strained muscles not accustomed to the repetitious movements.

Once the midday break arrived, they found a shady spot and slumped onto the grass. Alan gazed at the rest of the workers. "Hey, the kids aren't bringing us lunch today. What gives?" As was their norm, the Reaper crew sat together, passing food to one another. Alan stabbed a finger in their direction. "Look at them. Cal told us everyone had accepted us. Now this? I'm going to give them a piece of my mind."

"Take it easy, Al." Tess interrupted. "Look, the crew leader is motioning for us to join them."

The elder Reapers, wisps of white hair under his floppy hat, eyed them as they approached. He was an oddity in a village of mostly younger residents. What happened when Reapers grew old? Could they retire, or were they coerced into working until they dropped dead? He motioned for them to sit nearby, another unexpected gesture of friendship. As they sat on the soft ground, two children handed each of them a green wrap and a piece of fruit.

He still hadn't spoken, so Tess said, "Aren't you afraid of being seen with us?"

He shrugged. "They know you are here, so I guess it doesn't matter. If they wanted, they could use any excuse to penalize us." His smile widened. "And if it's true what some maintain, we need to feed you long enough to change all this." He motioned with his hand to the field and the Reaper village beyond.

She frowned. "Is that what you believed, that I will save everyone?"

He shrugged matter-of-factly. "Doesn't matter much what I believe. Those of us amongst us workers who do matter now support you."

"Like who?" Russell asked.

Sol took his time to respond. He seemed more interested in scrutinizing them by examining what they said, how they reacted rather than avoiding them. He took a bite of his wrap before continuing. "This may surprise you, but Cal, for one, has been your biggest supporter from the very beginning."

"What? He couldn't spare two minutes to explain this place to us during our first weeks here," she said. "We could have died for all he cared. Although, I will admit, he's become more helpful to us as of late. But that still doesn't excuse his rudeness."

Sol smiled. "You do not understand him as we do. Cal has experienced more hardships than others, suffered more than anyone deserves. Most Reapers have lived through the death of loved ones, yet it is never easy. We are all slaves to the Elite. He was only a child, maybe six or seven, when his life upended. His sister, Astra, was several years younger, and their parents both worked in the mill. It was a ghastly place where Reapers spun fabric into the fine clothes desired by the Elite. It still is a terrible work assignment. You might think it would be a safe craft, considering the dangers of other jobs. If you haven't visited the mill, it is a hellhole of swinging blades on levers and contraptions that most sane individuals wouldn't come close to. Cal and Astra's parents had chosen the craft to be together."

Sol's eyes watered, and the rest of the work crew had gone silent listening to the story. "The crew chief at the mill was a good person, a lady who had worked her way through the ranks. One day, an Elite entered the mill, as they do occasionally. Most times, the reason for their visit is to order a special fabric or color of cloth to suit whatever whim they desire. On this day, the Elite arrived to inspect a batch of cloth that was to be used for some event they were planning. The spun cloth did not satisfy him."

Alan, Tess, and Russell stared unblinking, intrigued by the account. Sol took a breath. "The fabric wasn't sheer enough, even though the crew chief explained the looms could not run fast enough for something that delicate. The Elite said he would accept no excuses."

Sol shook his head, knowing what was to come. "The Elite inspector ordered the crew chief to run the looms faster. Once the speed increased, it became too difficult for the workers to position the cloth and yarn. Everything moved too quickly. The looms severed several hands and fingers in the first few minutes."

Tess inhaled, but did not interrupt.

"Then the mechanisms failed. Cards and weavers ripped apart. They were not constructed to run at those speeds. Blades and belts whipped across the room. Some of the flying debris crashed into other machines, causing a cascading failure. A belt took Cal's mom around the neck and pulled her onto a spinning blade. His father dashed to help her, but by then everything was falling to pieces. The rupturing machines tossed him through the air like a paper doll before he came close to her. Neither survived. Nor did over twenty other Reapers. All because some cloth wasn't delicate enough."

He stared at the ground in front of him as if reliving the events of that day. The rest of the work crew remained hushed, sharing a sacred moment of reflection. Even the surrounding field had become still. Sol looked back up at them. "Cal became a man that day; it is the way with Reapers. Such is the necessity of our existence. He took responsibility for his younger sister, Astra. He still carries her quota even after the death of her mate while working in the fortress. The Elites never explained the cause of his death, rarely do they. At that time, Astra was with child with Mara. When she was born, well, Cal loves her as if she were his own daughter."

He lapsed into silence, studying the three. Tess cleared her throat. "I—we didn't know. I should have been kinder to him."

Sol recovered from his sad tale and smiled. "Nah. He thrives on the attention you give. Particularly a pretty young lady such as yourself."

A Reaper, someone not part of Sol's work crew, shouted at the other end of the field. He was waving as he ran toward them. "What's the matter with him?" Sol mumbled.

Everyone stood as the man approached. He took a minute to catch his breath. As soon as he could speak, he croaked, "They've taken her."

"Blazes, talk sense, Reed. Who?"

The young man gulped another breath, eyes wide. "The girl, Mara. Two Elite came. When Cal learned of it, he stormed out of the fields and headed toward the fortress. I'm afraid he is going to do something stupid."

Sol muttered a curse. Tess turned to her companions. "Come on, let's go."

Alan blinked. "What! Where?"

"To stop him, of course." She spun around and charged away, not caring if anyone followed.

TESS REACHED THE OUTSKIRTS OF THE REAPER village as Russell followed. Alan was further behind, trotting at his own pace, grumbling all the way as if arguing with an unseen person. Russell grabbed her by the shoulder to stop her from going further. "Tess, wait just a moment. Please think this through. What do you plan to do, storm the Elite fortress and get us killed?"

Her eyes darted from him to the fortress in the distance. "All I know is that he's been the only one who has helped us, and now, knowing how protective he is about Mara, who knows what he'll do? If we can overtake him before he reaches the fortification, maybe I can talk sense into him."

"I understand. But let's be smart about this. We don't have to go running blindly into trouble. If you keep this pace, the Elite guards will spot you."

Her breathing slowed. "Okay, but let's hurry. We have to reach him before he gets to that entrance."

They followed the well-worn road that the Reapers used to bring their supplies to the Elite. The path became a raised berm a dozen feet high as it cut across the flooded fields.

Looming four hundred yards beyond the fields stood

the Elite structure, a dramatic contrast to the rest of the countryside. Its surface looked like stone from a distance, but the closer they came, the building seemed to be fluid, swirling and moving as if alive. Like any living entity, it appeared to be sentient, as strange as that may sound. The three had avoided coming close to the edifice except for the first day here. Tess had already noticed that the fortress evolved by sprouting new balconies or levels that hadn't existed days before.

They passed the wet fields and were already closer to the Elite home than ever before. Alan was still somewhere behind. A constant stream of other Reapers moved in both directions along the path, making them less conspicuous. The Elites guarding the entrance took no notice of them even as they approached. Tess and Russell fell in line with a few others, imitating the Reapers' dispirited shuffle.

Russell pointed to a group of Reapers some twenty yards in front of them. "There he is." He whispered, as if the Elite could hear them from this distance. Who knows, maybe they could. The Elite were still an enigma to the three outsiders.

Cal walked behind a pushcart, shuffling along like the rest of the workers. "I'm going to speak to him. Alone," said Tess. Something in her expression forestalled an objection from him.

She approached Cal quickly, but not so fast as to stand out. By the time she reached him, they were a scant thirty yards from the fortress entrance with its Elite guards. He caught sight of her before she could say a word. "Don't stop me, Tess," he growled. "This is not some silly game."

She balled her hands into fists as if to punch him. "You think I'm playing a silly game? We've put our lives in danger to help you and your people. I'm dead serious. You take one step further right now and I'm going in there with you."

He opened his mouth as if to protest, then snapped it shut. She didn't give him a chance to object further. "I heard what happened to your parents; how you've channeled your life to protect Astra and Mara. But you can't keep everyone safe in this place." She jerked her head toward the fortress. "That's only going to happen when they're gone."

She reached out and brushed his bare arm with her fingertips, her voice turning softer. "Come back with me, and I'll fight as hard as I can to rid you of the Elite. You talked about a revolution. I'm in, but only if you turn around right now."

His eyes watered. She gaped, never having seen this side of him. "They took everything from me, Tess. Everyone I ever loved has died because of them. How can I walk away?"

"I'm not asking you to forgive them. Find an inner strength to continue living until you rid yourself of them. I know you can overcome—"

"No!" He shouted before she could say more. Tess winced, knowing he was making a scene in front of the Elite. "How can you understand? You drop down out of nowhere and you think you can make everything right. Things don't work like that here. Nothing is fair. We work till our hands are numb and every muscle burns. And I can live with that. We all accept it. Yet, now you arrive, and some of us believe maybe we have a sliver of hope. We wonder if a better life might soon come our way. That's what will get us killed. Hope is an illusion. It doesn't exist, not for us."

Tears ran down his cheeks. Tess stared, overwhelmed at his outpouring of emotion, her eyes watering as well. His voice lowered as he spoke again. "I never wanted you in my life, Tess. None of us did. Why did you have to give us a reason to believe we can improve all this? You saw what they do to us. We have no future. We never did."

Tess wiped her face with her sleeve. "Cal, we all need hope. Without it, life is meaningless. Please believe you can change it for the better, maybe not today or tomorrow, but one day. You just have to be smart about it. A time will come when you have that opportunity. And then, you take it. That day will never come if you throw your life away."

She looked at the fortress and then back at him. "Think about what you're doing, Cal. Use your head. One person going in there won't get anywhere. Maybe you can kill a lone Elite, but probably not. Do you have a death wish? Because they'll only wheel you out in a cart so your family and friends can dispose of your body. You'll end up just like all the other Reapers who displease them. You need a plan, and I bet you and Brent already have one, but aren't telling me yet."

He blinked, and a thin smile came to her, knowing her hunch was correct. She grabbed his wrist. "It's time to put an idea into action. You have my word that I will do whatever I can to help you."

She tugged at his arm while he looked down at the ground. Then he took a tentative step with her. And once they took the first step together, they continued to make their way back to the Reaper village. Neither of them noticed the sole Elite standing on one of the lower balconies, regarding them with intense curiosity.

The figure observing them was none other than Rowan Sarroff, ruler of them all. He had once observed Tess working in the fields and had allowed her to remain unharmed. Once again, he did not interfere. He continued to regard them until Cal and Tess became lost in the swarm of other peasants. Only then did he chuckle, a sound devoid of any humor.

15

OUR ONLY HOPE

Four days passed since Mara's abduction by the Elite. The three friends from Earth continued to work with Sol's work gang, seeing no sign of Cal during this time. Tess had asked the crew leader if he had heard from him. "Give him time to heal," Sol had responded. "His concern now is to support his sister. It's best that they deal with this on their own. If either needs help, they know we are here."

On this day, they harvested berries once again in the field on the north side of town. Tess jumped at the unexpected arrival of another Reaper next to her.

Cal smirked at her before giving his attention to the plant in front of him, blending in with the other workers as he pretended to pick fruit. She regarded him, waiting for him to speak. Outwardly, he was the same person she had known since her first day here, but a subtle change had taken place. His emotions poured from him in waves, swirling just below the surface, barely held under control. He grabbed bunches of berries, juice squirting out, staining his fingers, while he shook them as if they were his enemy.

Tess ventured a smile. "You're supposed to use this tool rather than grab them like that. I don't think many berries are going to survive if you keep this up unless you intend to make jam."

Her remark coaxed a bitter smile from him. "I've picked more damned berries in my life than I care to remember." He stole a glance around him, his eyes flashing as he scanned the outskirts of the fields. Tess knew that expression. He wanted to be sure no Elite were in the area. "I talked with Brent last night. We both feel the time is right to take action."

"Because of Mara?"

He winced. "No, but that was one more insult added to a long list of abuses."

Tess observed him, searching for some sign of his emotional state. "What will happen to her?"

He looked away, gritting his teeth. She wasn't sure he would answer, but she waited him out. When he responded, his voice had a hard edge. "They took her to the fortress where they will educate her as an Elite. She's not the first they've taken. After a few years, the children are so brainwashed they barely remember their youth." He made a fist with his hand, juice from the berries seeping through his fingers. "They kill those who cannot adapt."

He took a breath, relaxing his grip. "You saved me from acting foolishly, and for that I thank you, even though I wanted nothing more than to lash out at them." He leaned closer to her, letting his arm rub against hers.

Tess responded by leaning into him. "You had every reason to fly off the handle. What's surprising is that it doesn't happen more often."

He shrugged. "Many have tried, but we have learned how fruitless it is. I should have known better. Anyway, Brent and I have been speaking with others. More of them now realize we have to do something."

"And her abduction has convinced them?"

He turned to look at her. "No, you are the reason."

"Me?"

"More of us believe events will soon take place that will transform our lives. For better or worse, you are the driving force. We can steer you in the right direction, letting you know how to help us if you choose to listen to our advice. The Reapers trust you now, even though many still have different opinions about the good to come."

"I don't have any special abilities—none of us have. You realize this?"

"I never said you did. But we have a plan, at least the beginnings of one. And for our idea to work, you do not need any godlike talents."

She looked over at Russell and Alan, who were listening to every word. She spoke to them. "I believe our purpose here is to help the Reapers. The statue of Elthea brought us to this place for this reason. Are you in?"

"You don't even know the plan, Tess," said Russell. "We're in when we understand more."

She let out a breath, ready to argue with him, but Cal held up his berry-stained hand. "He has a fair point. But I have to get back to work. We will hold the Harvest Festival two nights from now. There we can talk more." Without another word, he jumped up and walked away.

Tess blinked at his unexpected departure. Alan sniggered and said, "Not the most communicative guy, is he?"

SOL'S WORK CREW NORMALLY LABORED UNTIL DUSK, but not today, the night of the Harvest Festival, as they packed their equipment early. "You will find us along the east bank of the village," he said to the three as he passed them on his way out. "Food is part of the festivities, so come with an empty stomach."

Alan beamed at the news.

"The Elites allow us this one celebration each year," Sol explained when Tess had asked him about the event. "You will join us." Even though he might not have meant it, he sounded more like an order than a request.

Tess, Alan, and Russell approached the festival grounds, not knowing what to expect. Standing on the edge of the meadow, they surveyed the crowd already assembled. Sol's crew was easy to spot now that they worked with them each day, although this was a side of their personality they hadn't witnessed before. Like everyone else, the workers were engaged in animated conversations, with laughter coming easily. "Are they on drugs?" Alan asked. Tess and Russell shrugged, befuddled at the transformation.

Music drifted through the air. Music! It came from the same people who had looked beaten into submission. Fires ringed the large grass fields, keeping the chilly evening at bay. A lady approached the three dumbfounded outsiders. She smiled at them. Smiled! "We are glad you could join us."

They gaped, unsure of themselves. It was rare for a Reaper to go out of the way to speak with them, even after Sol's acceptance. "Er, thank you," Tess responded.

"This is a joyous night," continued the lady, not the least put-off by their uncertainty. "You may not recognize me, but my mate is on Sol's crew. This seems like a good time to greet you properly. Help yourself to any of the servings at the stoves. No need to be shy tonight."

As the female turned away, a young girl of about twenty passed in front of them, catching Russell's eye. "I'm working at one of the serving stations," she said to him. "Would you care to help?"

"S-sure," he stammered as he fell into step next to her.

Tess frowned as she watched them walk away. "Who's that?" she asked Alan.

He snorted. "Really, Tess. How can you be so perceptive at times and then so clueless? They've been making eyes at each other since our first day on the crew. How could you not notice?"

She shrugged, still looking perplexed. "I guess other events have distracted me." Her voice increased a level as she added, "Like keeping us alive." She shook her head as if realizing something else. "Have I been going about this all wrong? All this time I've been searching for a purpose here —a way to liberate these people from the oppression they are under. I didn't take a second to live and enjoy the simple richness of life in this place. I was so proud of going native, but we haven't practiced it at all. Have we? Except for a few Reapers, we barely know them. Is that what the statue of Elthea was trying to tell us? That we should discover what is good here and nurture it?"

Alan shrugged. "Maybe we'll never learn what it expected of us."

She cast an appraising eye toward him. "This business with Russell makes me wonder. You're not seeing one of the locals, are you?"

He chuckled. "No, but I'll let you know if that happens." He looked around, breathing in the aroma of unfamiliar spices. "She told us to help ourselves to the food, didn't she?" He had one eye on the cooking stoves as he nudged Tess in the ribs. "Maybe you're right. It's time that we live and enjoy, and I'm going to follow that advice by getting something to eat. Join me?"

She smiled, but shook her head. "No, you go ahead. I'll join you later."

Tess strolled into the meadow, angling toward a cluster of stoves placed in the fields. She approached one with a boy of maybe sixteen who was cooking a mixture of meats and vegetables over a flat grill. He didn't notice her approach until she said, "Hello there."

His eyes shot up. "Oh, hello, Tess Armstrong." He turned his attention back to the grill. "Forgive me while I stir this. I have learned that there is a fine line between being uncooked and overdone."

She smiled. "Take your time. By the way, Tess is fine. You don't have to use my last name."

He wrinkled his brow. "I still do not understand that distinction in your vocabulary. Why is it you have two names? We only use one, which seems much more efficient."

Her smile broadened. "From where I come from, our last name is called a surname. All members of the same family use it to designate they are members of that family." She thought about it for a moment. "Unless you are a female and you marry. Then you can change your surname to take the name of your partner." She let out a breath. "Which, I now realize, is more information than you care to know."

He looked at her blankly for a few seconds before turning his attention back to the stove. "It is so much easier for us. Our Directives provide us with that knowledge."

"Well, since I don't have a Directive, what's your name?"

"I am Kenzi. Just the single name."

She watched for a moment as he mixed the food from one side of the grill to the other.

"I see you enjoy cooking. Is this your craft?"

"Not yet, but I hope someday to be selected by a cook as an apprentice to serve for the Elite in the fortress."

Her face soured as if she had tasted something bitter. "Why in god's name would you want to do that rather than work in the fields? I've seen the bodies of Reapers carried out of there."

He looked back up, his face unsmiling. "All of us live in danger. Workers in the fields are not safe either. Besides, those with a craft in the fortress receive more rewards." He glanced around to see if anyone else was listening. Lowering his voice, he added, "And it's been my observation that the girls are more attracted to men working inside the fortress."

"Well, I hope you succeed," she said weakly as she took the food he offered, a stir-fry inside thick bread. Others approached behind her, so she thanked him and moved on.

Tess watched a group playing musical instruments while she munched on her meal. Why did the food taste so good here? Maybe it was because of the weeks they had spent scrounging for whatever they could find in the fields. Whatever the reason, she took her time savoring each bite of this meal.

"You need a drink to wash that down," said a voice behind her. She was so intent on eating that she flinched at the sound, jerking her head around to see a middle-aged man holding a flask. He extended it to her. "It has a kick, so don't gulp it too fast, or too much, for that matter. We call it shine."

She studied him a moment before reaching for the container. "You're on Sol's work crew, aren't you?"

He dipped his head and gave her the jug. "Tonight, we are all family. My name is Grenn."

She took the flask, giving it a sniff and wrinkling her nose. "I appreciate this, but tell me, why the change? I've been working with you for weeks, and this is the first you've spoken to me."

He looked away for a few seconds, his forehead furrowed. "Please understand, when Reapers decide something, we do it collectively. Once decided, we stay united. In the beginning, we could not accept you, and I believe you know now the reasons." He shrugged. "But that has changed."

"Because of this major event you predict?"

Grenn narrowed his eyes. "Yes, but that is not the only reason." He grinned. "You and your friends are likable, which is another part of the explanation. But this is a night for merrymaking, not weighty talk." He glanced at the flask. "So, are you going to have a drink or not?"

Tess hesitated before taking a swig and swallowing. A second later, she gasped and coughed. "That's horrible," she said through clenched teeth. "It burns like hell." She shoved the flask back into his hands.

He chuckled. "It takes some getting used to. But you wanted to learn more about us. Right?"

Her breathing was still labored. "Not about this."

"Don't worry. Even we Reapers have a similar response with the first sip. The next one will go down much smoother."

She tried to catch her breath. "Not sure if there's going to be a next time."

Noticing Tess's reaction, a woman strolled over. She frowned, her hands on hips as she glared at Grenn. "Of all the things, man. Do not tell me you gave her shine. Speak now, did you?"

He winced. "Only a sip, just to be sociable."

The lady pulled Tess away from Grenn. "Come on, before he does more damage." She lowered her voice to a whisper as she led her away from him. "Grenn's my mate, and I love him dearly. But sometimes I want to throttle him." She let out a breath and continued in a more pleasant tone. "Come now, I want you to meet a group of women before another unsavory person accosts you."

Each of the women greeted Tess as if she was one of them. They barely gave her a chance to speak as they chattered, speaking over one another. Tess looked from one to the other, trying to speak, only to have another one say something first. She soon stopped trying and just took it all in. This was their evening, not hers. It was the single day each year they could enjoy the company of others without the fear that their loved ones would never return home from their workplace. A cork had been popped, and everyone here was going to relish this occasion.

The music ratcheted up in volume as more couples and groups of women danced. Children followed along, doing their own interpretation of a dance. A bottle of shine circulated amongst this group of ladies, and soon the female next to Tess handed her the jug. She was less tentative this time as she swallowed a gulp. Her face still contorted—earning her giggles from the others—but at least she didn't gag on it.

The knot of women moved toward a makeshift dance space, pulling Tess with them. She offered a feeble resistance, laughing with the others as they urged her along. The steps performed by the other dancers, both men and women, resembled those of a square dance, even though the music was much different. One lady quickly showed Tess the steps before they began the dance.

Tess giggled hysterically as she blundered her way through it, stepping one way and then the other, coming face to face with a partner for several steps, separating and falling in with another. The Reapers laughed along with her, seeming to enjoy her confusion more than the dance. After a time, Tess slipped away from the dancers, feigning the need to take a break just as the music shifted to a slower pace, allowing couples to team up with one another.

Cal blocked her retreat. "May I have the honor of this dance?"

She smirked. "You weren't around earlier. I had no one to protect me from these nefarious customs of yours, especially that dreadful alcohol your people enjoy."

"I hope someone told you about it." He reached around her as they shuffled to the slow tune.

Tess looked into his eyes. "Oh, they warned me, but it was a feeble explanation. With this group pressure, well..." She shrugged. "Maybe I'm trying too hard to become one of you. And that's never going to happen."

He lost his smile. "No, it is not, but you are someone special. And now, after the initial uncertainty, they have accepted you. Although you may not be a Reaper, you are more valuable than the lot of us. Only you can change our future."

She sucked in a breath, as if trying to draw upon an inner strength. "Speaking of that, you said you and your uncle Brent have a plan. Are you ready to tell me what it is?"

"I don't think you are going to like it."

She chuckled without humor. "Why am I not surprised? I've already witnessed too many horrifying things about this place. What's one more?"

He stopped dancing and took her by the hand. "Let's walk."

He slipped his arm around her waist as they left the festival grounds and walked away from the ramshackle houses that made up the Reaper village. They skirted the perimeter of the town as they reached a small rise over-looking the wet fields. Here they sat on a cushion of moss with their backs against a thick, squat tree. Both moons were full, flooding the land with a surreal light. Celeus, the larger of the two, had passed the mid-point in the heavens while the smaller, Halcyone, was still catching up to it.

Tonight was unlike all the other nights Tess spent in this town. The ground seemed to sparkle from the reflection of the moons, a promise of expectation hanging in the air. For the first time since her arrival, Tess didn't feel like an outsider. Maybe it was the shine, but her heart filled with awe, a wonder of what was to come.

Cal and Tess sat without speaking for a time, watching the silent fields as geysers spewed a nourishing shower of water onto the vegetation surrounding it. "It's so beautiful," she whispered. "Even with everything wrong about this place, there is much that takes my breath away."

"The beauty has increased tenfold since you arrived." He leaned closer and kissed her gently on the lips. She didn't resist, and a moment later, she wrapped an arm around the back of his head. He broke the kiss but remained close. "I never thought I would feel this way," he whispered.

Her face clouded, and she looked again at the fields. "It will never work out, you and I. One day, I'll be gone from here."

"Maybe, but that may be true for each of us. We live day-to-day with nothing promised." He followed her gaze. "Possibly in the fullness of time, this place will become a paradise for all of us who live here. Until then, we do what's necessary until we can change our lives for the better."

"So, tell me. How can I improve this society? I know you believe that somehow I will be the catalyst. What's your plan?"

Cal didn't answer right away. He opened his mouth to speak, but then closed it again. Toying with his fingers, he searched for the words. "I said you won't like it, and neither do I. But nobody has a better idea." He stared at her for a moment before continuing. "To kill a serpent, we cut off its head. So it is with the Elite. We must remove their leader." He fixed her with his gaze, not letting go. "You must kill Rowan Sarroff, the Prime Elite."

She shook her head. "Kill? No, I can't do that. I won't."

He grabbed her by the shoulders. "Listen to me, Tess. This is the only way. Please, just hear me out so I can explain."

She pulled away, a look of panic in her eyes. "I told you no." She jumped to her feet. He protested, but she extended her arms, palms facing out. Without another word, she turned and fled.

Cal stood as he watched her run off, his face set in a grim expression. After running his fingers through his hair, he took a ragged breath. "There goes our future."

16

ABDUCTED

"Impossible," Alan repeated once again, as if to make his point. He stood near the stove of their modest shelter, pausing as he heated a warm drink. The early morning light streamed into the room behind him.

This room, the village beyond their window, all appeared as it had since their arrival. But an unseen transformation occurred overnight. Cal's words could not be taken back, and that had changed everything. "You must kill him."

"It's out of the question," Alan now continued. "Don't even think about it."

Tess sat on the cushion of huge leaves which served as a bed, her knees drawn up. She was still in her undergarments as she rubbed her face, trying to come awake. "All I know is what I explained. Maybe I was too rash by running away. I should have heard him out." Her eyes opened wide in alarm and she jerked her head around to scan the room. "Where's Russell?"

Alan grinned. "I'm guessing things worked out better than he thought with that young girl. What was her name again?"

She flopped back down onto the bed. "Everything has gone to pieces. We were going in the right direction. And now—"

He poured steaming water into a mug as he mixed it with a dark powder already in the container and handed it to her with a frown. "Don't beat yourself up, Tess. Rusty's a big boy and he can take care of himself. This murder business, however. What makes Cal believe you would ever agree to it? Why you?"

She waved him off as she brought the mug to her lips. "Too many questions. Let me wake up first." She took a sip and set it down on the floor next to her.

Alan didn't give her a chance. "He can't ask you to do something like that. You could never kill someone."

Tess shook her head. "I don't know. Never gave him the chance to explain. I probably should have; we owe him that much at least."

"This makes no sense," Alan continued. "Say you agree and kill this guy. The Elite will replace him. Hell, we've heard the Reapers talk about the Sarroff family. So somebody must be next in line, ready to become the ruler of the Elite. Killing him won't solve anything."

Outside, someone whistled a tune. A second later, Russell pushed open the door and smiled at seeing them awake. "Sorry guys. I feel asleep after the festival ended. Too much shine, I guess."

"Uh-huh, is that right?" said Alan with a smile.

Russell blushed, but changed the subject. "Say, why's Cal across the road leaning against a tree? Is he waiting for you, Tess?"

She groaned. "I don't want to do this right now."

He shot her a puzzled frown, but Alan didn't give her a chance to answer. "I'll explain Rusty." Gazing back at Tess, he continued, "You should go speak with him. Make him justify this scheme of his."

"What's going on?" Russell asked.

Tess slipped into her jeans and motioned for them to turn around before removing her nightgown and pulling a shirt over her head. She laced her shoes and looked at Russell. "I'll know more shortly." She took a deep breath before opening the door and walking outside.

Cal straightened as he saw her approach. He stepped toward her, his jaw set, face expressionless. "I never should have asked you to commit such an act. I'm sorry," he said before she could speak. "It was foolish of me to put that on your shoulders."

She stood an arm's length in front of him. "I don't understand. Was that your idea? Is that why you've tried to help us survive here?" Her eyes watered. "I thought you were kind and caring, but was it just a ploy to get me to fall for you and go along with your plan?"

He reached out, but she took a step back. "Believe me, Tess, I love you. That's the truth." He rubbed his palm against his cheek. "It didn't start off with me feeling this way. But then you stopped me from entering the fortress when I was full of rage, about to kill any Elite I could find. I saw a side of you I hadn't expected. After my parents died, I was determined to look after my sister and then Mara. Keep them both safe from the Elite. It had taken all I had. Never did I suspect I would feel emotion for anyone else."

"Then if you cared for me, why did you ask me to murder one of the Elite? And not just any Elite, but their leader."

Cal looked down at his feet and let out a breath. "Because I gave in."

She furrowed her eyebrows, but he spoke without a pause. "We have a council made-up of certain Reapers. I'm on it, so is Brent. You don't need to know the others. Reapers formed the council ages ago to plan and implement the overthrow of the Elite. We add new members to replace older ones, or those who died. We nearly disbanded the council several generations ago when the Elite discovered its existence. They killed most of those members. Other than that unfortunate incident, we've kept it secret and continue to plan a way to depose the Elite even though we've never been successful. Our plans always came to naught because of one major flaw: the Elite would know if any Reaper harboring violence ever moved close to them. Our Directive would give us away; it's something we can't conceal."

"And because I don't have a Directive, you thought I could approach him without raising an alarm?"

He winced. "It was the unanimous choice of the council that I should try to persuade you to go along with our plan. Desperate times demand desperate measures."

Tess shook her head. "You're talking crazy, Cal. What good is killing him, even if he is the Prime Elite?" She repeated what Alan had said a few minutes ago. "They're just going to replace him with whoever is next in line and probably kill a bunch of you as an example. What do you expect to accomplish?"

His eyes held a hint of sorrow. "Yes, they will supplant him, but as the Prime Elite, Rowan Sarroff's death will create a temporary void. We will strike before his older son, or any other family member, establishes alliances and assumes the reins of power. It won't take long for that to happen, but until it does, confusion and panic will sweep through the Elite. Never have we assassinated a Prime Elite. I don't believe they can conceive of such a thing ever taking place."

She shook her head. "I still think you are hoping against hope. I've only glimpsed Rowan Sarroff one time. How will I ever get close enough to kill him? And for the sake of argument, say I did murder him. How can you possibly subdue the rest of the Elite? They won't let a bunch of armed Reapers waltz into the fortress. Leaderless or not, the Elite guards know enough to stop you."

His eyes turned cold. "Believe me, we have a plan for how we will overthrow them. But none of it matters if

Rowan Sarroff remains alive." He reached out to her and this time, Tess let him clutch her shoulders. "I should not have asked you to do this, but I had to try. Each one of us on the council, including myself, would sacrifice our own life to topple those bastards. Hell, every Reaper would. But we do not have a right to ask you, not myself, nor anyone else. And the reason we have no right is because, even if successful, it is a suicide assignment."

Tess stepped back and he let his arms fall to his side. She took a breath before speaking. "I came here because I thought I could help, never expecting that an assassination and getting myself killed would be part of the deal." She looked at the ground in front of her. "Give me time. I now understand why you want me to do this, but an act of premeditated murder..." She shook her head. "I don't know if I can do that, even if I agree with you."

She turned and walked away. He called to her. "Tess, I will never ask you about this again. If you ever decide you want to consider it, tell me. And if not, never again will anyone speak of it."

She nodded once and continued walking. Tess rarely stayed dispirited for long, her bubbly spirit always came through. But now, her shoulders sagged and head hung low.

For the first time since her arrival in this land, her demeanor mirrored that of a Reaper.

TESS'S VOICE QUIVERED. "THIS ISN'T FAIR, WHAT HE'S asking. How can I?" She sat cross-legged, facing Alan and Russell as all three huddled together on the floor of their ramshackle home. "But how can we fault Cal and the other Reapers? They want to get out from under the Elite. It's our purpose here that remains murky. Why did the sculpture back on Earth send us here unless it wanted us to improve the destiny of these Reapers? That has to be the only reason, because picking fruit for the rest of our lives makes little sense."

"I can't believe you're even considering it," said Russell. "Cal claimed it was a death sentence. Is that what you want?"

"You can count me out as well," said Alan, a pained expression on his face. "Whatever we are, we're not killers, regardless of how badly the Elite treat the Reapers. I understand why they need you to murder that Elite. Life is grueling for the workers." He shook his head. "But killing someone is not the answer. Nothing good can come of it. Even if the Reapers can somehow take control because of it, the very act will taint everything to follow."

Tess rested her face in the palms of her hands. "I remember the voice at the statue. It told us to set things right. What's taking place out there isn't right."

Russell took a deep breath. "No, it's not. But you have to decide if that voice would have wanted you to kill someone. It doesn't ring true, which makes me believe that killing someone wasn't part of the plan of why we're here.

You had better be sure this is the right thing to do before you even consider it. Don't risk your life on an impulse."

She shook her head. "Isn't that the way of things: flitting from one moment to another without knowing what's next? Whether we act on a whim or think it through, how can we be certain of our choices? Life is full of surprises." She looked out of the window at the brightening morning. Sol's Reaper crew would be at work in the fields by now. "What was I hoping to find here? Was it happiness or a need to prove myself? Maybe if I hadn't been so impulsive, I would have thought about it more before jumping head first after hearing the call."

Russell grinned. "You have many valuable qualities, Tess, but patience isn't one of them."

Alan grunted in agreement.

She chuckled and rose to her feet. Looking at them, she stretched her arms wide. "Come here, group hug." They stood and clenched each other, foreheads touching. "Whatever happens, I couldn't have picked better friends to help me get through this," she whispered. "Thanks for being here with me."

"You can count on us," said Alan. "After all, misery loves company."

As they broke the hug, Tess beamed. "Let's go to work before we get docked. We're already late."

Without protest, they left their home to begin another day laboring in the fields.

~

THE SUN HUNG LOW IN THE SKY, CASTING LONG shadows in the Reaper village as the three companions returned to their dwelling. With clothes stained by dirt and sweat, they trudged through the town. Despite their grimy appearance, they wore smiles and held their heads high, often nodding to other Reapers they passed; such was the dichotomy between today and the first confusing, unwelcoming days of their arrival.

They had a mission that still needed to be completed. The words spoken by the statue were always on their minds. But once the Reapers had accepted the three, even welcomed them, life had become more tolerable, almost pleasant, despite the hard work.

"I'm taking advantage of that tub tonight," said Tess as she gripped the handle of the entrance to their tiny home. Opening the door, she stopped short and gasped.

An Elite stood in the middle of the room, none other than Rowan Sarroff, the Prime Elite. He grinned as Tess stared with wide eyes. His smile wasn't a gentle expression of warmth, as much as a haughty, I-have-you-now kind of grin. "There you are," he said without introduction. Tess remained unmoving as he looked her up and down. "If I didn't know better, little pup, I would swear you were one of these Reapers."

Russell tugged at her from behind. "Let's run Tess."

She stood frozen in place, her eyes never leaving the Elite. "Y—you have no power over me. We are free of your rule."

He shook his head, "Tsk, tsk. I fear these uncivilized

animals have not provided you with a proper education. You have much to learn, and I believe it is time for your training to begin."

"You cannot control me as you can with the other Reapers. We have no Directive."

A complex stream of multicolored symbols burst to life around him, lighting the darkened room. "Obviously, I realize you are without one. Are you so dull-witted?" He smiled again. "Tell me, why do you think I am here, waiting for you in this filthy refuse heap of a place?"

Her back stiffened as she glared at him. "I don't care why you're here. This is my house and I want you out." She moved aside and held the door open to give him room. Her haughty response did little to mask the terror on her face.

He shook his head with feigned sadness. "You disappoint me, Tess Armstrong. Surely these savages have explained how important you are. Even their feeble Directives should detect the upheaval you will cause. When that time comes, you must be on our side of the turmoil. Which brings me to the purpose of this visit. I am here to open your eyes to the cornerstone of our society and the value of our rule. And for that to happen, you must know the Elite."

He held his grin in place as if plastered to his face. "I have granted you time here in this slum so that you could comprehend the limitations of these pitiful workers. Now, you will learn the reasons for the Elites' supremacy. Come with me."

Tess balled her hands into fists. "I'm not going

anywhere with you. I'll say it again. You have no control over the three of us."

His gaze raked over Russell and Alan for the first time. "These other two are inconsequential. Normally, we simply kill outsiders, but because of you, I will graciously allow them to live." He smiled more broadly, but the grin never reached his eyes. "Do not give me a reason to rescind my decision. I require your cooperation."

With their attention focused on Rowan Sarroff, nobody noticed the half-dozen other Elite who had slipped into position behind them. Only when Sarroff nodded to his troops, did Tess spin around to see them. Alan groaned, but they didn't dare to run. Each of the Elite held a two-foot long blade pointed at them.

"We have other means of enforcing our orders other than using our Directive." He appeared pleased with himself, but a moment later he sniffed as his face turned sour. "I have had enough of smelling this stench. You and I will leave. Now."

He elbowed past Tess, not bothering to see if she followed. Never turning his head around, he said, "Kill the other two if she resists." Several armed Elite edged closer to Alan and Russell, while another seized Tess by her upper arm. She stumbled as they forced her forward.

"Find Cal," she hissed as she passed her friends. "Tell him I agree to his plan. He'll understand. Have him somehow get word to me."

The Elite guards didn't give her time to say more. Only

after Tess was well away did the other troops surrounding Alan and Russell back off and sheath their blades.

"No, no, no," Alan wailed as he watched the others depart. His face had turned red. "This isn't good. We're in big trouble." He shook his head and wrung his hands, not knowing what else to do.

Russell grabbed his shoulders. "Calm down, Al. We'll get through this. Cal will know what to do." But even Russell, ordinarily the most confident of the three, could not hide the pain in his voice.

17

YOU MAY THINK ME A MONSTER

Tess sat in an ornate chair as she chewed on a fingernail. Half the room opened to a spectacular panorama of the countryside, yet her eyes remained unfocused, indifferent to the view. From this vantage, she could look down to see a lush green landscape with shimmering lakes and rivers. Periodic geysers dowsed the land with purifying water, as if cleansing the terrain.

The inside of her room was no less impressive than the outside. Everything about it was luxurious. Inch-thick carpeting covered the floor, an imposing bed dominated one side of the chamber, decorative vases held bouquets of scented flowers, and a private bath was accessible through another door. The space was also large, the size of a dozen typical Reaper homes.

Tess observed none of this as she brooded with her mind in a different place.

A sharp rap on the door interrupted her reverie. She

jumped to her feet in time to see two women open it and stand at the entrance. Their downcast eyes and lowered heads identified them as Reapers, but their clean red robes suggested otherwise. "We need to bathe and dress you, my lady," said the one who appeared somewhat older than the other. They continued to look at the floor in front of them.

"I don't need you to bathe and dress me," she snapped.

The older lady pursed her lips. Lowering her voice, she said, "Please, my lady. Otherwise, they will punish us."

Tess's face softened as she observed the younger girl shift from one foot to the other. The girl couldn't be more than sixteen. "You're Reapers, aren't you?"

Their eyes lifted for the first time. "Yes. The Elite prefer to call us servants, my lady. May we enter please?"

She nodded, and they hurried into the room and closed the door behind them, exhaling a breath as they did so. Each carried containers with a variety of brushes and bottles of lotions.

Tess continued to examine them. "My name is Tess. I'm not sure if we've met before. I lived with the Reapers."

The older woman continued to speak for both of them. "We know who you are, my lady. It would not be proper for us to call you by your given name here. All the Reapers are aware of you and your friends. And no, we have not met." She nodded to the child. "Del and I spend most of our time here in the fortress serving the Elite." She bowed her head. "My name is Glynn. Now, can we begin our assignment?"

Tess glanced at the door to the bath. "I know where the tub is. I can wash myself and you can take credit."

Glynn's face blanched. "No, you do not understand. We must complete the task. It is our responsibility. Anything else—" She could not finish as her throat tightened.

Tess held up her hands in surrender. "Okay, we'll have it your way."

During the next two hours, they washed her multiple times with a variety of brushes and sponges, rinsing her each time. The women paid special attention to her hair by applying an array of soaps and other lotions. At various points, other helpers, both women and men, barged into the room, some to take away her clothes—even though she protested—others to trim her hair while she sat naked in the tub trying to cover herself. No amount of complaining mattered to the servants. New attendants came and went as if she didn't have a say. Glynn allowed Tess to wrap a towel around her while she stood as a man took her measurements, presumably to fit her for other clothes.

Each of the caretakers went about their business with a sense of purpose, if not enjoyment. Nobody laughed or joked around. Neither did they engage in banter. They were here because they had no other choice. Whether it was picking fruit or vegetables in the fields, working in the mills, tending the livestock, or many other everyday chores, this was the lot in life for all Reapers.

After the washing, rinsing, hairstyling, and preening, she donned the new robes. Glynn inspected Tess one last time. Tess stood awkwardly, uncomfortable in the pleated gown she wore. The material hugged her bosom, flaring out at her waist and reaching to the floor. She frowned as she gazed at herself in a mirror, knowing she looked nothing like the grimy girl who had lived with the Reapers these long months. "What have I gotten myself into?" she muttered.

Glynn tightened her lips. "Whatever happens, my lady, always remember that we do what is necessary to survive. This is true for both you and the rest of us." Her eyes darted around the room before whispering into Tess's ear. "When the uprising comes, please do not forget the Reapers."

Before Glynn and Del left, the older woman said, "Another servant will be here soon to bring you to Rowan Sarroff. Be careful." The two hurried away, closing the door behind them.

A knock on the door announced the next attendant. Like the other Reaper servants, he didn't wait for a reply as he opened the door and bent his head in respect. "My lady, he is ready to see you now."

Tess took a breath, but didn't move. She had faced many dangers in this land, but the impending audience with the Elite leader seemed much worse. Her legs felt unsteady and for a moment she thought about sitting down.

The man in red robes at the door raised an eyebrow. "My lady?"

She cleared her throat. "Yes, I heard. I'm coming." Finding her courage, she stepped forward.

Once out in the broad hallway, the guide ambled ahead while Tess gawked at the ornate columns, colorful artwork on the walls, even the rich texture of the flooring. He stole a glance at her and smiled. "It is different in here, unlike the fields and the village, is it not?"

"Different? This is like entering an unfamiliar world. Once again."

A group of Elite dressed in white gowns came toward them and passed as they walked in the opposite direction. Tess flinched and drifted to the other side of the hallway, her head bending low. They paid no attention to her. "You do not have to fear them here in the fortress," said the Reaper guide.

She shrugged. "Other Reapers have warned me to avoid them. Seeing so many of them makes my skin crawl."

He studied her before responding. "Here's a bit of advice, my lady. You should not say something like that here, lest one of them overhears you. For the moment, the Prime Elite has granted you protection. But you never want to make enemies with any of them."

They continued walking in silence through the massive fortress. The inside appeared larger than she had imagined when viewed from the outside. Hallways were wide enough to fit fifteen people shoulder-to-shoulder, with ceilings twenty feet high. From the surrounding fields, the fortress was a mass of churning stone as if it had a life of its own. Here on the inside, the walls were transparent, like glass windows. An abundance of natural light brightened the area, making it seem as if they were strolling along an exterior walkway.

As they passed more Elite, the floating symbols of their Directives surrounded them. Unlike Reapers, who only occasionally displayed their Directives, the Elite appeared to flaunt them for others to see. Could it express a level of status in their community?

Some sights were incomprehensible. Tess stopped to gaze at a knot of about a dozen Elite as they gestured at what might be a group Directive, a massive display of lights and symbols floating in one of the larger rooms off the central passage. They appeared to be taking turns changing specific waves or patterns on the Directive. Tess's escort cleared his throat, urging her to continue.

Turning a corner, they walked into an imposing hall, even more majestic than the rest of the area. Round columns supported the high ceiling, while paintings of what must be Elite rulers or dignitaries adorned many of the walls.

Rowan Sarroff lounged on a thick cushioned chair at the far side of the room, a slight smile giving him a cocky appearance, as if he were happy with himself. His Directive surrounded him like antlers on a deer. A massive table dominated the chamber, laden with platters of fruits, meats, and an assortment of foods now familiar to Tess. Dozens of servants in red robes stood along the perimeter, ready to tend to the slightest need of the Prime Elite.

"I have been observing you for some time now," he

thundered. Tess winced as if hit by a gust of wind by his voice. Did he use his Directive to modulate the volume, or was it amplified by some unseen attribute of the hall?

Tess's guide moved to stand by the edge of the wall with the other Reapers. She stood alone to face a demon more vicious than she could imagine. Her courage wavered as she glanced back the way she came, wanting nothing more than to flee to her room. She clenched her fists and took several tentative steps forward. "If you intend to speak loud enough to frighten me, you'll need to increase the volume even more."

He smiled even wider and spoke in a normal tone. "I can see why you made such an impression on those Reapers out there." He nodded to the fields out beyond the transparent wall.

"They are my friends. The workers out there want to survive and live without fear of being killed for no reason. But you know nothing of that. Do you? They deserve better than what you've given them."

He wrinkled his forehead as if considering her opinion, or possibly to comprehend it. "An interesting assessment. Did any of these... friends tell you they have carried out over a dozen assassination attempts on my life since I was a child? Have they even explained to you that if they ever gained power over us, they would treat us the same, or worse? Do you know Elites do not risk taking a drink or eating a morsel of food unless a Reaper tastes it first?" He grasped his hands into fists and his Directive changed colors in rapid sequence. "No, I suppose they have not mentioned these inconsequential details."

A moment of uncertainty clouded Tess's face before her eyes flashed. "What do you expect? Your people kill them without the slightest regard for their life."

He tapped his index finger against his cheek, as if considering a different point. "Tell me, Tess Armstrong, is your homeland so perfect that nobody ever kills another? Does your race ever subjugate others for the benefit of themselves? Do you have different clans, some more powerful than the rest? Does no one take advantage of the disadvantaged?"

"That doesn't make any of this right!" she shouted.

He pursed his lips. "I am afraid that right or wrong has nothing to do with any of it. The universe contains an order to all life. You only have to look at the animal kingdom to confirm it. There will always exist some who are more powerful than the others. This is our society. The Elite and the Reapers are one, but we are unlike each other. Each group has our different mores, aspirations and dreams for a better world. We live in separate planes of existence. If the Reapers were in control of our community, chaos would be the result. They have no capacity to rule."

Tess shook her head. "That's not true."

He held up his palms to forestall her. "You may wish it so, my dear. But that will not make it so. The Reapers would not be better off if they ruled. It would be deadly for them and everyone else in this land."

Tess frowned, but didn't back down. "You made them that way. You never allowed them to control their own well-being." She lowered her voice in sadness. "You ensured they would never become equal with you."

He sighed. "Do you know why the Directives of the Elite are so much more robust compared to those of the Reapers?"

Her face brightened as she caught him in a deception. "Yes, it's because you force the Reapers to inbreed. You don't allow them to mate with the Elite. The strength of a Directive is hereditary. Theirs becomes weaker through the generations. It's how you keep them in their place." Her voice took on a cutting edge. "And not only that, you kidnap any child with a strong Directive. How can you be so cruel?"

"Part of what you say is correct, but it is not the entire truth. Genetics plays a role in the strength of the Directive, but only to a degree. Most of the power of a Directive is based upon the extent one uses it. A muscle will atrophy if one does not exercise it. We understand the importance of strengthening our Directives. The Reapers do not."

"They don't have the time to exercise it. You enslave them, give them quotas so they have to work day and night."

He waved his hand to brush off her objection. "Everyone works in this place, only in different ways and on unrelated tasks."

He took another breath. "You have so many false notions about life here. Did you realize we have no rule prohibiting Reapers and Elite from mating? Through the generations, those with stronger Directives sought and mated with those who were similar. So did those with Directives that were not as robust. It is a preference we carry forward to this day. A preference, not a mandate. I wonder if this is the same in your culture. Are attractive individuals drawn to others who are also attractive? Maybe physical beauty is not important in your homeland. Possibly, your society finds social values or mental capacity more appealing. You claim we coerce the workers to breed only amongst themselves when, in fact, they are more comfortable with their own kind. We are not like them, and they are unlike us."

Tess shook her head in frustration. "This is getting us nowhere. But for the sake of argument, let's say everything you claim is true. None of it, however, negates the brutality of the Elite, how you kill indiscriminately and force others into slavery. There's no reason to treat them like that. And nothing you can say will change that reality."

Rowan looked at her for a long time without responding, studying her. In a lower tone, he said, "You are not one of us. Yet, you must have gained a little understanding about the passion of our race. Our emotions run strong in both Elite and Reapers. It is who we are."

He gazed again at the fields beyond the fortress. Tess frowned, wondering if her audience with him had ended. But after a time, he looked upon her again and said, "Here inside our home, you may have noticed some of us who have joined our Directives together in a shared network. Do you know the reason for this?"

Tess furrowed her forehead at his sudden turn in direction.

"I will tell you. It is one example of the work we do for the good of both clans. We nudge events along when necessary. We guide activities so that our entire race continues to grow and prosper."

"Only the Elite prosper!"

"Would mayhem, war, famine, and disease be better for the Reapers?" His tone was sharp. "Would the deaths of millions from one generation to the next be better for everyone? The Elite facilitate a flourishing society. It is our guiding principle."

Her eyes flashed, but again, she had no answer.

He stared back at her as his face softened. "Believe me when I say I have tried to govern wisely. Governing is not always easy. The continuation of our race, the big arc of progress, drives all my decisions." His voice became even lower, and he looked sad for the first time. "I have discovered that for every righteous task I try to accomplish, I must rip something apart or cause harm. Maybe it is an unwritten law of nature, I do not know." He shrugged. "Possibly that is true for all rulers. Did my forefathers feel the same?" His tone took on a sharper edge. "Whatever the case, I am responsible for the preservation of our society. I cannot pay attention to every individual life or the feelings and dreams of each soul. By degrees, I stopped caring. I had no other choice."

He wiped his hand across his cheek as Tess stared, transfixed. He took a deep breath. "Tess Armstrong, you may believe I am a monster. But I am not."

ROWAN SARROFF WOULD SAY NO MORE. HE NODDED once at Tess's guide, who stood against the wall, and the Reaper stepped over and nudged her out of the ballroom. As they moved along the passageways back to her room, he glanced at her from time to time, seeing her in a new light after her audience. Nobody in his lifetime had ever spoken so boldly to the Prime Elite, nor supported his fellow workers as she had. Did the prophesies have merit after all?

She took no note of him, nor of the other Elite in the hallways, keeping her eyes forward, her mind somewhere else. "Why did he explain all that to me?" she mumbled, as if talking to herself.

He fixed her with his gaze. "You are important to him, my lady."

She turned her head to him for the first time. "Because he believes I will help him?"

The Reaper glanced around to be sure no Elite could hear them. "Yes, he wants you on his side. He has ambitions, as do all Elite, but he desires more than others. I believe he wishes to rule beyond this meager parcel of territory. Not satisfied with what he has, I imagine he hopes you will support him as he expands his realm."

She frowned. "But he said nothing about that."

"First, he needs you on his side. You will only assist him if you trust him."

She stopped walking and stared at him. "What do you know about me?"

He shrugged. "I have seen you working with Sol's crew as I passed the fields. You may not have realized this, but many of us sneaked a glimpse of you and your companions once we understood you were not a typical outsider. But you and I never spoke. Even within the Reaper community, a distinction exists between those laboring in the fields and those of us serving in the fortress. We spend most of our time in different locations. But in the end, we are all slaves."

Tess let out a breath. "Everyone thinks I'm some kind of knight in shining armor."

"A what?"

She smiled as they began walking again. "An expression from where I come from. Someone who will come to the rescue. The Reapers believe I'm going to save them, and now so do the Elite. I keep saying to both of you I have no superhuman powers, but nobody believes me." Her gaze went out of focus again. "My home is far away, and now I'm way over my head. I came here because I thought I could help, never realizing it would be this difficult or the cost of failure so high. My goal in life was never to become a savior or someone of importance. I've had enough of all this and just want to go back to my own life."

He frowned as they stepped together in silence for a time. "My lady, you may not consider yourself capable of achieving greatness, but it is not something bestowed on powerful leaders alone. Our Directive tells us that ordinary individuals will one day change our lives. I do not know you well, but I can tell that you are compassionate and have a good heart. Maybe that is all you need."

She returned the comment with a weak smile. "Oh, if it were only true. But I'm afraid that freeing the Reapers will take more than kindness. My heart tells me that blood will be spilled, and I fear I'm going to be the spark that ignites a firestorm." She kept her face forward. "And even worse, I have a premonition that the outcome will be more terrible than what now exists."

18

BEFORE YOUR TIME HERE ENDS

Tess woke with a start, her breathing heavy, a bad dream already fading from her memory. She remembered a group of Elite faces with their eyes wide, but nothing more. Taking in her unfamiliar surroundings fed her distress further. What was she doing here in these opulent quarters?

In another heartbeat, it came back to her in a rush: the Prime Elite, Rowan Sarroff, had taken her prisoner. Later, his audience with her was no less distressing. He would never allow her to return to her friends in the Reaper village; that much was clear from his discussion.

She closed her eyes, head sinking into the pillow. "My life is in shambles," she murmured. "How could I mess up so badly?"

Her racing heart had returned to normal when a loud blast sent her bounding out of bed, the stone floor still vibrating from the eruption. Was it an explosion? Had the

Reapers attacked, trying to free her? She lurched toward the exit, expecting to see Cal out in the hallway, a crooked smile on his face.

But she paused at the door, her gaze fixed on the latch. She tested it and found it unlocked. This had been her first night in the fortress, and she wasn't yet sure how much freedom the Elites would give her. Whatever liberty they granted, surely it would end at the front gate.

Still in her nightclothes, she opened the door to peer one way and then the other along the wide passageway. A few Elite strolled the hallway as if nothing was amiss. Nobody was running or shouting orders to evacuate or arm themselves. "I don't understand," she mumbled. "Why aren't they more concerned?" Without bothering to change out of her nightgown, she picked a direction and began striding forward as if she belonged here.

Before she traveled a dozen paces, someone shouted, "My lady!" Tess spun around to see Del, the younger of the two maids from yesterday, waving her arm as she balanced a tray with the other. Setting it on the floor, she dashed at Tess. The whites of her eyes underscored her panic. Maybe now she would discover the reason for the explosion. "Please," said the girl, "if they see you dressed like this, Glynn and I will be at fault." She grabbed Tess by the elbow, pulling her back toward her room. "I beg you, let me dress you first."

"That blast, you must have heard it. I'm trying to find out what happened. What the hell was it?"

The girl continued to urge Tess along. She glanced

around the passage before speaking. "I will explain what I know, but not here."

The girl's presence calmed Tess, and she complied. Once in the room, she demanded, "Well, was it some sort of explosion?"

Del concentrated on placing covered plates and utensils in precise positions on a small round table. She frowned as she glanced at Tess, worry lines creasing her youthful face. "You must understand they do not tell us everything. After all, I am a Reaper, and only a serving girl at that." She fell silent, turning her attention back to her task.

Tess stepped over to her wardrobe to grab a wrap hanging there. Her face softened as she looked at the serving girl. "It must be difficult working here in the fortress. You see and hear things the other Reapers in the fields do not."

Del tilted her head, puzzled by the comment. "I volunteered for this assignment. My parents who work the fields are proud they accepted me." She waved her hand to dismiss the thought. "But you asked about the bang. They are testing something, maybe a weapon, I don't know. I've heard a dozen different opinions about what it may be. It's controlled by their collective Directive. That's all we have learned."

"A weapon to use against the Reapers or others in this world?"

She shrugged. "It doesn't matter, does it? The Elite will do what they want."

"But somebody must have a clue. If the Elite intend to wage a war against others, think about how many more innocent lives will come under their oppression."

Del looked at her without expression. "There's no stopping them. You should understand that by now."

Tess pursed her lips. "You've probably seen more suffering than I ever will. But we're on the same side."

Del smiled a weak grin. "I didn't know we had sides."

"The Reapers against the Elite," Tess sputtered. "The way they rule you..."

Del waved her hand. "I grasp what you mean, my lady. They are the Elite and I am a Reaper. Some say we would be better off if we rid ourselves of them." She lowered her eyes to the floor. "The Elite do horrible things. It seems every Reaper knows of a friend or a family member killed by one of them. But if you ask any of us what should take the place of the ruling dynasty, nobody has an answer. If any Reaper has an opinion, it is to replace the rule of the Elite with the rule of the Reapers. We should treat them the way they have treated us." She looked back up at Tess. "I cannot wonder if that would be any better."

"But something has to be done."

The girl studied her for a moment. "Some say you will be our salvation. Is that true?"

Tess frowned as she stood still, hesitating before responding. "I honestly don't know. I came here to help, yet I have no idea how."

Del barked a laugh. "In that regard, you do not differ from the rest of us Reapers." She examined the table settings one last time. Satisfied, she held the back of the chair. "Please, before your breakfast becomes cold. Glynn will be here shortly so we can provide you with appropriate attire. You have another session with the Prime Elite."

Tess's shoulders slumped as she shuffled to the seat.

DEL AND GLYNN TOOK HOURS TO PREPARE TESS FOR another public appearance. "I hope we don't have to do this every time I leave this room," she complained. The two maids glanced at each other without responding. Tess did not lose the meaning of their expression. "Oh, I get it. This is about you as much as me, isn't it?"

Again, they didn't answer, but looked less troubled as they continued to primp her hair.

When Tess entered the great hall for another audience with Rowan Sarroff, he was nowhere to be seen. A few Reapers still lined the edges of the hall, but far fewer than before. Her guide motioned her to an outside balcony. As she approached, she saw him sitting at a round table upon which held more food than she could eat in months.

His face brightened as she walked into the sunlight. "You look exquisite this morning, Tess Armstrong. If you do not mind me telling you."

Her body tensed. "Is this another of your lies meant to convince me how charming you are?"

He pinched his eyebrows together. "I am disappointed

you believe that of me." He gestured at the other chair. "Please join me for a midday meal. That is all I ask. If you wish, we can sit here in silence and enjoy the food and the view."

She glanced at the magnificent vista of green fields and trees. A few small puffy clouds dotted the sky. Tess sat straight-backed while a young lady, wearing the typical red robe of a Reaper attendant, stepped over to pour a pale liquid into goblets in front of each of them. Tess frowned as she eyed the drink.

Rowan saw her reluctance as he lifted his glass. "To your good health, Tess Armstrong." When she didn't respond, he added, "Please, try it. You have my word everything here is safe. I have a vested interest in keeping you from harm."

She took a tentative sip and her eyes lit up. "This tastes fabulous. Made by the Reapers?"

He nodded. "Of course. Just be careful not to drink too much of it."

"Hmm, sounds familiar. I've been told the same by a Reaper offering me shine. Have you ever had it?" Her eyes shot up. "Oh, I hope that's not outlawed or forbidden. Maybe you should forget I mentioned it."

He chuckled. "I cannot say I have had the pleasure of tasting shine, but I understand it is quite disgusting. And no, you have not divulged a dark secret of the Reapers. Everyone is free to eat and drink whatever they wish." He nodded at the platefuls of food on the table. "Please help yourself. I am starving." He spooned a variety of items onto his plate. Tess followed a moment later by taking a much smaller amount.

"What do you want from me?" she said before taking a bite.

He finished chewing before he answered. "That is a fair question. I could say I want to know more about you. That would be true, yet I doubt you would believe me. The genuine answer is that I do not know what I expect from you. I explained how we presume you are the center of a crucial event that fast approaches. We have an inkling what will take place, but I am unsure of the role you will play in it." He leaned forward. "So, trust me when I say that all I really ask is you keep an open mind about me." He motioned with his hand to indicate the fortress. "I would like you to discover who we are. Your education in our community has been with the Reapers. I allowed you to learn about them. Now permit me to teach you about us."

"You allowed me? I've already seen enough of the Elite to know that you are heartless. You're cruel and care little for the lives of others, regardless of what you tell me about yourself."

His lips tightened. "You still see us through the eyes of the Reapers." He motioned with his utensil. "You see them as powerless, kindly, with no agenda of their own. Yet, you believe I want something from you. Tell me, what did they ask of you?"

Her eyes shot up, stopping before putting a piece of

food in her mouth. "W—what makes you think they asked anything?"

His smile returned. "We are the same, the Reapers and Elite. The differences you observe in us are minuscule compared to how much we are alike. You would be wise not to trust them."

"But you want me to trust you. Isn't that correct?"

"Ah, you are good, Tess Armstrong. May I suggest you mistrust each of us equally?"

She considered this for a moment before saying, "Okay, here's a chance for you to be honest with me. This morning I heard a noise like an explosion. What was it?"

"It was loud, wasn't it?" He delayed answering by taking a bite of food. "What you heard this morning was a test of an instrument we have produced for the next phase of our development. We have a plan for our future in which we expand to many worlds. If that destiny ever becomes a reality, our Directives must be strong enough to both protect us and deflect unknown enemies."

"So it is a weapon. One you could also use against the Reapers."

He swept his hand around the room. "You believe incorrectly that we are primarily concerned about the affairs of those serving us. Our goals are loftier." He leaned closer to her. "Consider a million worlds with its citizens all working together in harmony. A universe without wars or poverty. Think about the benefit we can bring to those beings stymied because they remain detached from society or because nobody has attempted to advance their intellect. The advances are limitless. Civilizations across the cosmos will know a golden age of enlightenment." His eyes were bright, and he held his head high as Tess looked at him with alarm.

"We are on the verge of bringing this new existence to others. You can be at our side as we sweep away the old ways and create an improved life for everyone."

"And this weapon, this explosive force, will exterminate those who oppose you?"

He leaned back in his chair as he regarded her while tapping an index finger on the table. "Please consider the remarkable advantages we can offer others rather than what we need to protect ourselves. Not everyone will see the benefits of what we wish to provide. The misinformed may attempt to harm us. By expanding beyond this small valley, we open ourselves up to unknown dangers. That is the only reason for this defensive tool."

She said nothing as her expression remained frosty. He sighed. "Perhaps I have left you too long among the Reapers. I can see you remain unconvinced." His Directive went through a rapid succession of changes in color and velocity. "You do not know me, so I understand your suspicion. But there is someone I am asking to join us, one you will believe."

Tess frowned, her body tensing. "What do you mean? Who?"

He sat back, smiling as if he had played a winning card. Holding up a finger, he said, "One moment. Please remain here." He stood to leave. "You can speak alone without fear that I am attempting to control anyone's opinion."

He spun around, robes flowing, and strode back inside the great hall. From her vantage on the balcony, she saw him dash across the room and exit the far end. The other Reaper servants remained impassive, as if they were deaf and mute.

Tess stood, looking left and right, hoping to discover an answer to his riddle. She whispered to some of the closest servants, "What did he mean?" They reacted the same as during her early days among the Reapers, when she might as well have been invisible. None of them so much as blinked an eye or offered a response. She paced back and forth, eyes glued to the inside of the great hall.

Before long, a lone figure strolled through the length of the hall toward the balcony. The person's Directive floated through the air, but Tess couldn't make out the face until she reached the entry of the terrace. A girl blinked as a ray of sunlight played across her face. Tess sucked in a breath. Unable to restrain herself longer, she rushed toward the child and wrapped her arms around her in a tight hug.

"Mara, you're safe," she gasped, not letting go.

The child smiled and returned the embrace. "And you survived too. I can't believe it." Mara broke the hug and held Tess at arm's length. "They didn't tell me you were here. I thought I would never see you again."

Tess's eyes watered. "I have a million questions. How are you being treated? Did they hurt you? What kind of work are they forcing you to do? When will—"

Mara held up a hand. "I am good. My life is well, and this is the best I could have hoped for."

Tess frowned. "The best you could hope for? Your abduction devastated me. Everyone felt the same: your mom, Cal, all the others. We all love you."

Mara clutched Tess's palm and led her to the chairs at the table. Once seated, the young girl said, "Nobody has harmed me. I spend most of my time training, often for long hours." She beamed. "Look at how much I have improved my Directive." Tess glanced at the lights and symbols circling her, seeing they were more vibrant and elaborate than previously. Mara continued with a quiver in her voice. "And I made new friends here,"

Tess studied her. "You didn't ask for this. How could they do this to you, take you away from everyone you loved?"

The girl looked down at her hands folded on her lap. "I miss them—Cal, mom, uncle Brent, others—and I think about them." She took a quivering breath, her face remaining calm. Was that a part of her training? "My choices were to either adapt or die. I learned that from my life with the Reapers. The lesson was true then, as it is now."

Tess hesitated before she spoke again. "So, you don't consider yourself a Reaper any longer?"

Mara looked at her without expression. "I once was, and I loved that life. But it doesn't exist for me now." Her lips tightened, a sign that she felt troubled by what had happened to her. "Please understand. I cannot return to the life I once had. That is not a choice. If I fail at what they teach me here, they do not send me back."

"They'll kill you if that happens." It was not a question.

Mara's eyes lowered again and she squirmed in her seat. "I grew up fearing the Elite, maybe hating them. But they are not as evil as I had believed." She looked up to see Tess's reaction. "Living here has helped me learn about them, to see the world through their eyes. They do so much I had never realized. The Elites are necessary to everyone's lives, including the Reapers." Tess was on the verge of interrupting, but held her tongue. Mara continued, "Before this, all I saw was the killing and the bitterness. There is more to them."

"Did Sarroff put you up to this, give you the words to say?"

She flinched. "No! Nobody told me to say anything. I didn't even know you were here." Her eyes watered. "You once believed in me and loved me, so why are you unable to do so now? Put yourself in my place. I had no future except as a picker in the fields, or as a seamstress, or doing some other menial role. Few Reapers ever break out of their appointed tasks. Now, I work hard, but I don't live in fear of my life. I have a future and a purpose here."

"What purpose?" Tess hissed, still concerned Sarroff might hear them. "And don't blame the Reapers for not doing more with their lives. The Elite have crushed them into submission."

She shook her head. "The Elite do not force the

Reapers to serve them." Tess inhaled, about to object, but Mara continued. "Anyone can leave here if they wish. Did you know that?"

Tess had nothing to say.

"We have no wars, no theft or looting, no anarchy. Everyone has to work hard, both Reapers and Elite. Except, the Elite work differently. They fortify their Directives, keeping all of us safe. They maintain an organized community for the good of all."

Tess stared, dumbfounded. "You've changed, Mara. I hardly know you."

The young girl frowned. "That is not true, but if so, I have only changed for the good." She held her head up, as any Elite would. "It is difficult for me to explain everything without being able to show you through the eyes of a Directive. You would see that I am happy—no, thrilled—at how much progress I have made in myself." She gripped Tess by the shoulders. "You may not believe it, but my life is better."

They hadn't noticed a middle-aged woman in Elite robes approach. She stopped at the entrance of the balcony and cleared her throat, startling Tess. "Time to continue your lesson, Quinn."

Mara glanced at Tess, seeing her furrowed brows. "They give us an Elite name once we begin our training. It signifies our acceptance into their society."

The lady at the doorway narrowed her eyes as she observed the girl. "You should have been mindful of my summons. Perhaps your Directive is not yet strong enough."

Quinn sighed. "Oh, I was aware of it, but I ignored you. I placed more weight on Sarroff's request that I speak with Tess Armstrong. In this regard, my attention to your call was secondary."

The lady didn't react. "Very well. Perhaps you are right. But you still have much to learn and my responsibility is to see that you gain the skills to be an Elite. Are you ready to continue?"

Quinn stood, her eyes on Tess. She hesitated, now unsure of herself for the first time. But then she straightened, shoulders back. "We each have a part to play in this kingdom, Tess. You, me, everyone who lives here." Her gaze went unfocused for a second, as if seeing something invisible. "Before your time here ends, you must determine the role you will play. I believe yours is the most important of all."

The Reaper girl once known as Mara, now an Elite named Quinn, marched away, never looking back. Her white robe billowed behind her, back straight, head held high, appearing like every other Elite. The shy little girl Tess had met on her first day here was nowhere to be seen.

19

CRIES OF PASSION

On the fourth week since her captivity in the Elite fortress, Tess waited for her handmaids to enter her room, as they had every morning. Today, unlike many of the past days, she sat on a plush sofa facing the door rather than forcing them to rouse her from her bed, too despondent to even rise. One finger tapped the arm of the chair as her eyes remained riveted on the entrance. She had dressed in the simplest clothes she could find among the elaborate gowns.

Without knocking, the Reaper maids Glynn and the younger Del opened the door. "What is wrong?" said Glynn in surprise once she saw Tess.

Tess came to her feet. "I'll tell you what's wrong. I'm useless here. My life is wasting away in this room while I sit and wait." She raised her voice. "And wait for what? Some imaginary catastrophic event that might or might not involve me? Or do I sit here and wait for this grand ruler to summon me for yet another audience with him? I'm sick of it. My life has meaning and purpose... at least it once did." She shook her head as if to clear it. "This is not who I am, and I will not accept it. These Elite may beat everyone else into submission, but they have never faced me before."

The two maids stood mute, eyes opened wide. Tess lowered her voice. "I want to escape, find a way out of here. The Reapers in the fields will help me once I get out of this fortress. I need you to do me a favor and tell me how I can get away."

"Do you a favor?" Del squeaked. Glynn hurried to shut the door.

Glynn turned to Tess and scowled. "My lady, what you ask is not possible. I do not believe you understand your importance to The Prime Elite."

"I'm under no obligation to serve him, as much as everyone else here believes."

"You have every right to have your own opinion. That is true of all Reapers. He cannot reach into your head and change your thoughts. But leaving here is not an option, at least as long as he orders you to remain." Glynn swept her hand through the air. "Nobody leaves the fortress unless the Elites agree. They find the Reapers who have tried, and they kill them."

"But I'm not a Reaper, that's the difference."

"Then they will kill every Reaper who served you here in the fortress or who aided you in an escape. Then they will kill every Reaper you ever associated with in the village. Is that what you want?"

Tess remained silent for a moment as her eyes flickered between the two maids. "Then tell me what you would do if you were me. And don't say that I should sit quietly like a good little girl."

Glynn put her hands on her hips. "The problem is that you need to recapture your ambition and zeal—emotions somehow lost when they took you here. You are under no obligation to sit here in this chamber." She pointed toward the bedroom. "Neither should you stay in that bed half the morning feeling sorry for yourself. You have the freedom to do whatever you want as long as you remain inside the fortress. Explore it. Learn more about the Elite. Make some other friends—Reapers or Elite. Live!"

Tess opened her eyes wide at the rebuke. She thought about it for a moment. "Well... I'm not happy about being here, but you may have a point." She pointed to the outside door. "But what about Jed, my guide? Whenever I leave, he's there to escort me as if I were a child."

"He is here to serve you, just as we are. If you would rather walk the halls without him, you only need to tell him."

Tess dropped her hands to her side in frustration. "Well then, what about those frilly gowns you have me dress in when I have an audience with Sarroff? I don't need to wear those. How's that? And by the way, I want the clothes I had been wearing when they captured me. Whatever ever happened to them?"

Glynn didn't back down. "We dress you in frilly gowns, as you call them, for your own benefit. You are vital to the Prime Elite. The manner of your attire amplifies that in his eyes. Although you don't realize it, we provide you with those clothes to give you an edge. You would be foolish to discard whatever advantage you have."

They both stared at each other while Del looked from one to the other, as if fascinated by the exchange. Tess finally relaxed her stance. "Very well then, I won't try to escape, at least not right now. But I'm doing what I want from now on."

Glynn bowed her head. "I would expect nothing less from you, my lady."

"Good, because the first thing I'm going to do is to explore this jail dressed this way without being primped and washed first." Tess moved toward the closed door, but turned to look back before she reached it, half expecting them to stop her. "And please get me some simpler clothes to wear from now on, at least when I'm not entertaining his holiness. Maybe something like what the Reapers wear."

A hint of a smile came to the maid's lips. "I will see what I can find." Before Tess was out of the door, Glynn added, "I have to admire your tenacity. For most of us Reapers, it is a quality we can only wish for."

Tess frowned at the maid as she reached for the handle. She was about to say more, but thought better of it. Any advice might only result in the Maid's death. And that was something she didn't want to put on her shoulders.

For the first time, she walked out of her room alone.

~

Tess frowned as she looked left and then right at an intersection in the hallway. Unlike many other areas of the fortress, this location was unoccupied by either Elite or Reapers. She shrugged, trying to hide her nervousness as she took the hallway to her right.

Natural light streamed in from the transparent wall on one side, allowing her to take in the view of the fields far below. Judging from their distance, this was one of the upper floors. The other side of the walkway was solid, with no doors. Unlike the central passage of the fortress, with ornate pillars and broad aisles, this was narrow, only wide enough for two people to fit alongside each other.

After a short way, the walkway veered away from the outside wall. She hesitated as she looked at the darker passage ahead. It ended fifty yards away with a cloth-covered door. The sheer fabric emitted daylight from the other side. "Strange," she muttered.

Taking a breath, she stepped toward it.

She paused for a moment before pulling the curtain aside to peek at what was behind. Plants and trees blocked her view and a puff of humid air washed over her. Was this a secret entrance to the outside world? Brushing a branch of a tropical-looking plant aside, she stepped through the opening. A quick look around dashed her hope that this was outside the fortress. The glass walls of the building still surrounded her and rose in a dome four stories above, with some of the taller trees nearly reaching the top. The twitter of birds and insects came from every direction as butterflies danced through the plants.

Her eyes sparkled as she looked around. "Who would have thought?" she said to herself. "Here in this prison."

A meandering stone path led away from the entrance, so she followed it. Her head swept from one side to the other as she tried to take in everything at once. A small yellow bird landed on her shoulder, and she froze, hoping the small warbler would remain close to her, even for a moment or two. The bird looked back at her, chirped, and flew off to join a friend on the limb of a nearby tree.

Tess strolled along the path, noticing the occasional stone bench lining the edge of the walkway. The tension and anger she had been feeling earlier today drained from her as she tried to look everywhere at once. The twittering of small wildlife sounded like a soothing musical melody. Her face brightened as she spun around, seeing birds take flight or perch on nearby limbs.

Looking up at the transparent dome high above, she noticed designs etched into the glasslike outer walls, unlike the clear transparency in the other areas of the fortress. The markings would prevent the birds inside from flying into it and killing themselves. The outside of the dome must consist of the same stone as the rest of the stronghold.

She approached a bench and considered sitting so she could continue observing the view. At the last moment, she straightened, her eyes fixed on something farther along the path. A man stood there, wearing Elite clothes, his back to her. His arm was outstretched, palm up, as birds swirled around, pulling seeds from his hand.

Tess was about to sit again and observe the man until

his face turned enough for her to recognize him. Rowan Sarroff smiled as he watched the birds battle over the seeds, spilling as much as they ate.

She stiffened, her eyes opened wide. Her feelings toward Rowan had softened this past month, but she was still wary of him. Yet he had been nothing but cordial with her whenever they were together. Lately, he had requested to meet with increasing frequency. Requested! How could someone be a monster yet treat her with such respect? The dichotomy between his public persona and her personal experience still bewildered her.

She had begun to feel comfortable around him, a sensation she tried her best to deny. But when they were together, she would laugh at his jokes and become disheartened to learn about his burdens. And whenever he looked at her, he had a softness in his eyes. She wondered if she too gazed at him with the same compassion.

She stepped back, but bumped into the bench behind her and lost her balance. Yelping, she grabbed onto a tree limb before falling into the dark loam bordering the path. Rowan turned at the sound of her cry, his face angry at the intrusion. But once he saw Tess, he smiled.

"My lady," he called to her. "Please come join me. This is an unexpected surprise."

Tess took a moment to smooth her blouse, which had become twisted during her stumble. "I—I don't want to intrude," she stammered. "I was just exploring."

"Then let us explore together, shall we? I insist. This is a magnificent conservatory, do you agree? It is my pride and joy, part of my contribution to our living fortress." He motioned to one of the nearby trees. "But please, our shouting only scares the birds." It was true. A flock of them now sat perched on branches several saplings away.

She murmured something unintelligible under her breath and plastered a smile on her face as she approached him. "What do you mean by living fortress?"

He raised his eyebrows. "Surely, you see the spirit inherent in this structure. We have not constructed this building with stone and wood, but with part of ourselves. It lives, breathes, and exists, as do you and I. Every Elite contributes to its growth, and over time, the life within has become tuned to our aspirations. I do not know if we could exist without it." He looked around with delight in his eyes.

Tess frowned at yet another explanation to puzzle over, setting it aside for later. "I didn't expect you to be here," she apologized. "My guide isn't with me today, and I discovered this place by chance."

He was more interested in the birds at that moment as he observed them rather than her. "They are superb creatures, so full of energy."

She studied him rather than looking at the birds. "Uh, I guess so, although I never thought much about them. I'm surprised you have such a fondness for these feathered friends."

He chuckled as he tore his gaze away from the tree and looked at her. "I suggest your amazement is due to you still not knowing me very well. You cling to an illusion, and I am not who you thought I was. In your mind, I am your nemesis, someone to hate and blame for all the wrongs you have observed. How can I possibly do anything right?"

She shifted from one foot to the other. "Well, maybe you are not as terrible as I had thought." She looked at the birds, suddenly concerned. "Unless you keep these pets for some perverted reason. Tell me you don't torture them."

He raised his eyebrows and then shook his head. "It pains me you have to ask such a thing. I had hoped you would come to feel differently about me once you knew me better. But now..." He didn't finish his thought as he continued to gaze at her. "You are strong-willed, Tess Armstrong. Maybe I always realized that about you. I admire how you cling to your beliefs, but there comes a time in one's life to consider another perspective."

He sat on the bench and motioned for her to join him. "To answer your question, no, I do not torture the birds."

She wore a sheepish expression as she settled next to him. An awkward silence followed for a moment until she said, "You're right. I don't know you, and I haven't given you a fair chance. Yet, I've seen the way the Elite treat the Reapers. It isn't fair, and I blame you for it." She looked down at her clasped fingers on her lap.

His voice softened. "We all live under the bane of inequities, Tess. That is true for anyone who has ever existed, an irrefutable reality of nature." His tone became more urgent as he continued. "But we provide a structure in their everyday lives and a way for them to exist with a degree of freedom. As long as they have hope for a better life, they will accept their place in the larger scheme of existence, as would any society." He wagged his finger in front of him, as if playing to an unseen audience. "Once the workers understand we will expand our dominion over the rest of the land, and then beyond our world, everyone will be a winner. When the entire community comprehends that we, as a whole, will become the dominant race, they will accept it and work toward that end in unison. Such is our state of affairs. And with your arrival, the pivotal point in our lives is nearly upon us—even they realize it—and you can bring us all forward."

Tess furrowed her forehead but didn't respond. He searched her eyes as he sat with his back straight, a slight smile on his face. "You can have it all, Tess, more power, wealth, strength, vigor, happiness—whatever your heart desires. And we can achieve this together, you and I. You will be by my side as an equal as we reach for a glory never known before. All you need to do is support me when the time comes."

Her resolve began to waiver. His voice was sincere, with no hint of deception. Although Tess wanted nothing of fame and glory, he moved her with his candor. This was the man she hated more than anyone, wasn't he? Yet somehow, she didn't feel that way any longer.

The indecision showed on her face. "You don't understand, Rowan. You talk about this impending event as if I had some hidden power. I don't! And neither do I want it. I'm not like you; I'm an ordinary human being from an average place I once called home—no, it's still my home.

This is not my place or life. I'm only here to help, but everything has become so confusing. I seem to have lost the ability to know who's right and who's wrong."

"You are here to make us a formidable society, even more so than we thought possible. That is your purpose; I can sense it. And when the time comes—and we will know when that moment arrives—then I believe you will manifest your hidden abilities as you bring us into the future. Trust me."

She let out a breath. "Oh, I wish I knew. I would love to have your confidence. Everything has been so confusing since the day I arrived here. I only want to do what's right. That's all I ever wanted."

He put his hand gently on her shoulder as they faced each other. "And so you shall. I have faith in you." He hesitated as he gazed at her face, taking a strand of her hair and twirling it around his finger. "This is not something I should tell you, Tess, but I have been thinking about you a great deal. I find you quite captivating. Never in my life have I met someone like you. In fact, I think—"

"No, no, no. Don't say this."

"I find myself falling in love with you."

Tess kept her eyes lowered, fingers clenched. "Rowan, maybe you mean well, but I can't deal with this right now."

His gaze never wavered. "I never realized what I was missing until I met you, Tess Armstrong. Your mere presence is intoxicating. And I can only hope that someday you will feel the same toward me."

She kept her eyes downcast, on the verge of tears. He

let go of the strand of hair and tenderly cupped her chin, raising her head. "I love you, and I always will. Believe me, that is the truth."

Without asking, he bent forward and kissed her on the lips. She didn't resist. All the emotions she had been feeling these past months came together at this moment. She had been devoting all her energies to staying alive, while also protecting Russell and Al. It was too much for her. For this one time, she was going to give in to her own needs. Nobody would be harmed because of her feelings. No one else would care.

After a moment, his kiss become more passionate as she moaned softly. Her hands reached up behind his shoulders, gripping him tightly.

Clothes soon tumbled to the ground. The colorful birds on the nearby branches continued to chirp, the only ones to witness their intimacy and hear their cries of passion.

2 0

THE SECRET POCKET

"I'm a prisoner in a gilded cage," Tess lamented a few weeks after her encounter with Rowan Sarroff in the conservatory.

This day, she strolled through the halls with her Reaper guide, Jed. He was the only escort ever assigned to her, just as Glynn and Del were her only handmaids. They shared a closeness with each other, an affinity born from their time together and a mutual respect. Each of them had a role to play, none yet aware of the cataclysmic events to come.

Tess was free to wander anywhere within the fortress by herself, but Jed would always offer to go with her. She only declined when she was meeting Rowan, which had become more frequent as the days passed. Her attitude toward the Prime Elite had warmed since her arrival in the fortress, as she observed his thoughtful and caring nature.

Maybe he wasn't as cold-blooded as the Reapers had made him out to be.

Tess glanced at Jed when he didn't respond to her comment. She frowned, seeing his eyes dart across the hallway. "You're on edge today. Is something wrong?"

He shrugged and put on the semblance of a smile. "No, my lady. Sorry if I appear distracted." He snuck another look around. "But I could use some fresh air. Would you care to visit a balcony?"

She nodded, her brow still furrowed. He continued to regard each Elite with more than his usual interest as he led her to an outside spot she had not visited before. It was on a lower level, facing away from the flooded fields and geysers. His eyes swept across the deserted platform before he spoke. "The Elite rarely visit this place. They favor the upper floors and locations with a better view."

He gazed at the barren landscape and rugged terrain beyond. The Reaper village and the Elite fortress were in a valley, with jagged mountains surrounding them. The location formed a natural barrier, leaving them isolated from the rest of the world.

Tess waited as Jed fidgeted until he licked his lips and moved closer, speaking in a whisper. "I have a message for you."

"From who?" she blurted.

"Shh. Please keep your voice down." He glanced around again. "I am a dead man if they ever discover I have spoken to you about this." He flinched as a bird the size of a hawk passed above, casting its shadow across both of them. "Cal asked me to tell you that the time approaches when you must complete your task."

Tess's eyes opened wide, but she did not respond.

"He said this is your destiny, to free the Reapers from our bonds. Only once in many generations will we have this chance."

She stood still, unblinking. After another moment, she responded, "I swore an oath that I would free the Reapers. Yet, what he asks is no small request." She gazed up along the dark walls of the fortress, seeing banners and flags high above. "The Elite are unsympathetic to the plight of the Reapers, but Rowan Sarroff believes he is doing what is right." She shook her head, eyes pleading as she turned back to him. "Maybe there's another way?"

"We have tried. Appealing to them has accomplished nothing. We have failed, from one generation to the next. The killings and suffering have only increased. There is no other way but to overthrow them."

She raised an eyebrow. "Is this Cal speaking now, or you?"

"You know us, Tess Armstrong. Our Directives unite the Reapers, whether it is the solace we give to others or the pain we all feel. We have the same purpose in life. One day, the Reapers will be free, and the Elite will be the ones slaving away at our feet."

Her eyes blazed. "And that will be better? You replace one overlord with another, one day treating them the same way. When will it end? You crush their spirits until one day they overthrow you." She let out a deep breath, her voice trembling. "I told Cal I would do this, but in my heart, I can't help but wonder if it will accomplish anything beneficial."

Jed lowered his gaze. "I wish there was a different path for us. But this deed must happen before the Elite crush whatever emotions we have left. I know Cal, and he would not have asked you if he did not believe you were capable of it, or if we had some other alternative. You are our best hope."

She frowned. "But not your only hope?"

He wasn't expecting that question. "If you fail at this, we have alternative plans, none as viable. You are already in the fortress and trusted by Rowan Sarroff. No others have that advantage."

A new thought dawned on her as she spoke with an icy edge. "What will you do if I am unable or unwilling to kill him?"

He hissed as his eyes darted around the balcony. "Do not speak of the act. You must never say it out loud. They hear more than you realize." Her expression remained hard as she stared at him, waiting for an answer. He relented. "If you cannot perform the task, we have enlisted your companions, Alan Sabrinsky and Russell Ingram, to do so."

Her body tensed, and he took a step back at her reaction. "You said Cal would keep my friends safe," she cried. "Was that just a lie to gain my support? You realize what will happen if the Elite discover you have entangled Rusty and Al in this scheme, or if they fail in the attempt." She answered for him. "They won't hesitate to kill them."

He held up his hands, palms out. "Please, my lady, I beg you to understand. We do not wish to involve them; they are only a backup of last resort. You have it in your power to end all of this." He swept an arm to indicate everything around them. "You control our future. Do as you will, but know we must take whatever steps we can to free ourselves."

Her jaw muscle quivered as she stared at him. With her body still tense, she said, "Tell me what you intend. What is your plan?"

He licked his lips again. Lowering his voice to a whisper, he said, "In three days' time, the Elite will celebrate Abhijit, their festival of good fortune." Jed gave out a snort of disgust. "It will be one of their larger celebrations. They will need more Reapers than usual during the event. We may even outnumber them. We can smuggle a blade into the fortress before then. Your handmaids, Glynn and Del, will secure it within your clothing on the day of the festival. Rowan Sarroff will surely have you by his side, at least during some of the time. Choose your moment and stick him with the blade. That is all. During the confusion, we will do the rest."

"And if I fail?"

He stared at her for a moment, as if measuring her allegiance. "You have always been honest with me, so I will speak truthfully. Although you are our best hope, we will also smuggle your two companions inside for the festival. Like all Reapers in the fortress, we will dress them in servant's clothes. With any luck, the Elite will have consumed enough wine to dull their senses so they do not recognize the absence of a Directive in your friends. Russell and Alan have already agreed to kill, or at least disable Sarroff if you cannot."

"I want to talk with them first."

He shook his head. "Impossible. The Elite will certainly notice it and raise an alarm. We cannot risk it."

"But you'll be exposing them to danger. I must explain to them how risky this plan of yours is."

"They are aware of the peril. We explained the threat to their lives and held nothing back from them. None of us are under any illusions about what will happen if we fail. Everyone who takes part in this rebellion will breathe our last breath if we are unsuccessful." He looked at her, unblinking. "Cal wants you to think about him, and the life he might yet have if you go ahead with this."

Tess chewed on her lower lip. "I had thought it would be easier before I met Rowan, when I still believed he was a monster."

"He is a monster, a beast that has no right to live."

She scowled. "And that is the reason none of you will ever find peace in your lives, neither Reapers nor Elite. Mark my words, whatever happens here with this plan of a rebellion, it will not end the bitterness you all harbor within you."

~

GLYNN HANDED THE BLADE TO TESS, HILT FIRST. THE five inches of polished steel gleamed as a ray of sunshine from the window reflected off it. The smooth green handle was ceramic, with several rubies inlaid in it. Tess hefted the weapon in her hand, feeling its weight. "This is no common knife, is it?"

The two handmaids, Glynn and Del, were more somber than usual as they prepared Tess for the Abhijit celebration. "No, nothing is ordinary about it," said Glynn as she glanced at it. "A master Reaper blacksmith, now long gone, crafted it. The blade has one purpose: to spark a revolution. Reapers have passed down this artifact through the generations, hiding it away, a reminder that one day we will strike against our oppressors and overthrow their rule."

"And if I fail in the attempt."

Glynn pursed her lips. "You are not like us, Tess Armstrong, but we share more similarities than differences. A fire burns in your emotions, creating a bond between us. You care about us and the conditions under which we must live. When the time arrives, I believe you will strike a blow against our enemy."

Tess looked uncertain, but didn't respond.

"Come now, my lady. It is time for you to dress for the big event."

Unlike her other gowns, this was extravagant. Nothing she had ever worn in her life compared to it, with folds and layers of fabric forming a dress reserved for pageants.

After helping Tess into it, Glynn and Del showed her the hidden pocket to sheath the knife. "The Elite are cunning and can react quickly, so do not pull out the blade until you are about to strike," Glynn warned.

Tess's eyes watered. "My lady?" Glynn questioned, seeing her reaction.

She tried to shake it off as she blinked away the tears. Her voice cracked as she said, "It's just that, when this is over, whatever happens, I may never see you again. Even if I do what's expected of me, many of us are going to die today. Both of you have been a friend to me when I needed it most."

"You are one of us, Tess Armstrong," said Del, the soft-spoken of the two. "Friendship does not flow in one direction. I believe we have gained as much from you as you have received from us—from all of our people."

Tess smiled through her tears. "Why does it always come down to violence? The Elite, the Reapers, you're all part of the same community. I wish there were another way."

"As do we," said Glynn. "But there comes a time in everyone's life when extreme measures are necessary. We cannot, we will not, continue to live as slaves. After this day, we will be the rulers, or we will be dead. There is no other recourse."

Tess reached out to take their hands, one in each of hers. "If I never see you again, I hope you both survive and live a happy life. But I have one request of you."

The two women glanced at each other. "We will do what we can, Tess," said Glynn. "But please do not ask us to jeopardize this plan."

She shook her head. "No, I don't expect you to be disloyal to the Reapers. I love them, as do you. But I also care deeply about the two companions who came here with me. Please, I need you to pass a message to them. Jed explained they are the backup if I fail. I don't want them to strike against Rowan Sarroff unless I am killed first. They must wait until then. Can you do that?"

The two girls looked at each other again. Moments passed. Were they communicating with each other, or with other Reapers through their Directive? Tess would never know the extent of its capabilities. Glynn finally responded with a terse nod. "You deserve that much. We will be sure they receive your request."

Tess let out a breath as if someone had lifted a weight from her. "Thank you." She ran her palms down her side to smooth out the folds of her gown, pausing at the hidden pocket that concealed the knife. "Whatever happens, I'm ready." She furrowed her brow as she gazed at the two Reapers.

"I pray you are victorious," said the younger girl.

"I fear nobody will win today." She walked toward the door, never looking back.

21

THEY WILL BE BORN AGAIN

Jed stopped short at the entrance of a large ballroom as the soft melody of stringed instruments filled the air. He gazed at Tess. "This is your day, my lady. Thank you for allowing me to be your guide."

She brushed a piece of lint from his shoulder. "It is you I should thank. Stay safe, my friend."

He inclined his head as she continued into the grand hall alone. Once inside, she paused, unsure of where to go next. A riot of colored garments greeted her, so unlike the simple white robes with gold trim worn by the Elite. All the females wore gowns as elaborate as hers, while the men dressed in billowy pants and loose-fitting jackets. Everyone proudly displayed their Directives adding to the medley of colors.

Tables, positioned around the edges of the room, over-flowed with a variety of foods, many in steaming pots or sizzling on grills. Reapers in red gowns stood behind the counters, ready to dole out whatever an Elite wished.

Music came from Elite playing stringed instruments, and many danced in the center of the great hall. Unlike the wild, almost frenzied motions of the Reapers during their harvest moon festival, the Elite swayed with fluid steps and sinuous sweeps of their arms and bodies. As the dancers glided around the floor, their Directives intertwined with one another, becoming part of the movements. It was beautiful, although it lacked the spirited steps of the Reapers' dance.

As Tess stood at the edge of the hall, many of the Elite turned toward her, smiling as if recognizing an old friend, even though she had spoken with very few of them.

Seeing her, Rowan Sarroff strode forward, his face gleeful. "Welcome to our celebration, Tess." He took her hands in his as he looked at her with piercing eyes. Did he suspect anything? "We have much to celebrate on this day, and I'm so happy to have you by my side." He clenched her hands tighter and pitched his voice for her alone. "I couldn't imagine a better person to be with today. On this occasion, we pay homage to all that is important in our lives." He spoke with no hint of deception.

Keeping hold of one hand, he guided her further into the hall as all eyes followed. Was she the center of attention, or was it because of Rowan's response to her? Among the crowd, Tess glimpsed some who glared at her, particularly the young, attractive maidens. Whatever the emotions of the other Elite, the machinations of their politics were the furthest thing on her mind right now.

Tess plastered a smile on her face, but anyone who knew her well enough would understand that it was an illusion. The blade hidden in her pocket felt like a weight around her neck.

Rowan sensed her uneasiness and frowned. "Be happy, my dear. More than any of us, this is your day to rejoice. We are all joyful on this occasion." His eyes scanned the other faces before he fixed his gaze back on her. "Normally, this is a day of celebration for all that we have achieved. But today, because of you, it holds the promise of our future destiny."

She winced. "What do you think I can accomplish, Rowan? I'm only a single person without your powers of the Directive. How can I bring about any change?"

He gazed at her, his smile never fading. "In the short time you have been here with us, I can see you are a wonderful individual and you have a fire in your heart, as do we. I don't need the Directive to discern your compassion. You will make the right choice when the time comes. I know you will do what is best to carry us forward to the next stage of our lives."

She pulled her hand away from his. "What if you're wrong? What if I have to do something terrible to help you move forward?"

He fixed her with a gaze as if he understood. "We each face demanding choices in our lives." He tapped his chest. "Follow your instinct; it will never steer you wrong."

"What will happen when you reach this nexus of events that you believe will change your future? With all the power of your Directives, you must know, at least have some idea."

He held her gaze. "As powerful as our Directives are, they do not give us total omniscience. We perceive that an eruption of something wonderful will soon take place. We understand you are at the epicenter of whatever will happen. And most importantly, I recognize you are a good, loving person. Your heart and intentions are honorable, and you will do what is best. That is all we know."

She winced as her breathing became forced. Her right hand slid to the hidden pocket in her gown. She moved with care so as not to raise suspicion about what she was about to do. Rowan didn't react to her movement as he focused on her face, fascinated by what he saw. The beat of the music came faster as the revelers on the dance floor increased their pace.

Tess's hand slid into the hidden pocket. The convergence of events had arrived as she tensed, never taking her eyes off Rowan.

"My, my, Rowan, dear. Won't you introduce your friend?" came a voice behind her.

Tess spun around, hand still inside her pocket. One of the young Elite girls stood pouting, her blond hair cascading in curls below her bare shoulders. It was the same girl who had walked with Rowan back when Tess still lived and worked with the Reapers. The day she first glimpsed him.

Rowan cleared his throat. "Ah, of course, Ezara. Surely you have heard of Tess Armstrong?" He nodded at Tess.

The girl tapped her index finger against her cheek, smiling. Her Directive changed colors as if she were excited. Tess took a moment to withdraw the hand from her pocket, fingers empty.

The female responded with a throaty voice. "Yes, of course, the outsider. You are such a mystery to us, my dear." Her eyes shifted to Rowan. "I can see why she demands so much of your consideration, what with this impending calamity about to descend upon us."

"We believe it will be a boon for us," he said, an edge to his voice.

"Oh, of course it will," she said, her tone dripping with acid. "What, with you taking care of her, how else could it end?" She shifted her attention back to Tess. "Tell me, my dear. What do you hope to gain when—"

"Ezara, this is not the place to interrogate our guest. Do you want something?"

She glared at him. "I want to be sure you know what you are doing, *my Prime Elite*." She emphasized his title as if to mock him. "Not everyone believes she will usher us into a brighter future. Be aware that your adversaries increase by the minute, and I am telling you this because of our *relationship*." She put an emphasis on the word relationship. "Unless we soon see proof we are on the right path, we will demand another approach."

"We? Demand? How dare you speak like this? I had thought you and I would one day rule together, uniting the different factions. Are you so easily troubled by another woman?"

She took a step closer to him. "Yes, I am concerned. That woman is an outsider. You should have killed her from the very beginning rather than having observed her from a distance. You have a duty to follow our customs. Instead, you take her to your bed and treat her as—"

"Enough!" Rowan's Directive crackled as it came into contact with Ezara's. She stumbled back a step, the first sign of fear in her eyes. He took a deep breath. "I am the ruler here, not you. What I do is for the good of all. Nobody cares if you agree or not. I alone will decide our path forward, and your role is to follow."

His Directive continued to intrude upon hers. The room had gone still, the music silent as everyone focused on the confrontation. Ezara licked her lips and lowered her head in capitulation.

Rowan smiled, his anger spent. He had won the argument. "I will have your belongings removed from my room and returned to you. You are dismissed."

She backed away a few steps but did not leave the hall, choosing instead to join a group of other Elite.

He motioned with his hand, and the music began playing again, and conversations resumed. He took a breath. "I apologize for that display," he said to Tess. "Our people often have forceful opinions about certain issues."

"And I seem to be one of those topics. I'm sorry to have interfered with any of this. I came to this place not knowing what to expect, believing only that I could make things better. Why is it that the noblest of intentions can make such a mess of everyone's lives?" She shook her head. "I can't win, Rowan. I hope you believe me when I say that I never wanted to hurt anyone."

She glanced away, her eyes falling on a line of Reaper servants against the wall. She spied Jed, located among them, worry lines on his face. Tess tensed as she saw who stood next to him. Russell and Alan wore red gowns like all the other servants. She hadn't seen them or spoken with them since being taken into the fortress. Russell, careful not to attract scrutiny to himself, nodded discretely when they made eye contact. Was it a signal? Did he want her to know they were safe, or was it something more? Maybe it was a sign that he was prepared to commit the murder if she failed.

Not wanting to draw attention to her friends, Tess looked back at Rowan. "Believe me, I never wanted to hurt you."

He frowned. "I have suffered no harm from you, nor anyone else. You have been my salvation, Tess. I can see clearly now; my rule has come into focus with you. I will lead our people to a new stage of existence, and you will be at my side. We will gain more power than we ever dreamed possible."

He leaned forward and wrapped his arms around her. She tensed, knowing this was the moment.

"I'm so sorry," she whispered.

The knife was in her hand and out of the hidden pocket before she realized it.

Rowan couldn't see the blade because his hands were on her shoulders. A guttural cry came from her lips. Rowan's puzzlement turned to shock as he spotted the weapon.

One jab into his gut and the deed would be done. This was her moment. The Reapers would have the freedom they sought.

Instead, she hesitated, her eyes locked onto Rowan while he stared at her. Lives hung in the balance as time seemed to stop.

Tess went even more rigid, as if bracing for the thrust. And then the metal blade slipped from her fingers and clanked against the stone floor. "Killing is not the answer."

Several events happened at once.

Rowan's former girlfriend, Ezara, shouted a warning. Or was it a command?

Tess's guide, Jed, overturned a serving table and grabbed a sword concealed under it.

Another Reaper holding a circular metal container dashed to the center of the dance floor. Before he even reached it, a detonation of light and heat erupted from the vessel, knocking Tess and Rowan off their feet. The blackened bodies of both Elite and Reapers near the explosion littered the ballroom.

From far away, another concussion shook the fortress. Reapers had begun their revolution.

And then, adding to the confusion, a knot of Elite led by Ezara charged forward with her shouting, "Kill them both!" Tess realized with horror that she was speaking of both her and Rowan.

Everyone in the hall began running, screaming, or stabbing one another.

Ezara's cohorts were the first to reach Rowan and Tess. He staggered to his feet, his Directive flaring brighter than she had ever seen. The attackers came to an abrupt halt, struggling against an unseen force. "You will die for this," Rowan growled through clenched teeth.

Ezara's face twisted in a snarl as she tried to ward off his Directive with her own. "You were a fool to trust her." Her eyes flicked to the discarded blade at his feet. "Your regime is over, Rowan. I will rule the Elite from now on." He snarled and enlarged the size of his Directive forcing Ezara back. "Even you cannot fight off all of us," she declared.

Tess picked herself off the floor and braced herself on hands and knees, her eyes glassy. She took a shaky breath, trying to overcome the impact of the explosion. Armed Reaper servants moved through the room, slitting throats or thrusting blades into confused Elite. One Reaper bashed the head of an Elite with a metal plate, cracking his skull open in a shower of blood.

The Elite fought back with their Directives, sucking the life out of Reapers. Screams of agony came from both sides.

Russell and Alan were suddenly at Tess's side as they

grabbed her and hauled her to her feet. "We'll get you out of here," said Russell. He jerked his head at Rowan. "What about him? Don't you want him dead?"

She clutched Russell by his red robe as she scanned the room, unable to look away from the horror taking place around her. "No, that won't make any difference. Both the Elites and Reapers are stark mad. They're trying to kill or control the other, and we can't fight their conflict."

Alan looked like a lost child. "We're going to die here, aren't we?" Even Russell, the unexcitable of the three, scanned the scene with wild eyes.

More Reapers wearing their dirty and ragged work clothes rather than the red servant gowns streamed into the hall. They had breached the gates of the fortress.

Rowan moved with the speed of a man possessed as he fought off both an Elite and a Reaper at the same time. He strangled the Elite with his hands while used his Directive to take the life from a Reaper.

Cal appeared next to Tess. Blood streaked his tattered shirt and dripped from the sword he held. He wore a crooked grin, as only Cal would at a time like this. "The bastard Elite are fighting each other. This is better than I expected." He glanced at Tess for a second before lunging forward to stab an Elite in the side. This battle was more important to him than her well-being.

A larger mob of Reapers charged into the chamber. The entire village must have taken up arms. Cal's uncle Brent arrived, followed by Astra, Cal's sister. Even gentle Sol, leader of the Reaper work crew from the orchards, barked orders to the rest of his team as they accompanied him.

Mara stood in the center of the hall, arms outstretched, her Directive more brilliant than most others. A slew of Reaper bodies lay motionless around her feet. Cal saw his niece and rushed toward her, his sword at the ready. Mara's mother, Astra, was right behind him.

"Fight with us," Cal yelled as he faced her. "You belong to the Reapers, not the Elite. Kill them."

She shook her head. "You are wrong, uncle. Do not force me to do this."

He let loose an angry screech as he raised his weapon over his head and lunged toward her. Astra screamed, "Cal, no." The young girl hurled a small portion of her Directive toward him and he spasmed as if struck by an electric shock. He crumpled in a heap as his blade dropped to the floor.

Mara's face was heartless as stone as she looked at him. Was any of the little girl still alive within her, the child that Tess first met on those flooded fields? "Because of the compassion you have showed me in the past, I will not kill you, Uncle. That is all I can promise." She shot a glance at Astra. "Goodbye, mother. You did your best when I was younger, but now I have a new life."

Astra slumped as tears dripped from her face. "I will always love you."

Mara didn't respond as she turned her attention to another Reaper, who rushed toward her with a thin blade in his hand. Her Directive wrapped around him and pulled the weapon away. The Reaper screamed before his life ended, his lifeless body dropping to the floor.

Tess ran toward Cal's prone form and hugged him on the floor as if trying to shelter him from the brutality taking place around them. He had a bewildered look in his eyes, as if he didn't know what had happened. Brushing her away, he jerked his head around, searching the room. "Where is she? After all I have done, I will kill her."

Tess grabbed his shoulders. "Cal, this isn't right. None of this is going to help. What do you hope to accomplish? Everyone is killing each other."

Dead bodies had piled on top of each other on the floor, many soaked in blood, others without a scratch, but dead just the same. Shrieks of agony mingled with shouts of rage. The hall was in shambles, with overturned tables and heaps of debris scattered everywhere. Curtains and tapestries burned, pouring smoke through the room. The steady burst of explosions sent bodies flying.

A Reaper crashed into Tess from behind as he ran for his life. Her head slammed onto the stone floor as he scrabbled to get his footing. Russell and Alan pulled her up before the mob trampled her. Blood flowed from a gash on her forehead.

Russell looked around, his expression frantic. "This is hopeless, Tess." He grabbed a discarded cloth and held it to her brow. Her eyes remained unfocused as he urged her to walk. "Let's get out of here. Alan, help me carry her."

Together, they supported her and moved toward an exit. But Rowan blocked the way before they had gone a few feet. "Where do you think you are going?" he shouted. "Tess Armstrong, you are our salvation, and I will not allow you to escape."

Russell screamed, "Look around, you idiot. Can't you see it's over? You're going to kill each other until no one's left alive. Is that what you want?"

Rowan's eyes flashed in anger. His voice was menacing. "Our destiny is to rule. You have no right to take her. I will—"

"You bastard!" Cal shouted. He held his sword a foot away from Rowan. "You took everything from me, and now I am going to kill you."

Rowan growled back. "You insolent fool. Watch while I rip your beating heart from your chest."

The Elite ruler swung his sword, aiming for the Reaper's head. Cal parried, just missing a blow.

Russell and Alan pulled the dazed Tess away from the fighting. "No," she groaned. "We have to stop them." She tried to pull free, but her friends gripped her firmly.

Cal and Rowan continued to strike each other, neither willing to relent. Each opponent landed blows on the other, yet they persisted. Blood flowed from their wounds as they fell to their knees, too weak to stand.

"Oh, hell," muttered Rowan. "One way or the other, I will kill you." His Directive was now less pronounced than before, but still stronger than Cal's. The Elite focused his gaze upon Cal, pulling the Reaper's Directive away from him. With a guttural scream, Cal lunged forward, sinking his blade deep within Rowan's chest.

Rowan's eyes glazed over, but he struggled to stay conscious, turning to look at Tess. "The Elite must continue to rule," he said, blood oozing from the corner of his mouth. "Our destiny will endure. You three will find a way."

Tess frowned as a small segment of Rowan's Directive floated away, split into three smaller subsets, and disappeared into the heads of Tess, Russell, and Alan.

"No," Cal hissed as he saw what had happened. Barely alive, his Directive sputtered on and off. In a moment of clarity, he too pushed some of his Directive into each of their heads. Alan tried to swat it away before it reached him, but to no avail.

Once they accomplished their task, both Rowan and Cal slumped on the floor, unable to raise their heads. And then, their Directives went from a soft white to the color of the sky at twilight, until sputtering out. Their bodies moved no more. The only two men Tess had ever loved were gone.

A firestorm still blazed around the room as more explosions detonated. The entire fortress spewed flames and thick, black smoke while Elite and Reapers continued to fight. Russell searched for a way out, fire and smoke blocking their escape.

And then, a female voice from long ago spoke to them again.

Come, your time in my Realm is over for now, your task completed. Alas, this is not an outcome I had hoped for, but you could not have averted their collapse. Their hatred prevailed, overshadowing any ability for them to reach a peaceful accord. Unfortunately, they will be born anew from the seeds they have planted. Their story does not end here.

The flames consumed the hall within the fortress, but Tess Armstrong, Russell Ingram, and Alan Sabrinsky were no longer in the land of Elthea.

22

AN INSATIABLE PASSION TO RULE

Every vision that had unfolded during Tess's Farseeing had taken place in the land of Elthea, whether the lush gardens and fields of the Reapers, or the resplendent luxury of the Elite. During these visions, Phil Matherson had witnessed each event as Tess had lived it.

And now, even with their time in Elthea over, Phil continued to relive her past life.

Fluorescent lights illuminated a small room jammed with an array of rack-mounted computers in metal frames. A hodgepodge of wires twisted around the backs of the units, spilling onto the floor and snaking to the front. Beeps and whirs of fans emanated from the equipment as red, green, and white LED lights blinked.

Tess and Russell sat at an immense square metal table in the middle of the room, their attention focused on the screens of large terminals in front of them while their fingers raced across the keyboards. Neither of them spoke.

A steel gray door to the room flew open as Alan stumbled forward, face grim. "It's gone," he blurted.

Neither Tess nor Russell looked up; their attention remained locked on the screens, their fingers striking the keys. Still focused on the computer, Tess asked, "What's gone, Alan? And it had better not be the leftover pizza. That's my dinner tonight."

Russell barked a laugh. "You're the one who used to eat healthy. Now, you're worse than him."

Tess sighed. "The life of a computer geek. You two have corrupted me."

Alan raised his voice. "Guys, this is serious." Something in his tone made them pay attention as both Tess and Russell stopped typing and looked up. He hesitated, now unsure how to break the news. "One of the rogue virus programs is missing. It disappeared."

Russell smirked. "That's impossible, Alan. I think you might be losing it. Maybe you've been working too hard and forgot that we isolated those programs on a secure server."

"I'm telling you, I checked the logs. They show an exit of the program with no details."

Russell frowned. "Let me look." He sprang from the table to use the keyboard at another terminal along the wall. Tess watched him as the worry lines on her face appeared.

Russell swore under his breath. "He may be right,

Tess. Somehow that code jumped the closed network. I can't find it anywhere."

"Maybe one of you deleted it by accident," she said, her voice cracking.

Alan grumbled. "Tess, you understand we're computer engineers. Right? And even if somehow we made that mistake, we have recovery algorithms. I've already run them. The disk is empty. It's as if the program vanished."

The three stared at each other, eyes wide, the ramifications dawning on them. Tess rubbed her forehead. "That rogue virus was one of the failures, wasn't it?"

Alan and Russell nodded, heads downcast. Without warning, Tess slapped her palm on the table. Alan and Russell flinched at the clap. "God dammit," she cried. "We should have destroyed it from the start rather than keep it."

"But we all agreed," Alan said. "It was the best way for us to test the effectiveness of our antivirus code. We had to find out if it could withstand an attack by a malware virus."

"Which of the rogue viruses was it?" she asked. Tess held her breath, as if fearing the answer.

"The worst of them," answered Alan. Tess leaned back in the chair and rubbed her temples.

"Should we report this?" asked Russell. "Tell someone what happened?"

She responded with a snort of derision, "Oh, yes, by all means. Here's how that conversation will go. We explain how this stone statue on Cape Cod mysteriously whisked us away to a strange world where we find this race of people who had something called a Directive. And just before the voice from the statue inexplicably brought us back to Earth, this race planted some of their Directive in our heads, which gave us this miraculous ability to create some of the most effective antivirus software on the market today. But we also ended up producing these failures, which we kept so that we could test our successful programs against them. And one of those nasty viruses, beyond all safeguards, is gone." She gestured with her hand. "Poof. It's gone."

Russell squirmed in his chair. "We don't have to get into all that detail."

Tess shook her head. "No, we're better off not saying anything. Besides, nobody's going to discover where that virus came from. Hell, we don't even have validation it ever existed." Her eyes blazed. "It was never here. Understand?"

"But it survived," said Alan, his voice squeaky. "And it's still out there somewhere on the web."

She nodded. "Yes, it is. And we know what it is, don't we?" A moment of silence followed as they looked at each other, hesitant about speaking it out loud. "Oh, come on. We've never discussed it, but we know the real reason Rowan Sarroff and Cal put bits of their Directives in our heads. Maybe other Elites or Reapers did also in those final, crazy moments, but we'll never know."

Tess took a breath before continuing. "Their purpose wasn't to make us super engineers and function beyond our normal capacity. That wasn't it at all. Was it? Did any of them even care about us?" She glared at them for a second and then shouted, "They wanted to continue to exist. And we've helped them accomplished it. They've reincarnated themselves, and now they're free."

Russell raised his hand for her to stop. "Tess, this is software we're talking about, not some living, breathing being. Aren't you reading too much into it?"

Her lips tightened. "We've all read about the advances in artificial intelligence. It's still decades away, but some scientists say it's the way of the future. And here we've accidentally created the worse AI imaginable."

Russell didn't relent. "But you don't know that, not yet."

She glared at him. "Was the land we visited real? We both know it was. I can't explain any of the events that happened to us, but I know it existed. We became caught up in something that we can never disclose. But that didn't mean it wasn't real."

She brushed back a few red locks of hair that had fallen over her eyes as she let out a soft breath. She lowered her voice. "I knew what that virus was; you both knew it. We tried to fool ourselves into believing the Directive in our heads were gifts to help us become better people, allowing us to keep one step ahead of everyone else—their ultimate gift because of what they put us through. That wasn't it at all, and now what remains of the Elite and the Reapers endures in this world."

"But they're not really alive," Russell said. "I mean, what disappeared is only computer code."

Tess had a faraway look in her eyes, as if she hadn't

heard him. Finally, she said, "It didn't disappear, it escaped. And it is cunning and dangerous. Mark my words, that code will do what viruses always do, whether computer or bacterial. They first attach themselves to a host and multiply. Then they execute the parameters dictated by their DNA. The virus will cause havoc, destroying beneficial programs. And just as this code freed itself from our secure server, I suspect one day it will overcome the limitations of its digital bonds, maybe even spread beyond Earth and return to Elthea."

Alan took a seat in front of another terminal at the square table. Nobody felt like speaking for a time, each lost in their own thoughts. The whir of computer fans and the blinking of LED lights continued as if nothing had changed. They each understood the ramifications of what had taken place. An imperceptible shift in the world's dynamics had occurred. Yet, even they did not know the violence and misery that would follow in the wake of what happened here.

Alan looked up from the terminal in front of him. "What about our antivirus software—the beneficial programs? Isn't that the same as what escaped? I mean, we created both. Didn't we?"

Tess shrugged. "We built both, although I think you were the mastermind behind much of it." She considered the question, shaking her head. "I don't believe our antivirus program is a product of the Elite and Reapers. It doesn't behave as they did by trying to tear things apart. I suspect—hope—it's what we intended, a beneficial tool that will do a lot of good. Who knows, possibly we created an entirely new AI. Maybe one day we'll find out for sure."

Russell lifted his head as if he had a new idea. "Maybe so, but we created our antivirus software with the help of the Directive in our heads. Couldn't it also go rogue and become harmful?"

Tess looked at him for a moment before answering. "I don't know. But I believe we put something of ourselves into that code, at least enough to make it different. Possibly, it's unlike the Elite and Reapers. Maybe we'll never know. There's so much of what happened that I can't explain."

Alan nodded, but did not respond.

The three lapsed into silence again until Tess asked, "Do either of you sense the Directive within you? When we first came back to Earth, and for a long time after, I understood it was there inside me. Like an elusive memory, it was always in my thoughts. And now, nothing. I'm not aware of it at all."

"I know what you mean," said Russell. "I can't feel it either."

"Maybe it lapsed with time," Alan offered.

"Or it vanished because it fulfilled its purpose," Tess countered.

"Whatever the reason, we're done with it," said Russell. "Thank God. I don't know about you, but I'm happy to put that entire episode behind us. I never want to see or hear about a place called Elthea ever again."

A melancholy smile came to her lips. "Oh, I don't

know. There was such beauty and wonder there. I never felt so alive as during that time in my life."

"No!" Alan bellowed. "I'm with Russell. Not me. No more stone sculptures with the name Elthea. I'm done."

Tess laughed, stepping over to tousle his hair. "Okay, Alan. You win. I promise I will never again show you anything that looks the least bit mysterious. The three of us can spend the rest of our lives on this spinning rock we call Earth."

I BLINKED AS IF AWAKENING FROM A DREAM. THE room was dark, save for the dozens of flickering candles chasing away the gloom of night. We had begun the Farseeing early this morning, sitting here in this garden chamber the entire day. An older Tess from the visions sat across from me, eyeing me curiously.

I stretched my limbs, giving myself time to absorb all that I had witnessed. I said the first thing that came to me. "You have nothing to be ashamed about in your past. From your reluctance to go through with this, I had thought you had a monumental lapse in character or a complete melt-down. You did as well as anyone."

"Yet, they're still out there." She tipped her head to indicate the outside.

The Bots were such an aberration from everything I had known about the evolution of living beings: beginning as biological beings, then becoming electronic code, back again to corporal entities. Tess needed assurances they were not her fault. "They would have eventually become the Bots. The Elite were preparing to expand beyond their home. It's who they are."

"Until recently, they left those of us in Haven alone. At least I can be thankful for that. I always wondered if it was because of my friendship with Rowan and Cal. But now I don't know what they're planning."

My stomach twisted. "I've changed all that, haven't I? My powers threaten them, and they won't have it. They've taken my friends, and next they'll take me, regardless of who stands in the way."

"If they wanted to kill you or make you one of them, they would have attempted it by now. They're massing out there for some other reason."

Feeling as if I had asked the same question a thousand times over the last few days, I repeated myself. "But what do they want?"

She didn't answer right away. "I honestly don't know. I've long ago given up trying to understand their motives."

The juxtaposition of this Tess compared to the younger from the Farseeing was still disconcerting. In the Farseeing, she had been only slightly older than her daughter, Rae. And in a blink of an eye, she sat before me as an adult woman in her forties or early fifty's. I considered this for a moment. "Something about the timeline doesn't make sense. You should be older than what you are."

She grinned. "You had asked that once long ago; I

guess you've forgotten. The powers of Elthea cure many ills, old-age being one of them."

"You'll live forever here?"

She shrugged. "Like other diseases, we are free from the ravages of aging, at least to a degree. Did you know humans do not have a gene that makes us grow old? Aging is a byproduct of our evolution, and as with any other sickness, the Spirit of Elthea can remedy it, or at least forestall it."

I put this thought aside as something to ponder another time. We needed to discuss more pressing questions from the Farseeing. "At the very end, when the three of you were in the computer lab, you all agreed that you would never return to this land. What made you change your mind?"

Her smile faded. "Ah, a good question, since we're talking about ill health." Tess winced, as if considering something she'd sooner forget. "Some thirty years after that day, doctors determined I had terminal cancer." She shrugged. "My time was up; at least I had thought so. I was saying my goodbyes to my family, but still not ready to accept death." She had a faraway look in her eyes. "Is anyone ever prepared for the end of life?"

She hesitated, as if stalling to finish the story. "Anyway, that was when the Spirit of Elthea came to me again, at least her voice. Like the first time at the statue called Elthea, I was on the shore of Cape Cod, looking out at the ocean, thinking about how my life was about to end." She stared at me with an intensity I rarely saw from her. "Do you know what that feels like, knowing you're going to die but unable to do anything about it?"

I didn't know how to respond. Who would? So I waited, giving her the space she needed.

Tess took another breath. "So that's when the voice called upon me again. 'My realm needs you once more,' she had said. 'In return, I will heal your ills and make you whole. Others also I will gather, including your mate and child.'"

She remained lost in thought until taking a breath. "I was reluctant to return, not after all the trouble I had caused the first time. But neither did I want to die. My dear Evan convinced me that if I could continue to live, it was worth it. And he would give up his life on Earth.

"Surprisingly, Russell and Alan agreed to come as well. The voice had also spoken to them, and even though they were not ill, the spirit offered them the same choice." Tess smiled as she recalled it.

"The Spirit of Elthea brought over five hundred of us from all around the globe, young and old, healthy and ailing of body or mind. How she accomplished such a thing without a global commotion was a mystery to me. She is such an enigma, so much I still can't explain."

Tess shrugged. "Once here, I expected to have to deal with the Elite and Reapers again. But that didn't happen. Elthea needed us to forestall the Bots in their war against the races of Elthea. During that pivotal time in the history of this land, the noble races were about to be annihilated by the more powerful Bots. Our unexpected arrival puzzled the Bots as they paused in their war to make sense of our appearance. Back then, I still didn't realize that the computer virus that escaped from our lab had transformed itself into those creatures."

"The Stonewraiths were already here to assist us with shelter and food. We lived in caves for months as the ultimate battle between Bots and the other races nearly destroyed the land. The noble races almost obliterated the Bots, but not quite. It seems those beings have more lives than those of a cat." Tess looked around the room, fixing her eyes on the outside. "Over time, the hurricanes, volcanoes, and quakes subsided—the aftereffects of the powerful magic released by the ruling races. We could venture out and the Stonewraiths soon built us this fortress."

Tess exhaled a weary breath. "But I prattle on. You knew all that already. I seem to recall telling you this bit of history when I first met you as we sat in the gazebo in our garden. Also, the Astari explained it to you once, didn't they?"

I nodded, remembering the account from the Lady Grandmother Elderphino, a conversation that seemed to take place a lifetime ago. "I don't know if I ever absorbed the details until now. The telling of it was always a story, like fiction from a children's tale. Now, it seems more alive after experiencing events through you."

She studied me with piercing eyes. "Of all people, you needed to understand them—both sides of their nature. I've repeatedly tried to explain that the Bots are not all evil." She shook her head. "Nobody ever believed me, of course, outside of Alan and Russell. But make no mistake, they will kill you or anyone else who gets in their way."

"Get in their way of what? I know them better, but I still don't understand what they want."

"If you learned anything from the Farseeing, you realize they need to rule. It's in their makeup. All the strife and conflict between the Elite and Reapers was about control over the other. One had it, the other wanted it."

"But they'll never be happy. Other races will always exist outside of their influence. They even once said their intent was to rule the galaxy. How can I satisfy beings that have an insatiable need to dominate others?"

Her lips tightened. "I don't know. If I did, I would have told you long ago. You are the only one who can stop them now. The Spirit of Elthea has gifted you, and whether or not she made the right decision, it is on your shoulders. I wish I had some wisdom to offer, but I don't have the foggiest notion."

And once again, we reached a stalemate, a place I found myself so many times before. Why me? What did I do to deserve this?

I rubbed my palms against my cheeks. God, I was tired. "I don't know about you, but this Farseeing has drained me. Tomorrow, if we're still alive, I'll be able to think more clearly. Maybe I can find a way out of this problem and also save Cass, Diane, and Matt. The thought of them remaining a Bot for the rest of their lives, well, it's one thing I can't live with."

We each stood, me with weak legs, as I braced myself

on the arm of the chair. She put her hand on my shoulder, more in sympathy than to steady me. "You'll find a way, you always do. Believe in yourself. I know that's not much to offer, but I suspect it's the only path to overcome this darkness."

I gazed absently at the flickering lights of the candles in the room, wondering how long it would take before the hatred of the Bots extinguished all the kind-hearted races in this world.

23

THIS ENDS HERE AND NOW

I sat bolt upright, waking from a deep slumber, feeling an unseen presence enter the room. My senses had become more aware of aberrations such as this, something I wouldn't have noticed before. Pre-dawn light filtered through the open window as the curtains stirred in the windless night. I pulled a weave of energy, ready to hurl it at the intruder.

—*I'm growing dim, my love. My past life has already become a wisp of a memory, relegated to shadows, never to return. You must help us.*

"Cass, is that you? Once before you spoke, but only briefly. Stay with me this time."

—*I don't have the talent for this, casting my voice this distance. Your skill far surpasses mine, greater than all the Bots. That is why they gather.*

Glancing outside the window, I wondered how many were out there now. "Help me get through this, Cass. Tell me how to stop them. How can I convince them to restore you? Only they are able to free you. There must be something I can offer them in exchange for your freedom."

She didn't respond. Had she left me so soon? Maybe I should use a thread of Elthea's energy to capture her so that she could remain here with me. But she finally spoke, a whisper of a voice.

—*They want you most of all. Your power and ability to command worlds. That's their greatest desire.*

I winced, knowing from Tess it would be the answer. "It's the one thing I can't give them. You will still be their hostage, as will I, and they will eventually destroy the Spirit of Elthea. In the end, with her power extinguished, they will still have nothing. Right now, she's the a source of their strength."

—*Yes, Elthea's powers will fail them, but by then they will have overtaken most of the universe. That is all they care for.*

My breathing became shallow. I was running out of options, wondering if I ever had a way out of this. My mind raced, knowing I should suggest something else now that I had her with me. But all I could think of was how much I wanted to see her—the real Cassie as a human—and caress her face. She needed me now, more than ever. And so did the others. "How are Matt and Diane doing? Are they holding up okay?"

Was it stupid to even ask? Of course they can't be doing well, realizing they had become a Bot.

—*They live. However, our time is short. You must do all*

you can. Remember, seek aid and support where you can find it. This may be your only hope. We cannot be the only beings who oppose them. Surely, there are others.

I didn't have the heart to tell her nobody else had my strength. The Spirit of Elthea had entrusted me alone as her savior. I recalled our high hopes when we had set out with Damek and the other Astari to bring together the once ruling races of this land to fight the Bots. "We tried that once, Cass, and it ended in failure."

—A single defeat doesn't mean you should abandon hope. You will find a way, as you always have. And now, my dearest, I must leave. I don't know if I have the strength to return. Farewell.

A shout formed on my lips for her to stay, but she was already gone. I covered my face with my palms, too shattered to cry. Cassie and the lives of my only friends were on my shoulders, and I had no idea how to save them.

THE SUN HAD RISEN HOURS AGO, YET HERE I REMAINED on the small balcony attached to my room, replaying every word Cassie had said. Shielding my eyes, I studied the fields beyond the once massive wall, now a pile of debris. The Stonewraiths had not begun working on this section of the wall, and I knew they did not have enough time to rebuild the entire structure before my next battle against the Bots would begin.

Was there some sign in their movements that would

give me a clue to their intentions? I was grasping at straws, but that was all I had. The Bots could have attacked days earlier, if that was their intention. The size of their force was formidable compared to The Guard of Haven. But size alone mattered little to them. They were fighting machines, each one capable of fending off a dozen or more humans at once.

Why were they waiting? What did they hope to accomplish? And what did I hope to discern by looking at them? Did I expect to discover a pattern in their movements that would give away their intentions?

If I was going to be honest with myself, I would have admitted that was not my purpose here this morning. Out of the throng of figures, I searched for three who might look out of place, possibly milling around by themselves, shunned by the rest.

It was a hopeless undertaking, something I already knew. Even with my augmented senses, I could perceive nothing unusual. Besides, I could only see a small slice of the assembled army from this vantage. This brooding was only pushing me into despair, a feeling I knew all too well.

Clenching my fists, I muttered, "Stay positive, Phil." Turning my attention back to last night's encounter with Cassie, I tried to puzzle out her words, anything that might help me. *Seek aid and support from others. It may be your only hope.*

Should I have dismissed this recourse? The Astari failed when we set sail with them, but races like the Oakenrill, as odd as they appeared, had helped me oppose the Bots. Without their guidance, I would never have honed my skill using Elthea's powers.

With the magical forces within me, it was now possible for me to travel anywhere in this land to seek help from others, even with the Bots surrounding us. But where to go? Who would oppose the Bots? Besides, this wasn't the time to begin traipsing around the world while the Bots surrounded the village. And without me here, the people of Haven had no chance of surviving an attack.

Activity near the base of the fallen wall caught my attention. A group of Stonewraiths had begun their daily task of rebuilding the fortification surrounding the town. They continued their work even in the face of a Bot assault. Maybe I should have a discussion with Torermak.

I headed out the door.

Bevon fell into step next to me. "The Bots continue to mass out there, Earthfriend." He scrutinized me for a moment. "Have you found what you sought with Tess Armstrong?"

When my Farseeing with her ended late last night, I had gone straight to bed without speaking with anyone else. "Well, not exactly. Maybe. I'm not sure." Grimacing, I searched for the right words. "Perhaps we will never have one simple answer. She showed me a great deal about the Bots, mainly who they once were. Knowing their mental makeup can only help." I took a breath. "At least, I hope it will."

He raised an eyebrow. "In times like this, I have observed that humans have a saying they use for getting out of difficult situations." He tapped his lips with his index finger. "Now, what is it? Oh, yes, you need to pull a rabbit out of a hat." He tipped his head up, staring at me, speaking in a serious tone. "Maybe I should find you a hat, Earthfriend."

I barked a laugh at the absurdity of it. Try as they may, Astari would occasionally miss the mark with humor. "If only it were that simple, Bevon." I placed a hand on his shoulder. "But I can always count on you to lighten the tension. Which, I suspect, was what you were trying to accomplish. And thank you for not faulting me for wasting time on the Farseeing with Tess."

"Well, in case anyone criticizes you, my advice is that you prepare yourself with a better response than the one you gave."

I chuckled again, keeping my hand on his shoulder. "Excellent suggestion, my friend. Now, come with me. I want to speak with Torermak and would like you to join us."

A team of about thirty Stonewraiths had already completed a hundred yards of the new wall, with the far end standing as tall as the original barrier. The side we approached was still waist high. Even though they were the size of giants, I marveled over how they could accomplish such a task. The process involved first clearing the rubble left by the collapsed wall before fitting each boulder into place to build the new structure. They were masters of stone lore, able to use Elthea's powers to mold stones to an exact fit.

"Master Philip," Torermak shouted, waving an arm from the top of the scaffolding. "I will be right down." He moved a short distance along the battlement and slid down a pole, much like one used at fire stations on Earth.

"Have you come to inspect our work?" he said with a smile as he approached. "We are making good progress, would you not agree?"

I stared up at the completed stretch of wall, squinting in the bright sunlight. "Your talent never ceases to amaze me. But we must discuss other issues."

"Ah, I should have realized. You have your serious face on today." He scrunched his face in an attempt to imitate a thoughtful expression.

I smiled for only a moment before blurting, "Cassie spoke to me this morning. She said that she, Matt, and Diane don't have long before their memories vanish and they become Bots in every respect. I need to act soon."

Torermak's face returned to normal, and Bevon asked, "Can you identify them from the other Bots?"

I shook my head. "I've tried, but no."

Torermak rubbed his chin as he observed the assembled Bots a hundred yards away. "I find them disturbing, seeing them standing out there. It is unnatural. Normally, they are heartless, killing without hesitation." He looked back at me. "What else did she say?"

My eyes watered as I thought about her. "She said they are obsessed with controlling and ruling over others. I learned as much from the Farseeing with Tess. But none of that helps me. We already knew that. I'm hoping either of you may have some ideas."

Bevon and Torermak looked at each other. The giant spoke first. "Your abilities have surpassed anyone I know." He glanced at the Bots for another moment. "They must want something. Otherwise, they would not linger here. You gave them a soul." He chuckled and shook his head in disbelief. "That is a feat beyond my understanding. Yet, it was not enough. I fear they now need you to join their cause and use your talents in their service."

"Your skill at weaving Elthea's powers would be a boon to them," said Bevon. "With you at their side, they could conquer untold worlds."

I tensed, ready to shout that I would never agree, but Bevon held up his palm to forestall me. "We all realize you will not willingly join them. The crux of your dilemma is to give them something as valuable as that so they will restore Cassie, Matt, and Diane to their former selves while also not harming anyone else."

I threw my hands up. "I'm looking for answers. You each have more knowledge about the Spirit of Elthea than I do. If anyone can come up with an idea, it's the two of you."

Silence followed as the Stonewraith shifted his weight from one foot to the other.

I leveled a stare at them. "Any idea will do."

"Earthfriend," said Bevon. "You may think we know more than you, but you surpass our capacity to draw upon the powers of this land. To give the Bots a soul is something I would never have thought possible."

Torermak nodded in agreement. "Ask me about stone lore, Master Philip, and I will talk about it until you beg me to stop. That is what I comprehend. The magnitude of your skills is beyond my understanding."

The admission from both of them hit me like a thunderclap. Regardless of the Oakenrill's training, I still felt inferior to their abilities and their knowledge of the supernatural powers inherent in this land. Had I gone from neophyte to a master without realizing it?

"You may not realize it yet," continued Torermak, "but the answer you seek may lie within you. Only you understand your capabilities, and only you can decide the course to take. Stay true to yourself, and I believe you will find a way."

I looked from one to the other and then at the legion of Bots. "If I could only kill them and be done with their race forever, I would. That would be easy. But stopping the cruelty within them..."

"We trust you will make the right decision," Torermak added.

If anyone said that one more time, I was going to scream.

THE SUN WAS OVERHEAD BY THE TIME I STEPPED DOWN from the pile of rocks that had once formed a section of the great wall around the town, my mind made up. After talking with Torermak and Bevon, I had sat up here, struggling with my indecision and uncertainty. They consented to my request to be alone for a while, as Torermak had joined his fellow Stonewraiths, working without a break during the daylight, reconstructing the fortification. Bevon wandered off, but I knew he or one of my other friends would be nearby.

All my companions still believed they had to protect me. Or was it a feeling of kinship they felt? We were so different, yet had bonded together. I spent most of my life in another world, yet somehow I had become a vital part of their lives, and them of mine.

Their love and devotion helped sustain me during dark days, but now they could offer no guidance. Their hearts were in the right place, and that would have to suffice. Only one entity could tell me what the Bots wanted.

I had to ask them.

Jumping off the rocks, my heart beat a little faster knowing what I had to do. After only a half-dozen paces, Bevon and the Valnorian, Ja'Krill, approached to stand on each side of me. I eyed them with a sideways glance. "Who's gonna save both of you if the Bots become angry?"

Ja'Krill chuckled. "You, of course. That is why we want to be as close as possible, Earthfriend."

Like many of my friends in this land, he could always make me smile. "Lucky for you, I'm here."

Bevon smirked. "It remains to be seen if your presence is a boon or not."

Even spoken in humor, I knew he was right.

My good spirits faded the closer we came to the Bots. It was difficult to see them as anything other than killing machines. My opinion of these monsters still hadn't changed from my Farseeing experience with the Reapers and Elite. How much of their former lives remained in what they had become? Did it even matter? Was the time I spent learning about their past going to help?

Fifty yards away, a single Bot strode forward. It stopped a dozen paces before me, while I stepped closer until only an arm's-length separated us.

It towered over me; its mask of a face contained only the slightest indentations and protrusions showing facial features. For the first time, I noticed that the gold trim around the joints of its elbows, shoulders, waist, and knees was the same color the Elites used to adorn their white robes. But there was no white visible on the Bots.

The creature stood still, giving no sign of its intention. Without expressions, the Bots were impossible to read except by their actions.

A ripple of uncertainty came over me. What did I hope to accomplish by confronting them? Asking them what they demanded would elicit the same response. They wanted me, and thus our stalemate.

Steeling myself, I spoke with a clear voice. "Return my friends to the way they were. You took them without provocation when I only tried to help you."

The words began pounding in my head before I could take another breath.

—Your meddling in our lives has consequences. We have no intention of returning them, at least not yet.

My neck muscles tightened. "Restore them to what they were, and we will work together. I will do what I can for you."

A screeching reverberation in my head caused me to flinch. They were laughing at my offer.

—You know what we hunger for. Join our cause, use your power to help us conquer worlds. That is our only wish.

"No, it is not." I waved my hand across the army of Bots behind this one. "You are here because you yearn for something more. You wait. For what?"

The Bot was slow to respond, unusual for them.

—Another inflection point is about to take place in our existence. You, Philip Matherson, are the trigger of this approaching event, just as Tess Armstrong was the spark for our last transformation. We wait for you to perform the deed to launch us forward.

Tess had experienced the pain and suffering of the Reapers and Elite during the battle in the fortress. Another cataclysmic episode would not be good news. "You now have a soul. Wasn't that enough to transform you into something more human?"

Again, the beast laughed inside my head.

—You know so little. The act you committed may be monumental, but it did nothing to change us. We still hunger for more.

It always came back to this with the Bots, as with the

Elite and Reapers. They were never happy with what they had. I shouted, "Your hatred consumes you, blocks out everything else. You never improve as you go from one conquest to another, believing that each time you are gaining something valuable. Instead, you become more empty, never satisfied." I softened my tone. "Deep inside, even you must understand this will not end well for you. One day, somebody stronger will end your existence."

—Your paltry appeal serves no purpose. Give us what we want and we will restore your companions. You can be together with them, spend the rest of your lives as humans. All you need to do is to join us, become the weapon we desire. If you delay much longer, they will turn into one of us forever, and you will never see them again.

Once more, I stood on a precipice. This time, it was too much for me. Why was I responsible for keeping everyone safe in this world? When did I volunteer for the responsibility?

Damn everybody else. What did I ever receive from life except pain and suffering? The time I had with Cassie was too short, and I deserved more—we deserved more. We should be together again: her, Matt, and Diane. Just like our college days. Each of them would give their lives for me, so shouldn't I do the same for them? Maybe I should listen to the Bot for a change.

A flicker of movement from behind the Bot caught my attention. Of all things, it was a tiny bird flitting back and forth, a stripe of red across its back. For a second, I silently chastised myself for letting my mind waiver on something so trivial. But then I remembered the mechanical bird of the Draas.

Unbidden, Cassie's message from this morning replayed in my thoughts. *We cannot be the only beings who oppose them. Surely, there are others.*

She was right. Other powerful forces existed who would defy the Bots. The simulation named Enia had once said that she would come to my aid. She was giving me a signal with the bird, letting me know she had my back.

I focused again on the Bot. "I am done with you. This ends here and now, one way or the other."

24

LIVE TO FIGHT ANOTHER DAY

A low rumble shook the ground. The tremor came from a great distance, much like the rat-tat-tat of a far off helicopter back on Earth, a vibration that you knew would soon become louder as it moved closer. The Bots felt as I did: the time to play nice had ended.

Without realizing it, my senses sharpened, ready for anything, my fingertips glowing with energy. However, the sensation differed from the other times I had wielded the force of Elthea, giving me pause. Understanding came to me. The spirit was feeding me with more power, knowing it would take all my strength for what was coming.

Ja'Krill and Bevon drew their blades and moved into defensive stances. Behind me, commanders of The Guard began shouting orders, causing me to consider the people of Haven. Without a wall, they were defenseless. Then again, a fortification hadn't stopped the Bots during the last conflict. This time, my presence would have to serve as the bulwark against another attack. Would it be enough?

My hand grasped the pendant hanging around my neck, a constant companion that had been a gift from the Draas named Enia. She remained in an underground fortress after the rest of her species had moved onto a different reality. The medallion had become a part of me. Enia had told me she would provide aid should I need it.

A warmth now emanated from the metal and stone. At other times, it felt cold and inert. I gripped the pendant, the world slowed to a stop, frozen in the moment. My vision blurred and there stood Enia, with skin the color of gray scales and eyes too large to be human. "We meet again, Philip Matherson. You have done well in your travels."

This was no time for pleasantries. Words fell from my lips in a jumble. "The Bots are holding my friends hostage unless I do their bidding. I don't have the skill to save them and I can't overpower the Bots without killing my companions. If ever I needed your help, it is now."

She nodded. "Elthea has gifted you well. It is wise you avoided doing harm."

With the time bubble surrounding me, the need to rush my words subsided. I took a deep breath. "A shred of humanity still exists inside my friends even though the Bots changed them, and I'm going to get them back or die trying. My life matters little if they live as Bots." I raised my arms, imploring Enia to help. "You saved me once before; please save my companions now."

Enia's brow furrowed in thought. "My capabilities are extensive, yet I have limitations. The ability of the Bots to transform your friends into one of their own is astounding, much like you giving the Bots a soul. Only your enemy can undo what they have done, but we will deal with that in due time." She raised her hand to forestall my outburst. "Hear this, Philip Matherson. You must first stay alive to have any chance of freeing those you love most. The Bots have determined that you will not bend to their demands. They have unleashed a force that will extinguish your life and the lives of those in the village behind you. Its intensity is greater than anything you have experienced before. You alone cannot save both yourself and the people you hope to protect."

Regretting now that I had provoked the Bots, Enia gave me no chance to ask for advice. She motioned with her arm to a space in front of me. "You must first be concerned with what is before you. Shield yourself and the villagers. Even that will not be enough. I will aid you, and together we must hope it will be sufficient. I cannot keep us in stasis much longer. Once I release you, the storm will crash over you in moments. Use every ounce of your strength to fend it off. Anything less will end with your demise."

"And if we stop the attack, what next?"

"If you live, we can discuss it. Ready?"

I steeled myself, preparing to raise a shield to defend us against the onslaught. I had practiced this skill many times under the Oakenrill's tutelage, but had never produced a barrier so large. The Bots would hold nothing back, and I would need to make it strong enough to with-stand whatever they threw at us. "Ready," I responded.

The wind and noise took me by surprise once Enia released me from the stasis bubble. It sounded as if someone was smashing a giant hammer against the ground, going faster and faster while getting closer and closer. Standing feet apart to keep my balance, the soil shook and the gusty winds threatened to topple me.

The disturbance sent shock waves toward us before the giant tsunami became visible. Its billions of razor-thin energy streams were more deadly than any blade. I had made a terrible mistake underestimating the Bots. The last few days, with their docile behavior, had lulled me into complacency. Why had I been so absorbed trying to under-stand them and what they wanted? No way would they agree to the return of my companions.

How foolish was I?

If only I had more time. But the Bots were angry with the world, especially with me. No amount of time was going to change that.

The deadly wave came closer, an ominous darkness on the horizon, sprinkled with glitters of red sparkles. It moved with incredible speed, giving me no chance to consider other options. I prepared to launch a shield as Enia proposed. At that moment, all the Bots surrounding Haven vanished. One minute they were there, the next gone.

"Earthfriend," Bevon shouted. "Can you safeguard the

village?" Neither he nor Ja'Krill witnessed my discussion with Enia.

I squinted at the massive surge, probing it for signs of weakness. It was more powerful than anything I had encountered before. A tinge of uncertainty seeped into my thoughts. This force was more immense than I had imagined. How would I stand against it? Steeling a glance at Bevon, I put on a brave face. "Enia from the Draas will assist. Stand behind me. Swords are useless against this."

The force of the wind threatened to overturn everything in its path. All other thoughts fell away. The townsfolk had placed their trust in me, and we would now discover if it was justified. I studied the wave as it drew closer, finding no weakness in it. Dirt and debris sailed through the air, blocking the sun. Trees cracked as they fell to the ground, uprooted stumps flew like tumbleweeds. Red streamers ripped across the sky.

For the millionth time since coming to this land, I thought, why me?

I readied myself, opening my senses to pull on more energy than ever before. "I hope you are going to do something soon, Earthfriend," Ja'Krill yelled over the din.

My fingers burned from holding onto the power within me. Enia had not yet bolstered my strength. My eyes hurt from grit; I could barely breathe. Still, I waited.

Just when I felt sure time had run out, another rush of vigor flowed through my veins. Enia had provided the extra boost needed.

The maelstrom was upon me as ribbons of light

scorched my skin. I opened my mouth to scream, never knowing if any sound came. The energy poured out of me, creating a protective barrier and extending around the entire village. The unrelenting force still continued to pound against me.

Was it destroying the town? How could I tell if I had failed?

Reaching deeper, perceiving I needed more, I wondered which would kill me first: the attacking force hurled by the Bots, or the supernatural energy flowing through me. My insides were on fire. How could I endure this much intensity?

Every fiber of my awareness focused on drawing more power as I released it into a protective shield around the village. When would it end? How long could I continue? Was I wearing down the attack, or did they have reserves enough to go on forever?

With my body aching from cuts, clothes shredded, eardrums almost bursting from the concussions, it was unclear if I had done any good. Dreading to see the damage to the town if I looked, I persisted, knowing death was preferable to failure. Too many innocent lives hung in the balance.

Had minutes or hours passed? A fog hovered over my thoughts as my body ached from so much exertion.

Thankfully, the stream of power ran dry. A spigot tamped closed in the ethereal world, a place between temporal and mystical. The source of powers within this domain was still a mystery to me.

My knees buckled as the energy dissipated. The ground came up to meet me.

~

A GHOSTLY MIST FILLED MY VISION, WITH NOTHING else existing in this reality. Somehow, since the time I had clashed with the Bots, my world had shifted from the tactile to the unreal. The sensation should fill me with fear, but after all that had happened to me, I remained calm... waiting.

Everything in life has a purpose, and this was no different.

Maybe this was a dream, I thought, or at least another reality. And then, a new concern intruded: was I even alive? Had the tempest launched by my enemy destroyed me, along with everything else in its path?

As I considered this, a voice intruded.

Phil, they need more than a soul, and only you can provide it to them. Don't give up now just because they're angry with you. They are a passionate group and are often hot-tempered. Regardless of what they do, rely upon your instincts. Your sixth sense has served you well in the past.

This was not Cassie's voice, much to my disappointment. Shouldn't she come to say a goodbye before my life faded? I reached out with my thoughts. *Who is this?*

It's me, Matt. Have you forgotten me so soon? Take my advice for what it's worth. At least it may help.

I wanted to shake my head in response to his question. But the reflex had no significance here.

Matt, of course I haven't forgotten. Every day I agonize over you, Diane, and Cass. I was foolish in thinking I could outwit those monsters. You must hate me. How can I tell you how sorry I am?

He chuckled. It was a sad sound. Turning into a Bot had to be difficult for each of them, but more so for Matt. He was the eternal optimist, always taking life in stride. Memories of our days together washed over me.

One chance meeting between the two of us came to mind. I didn't yet know the members of the utopia team very well and was still feeling my way. The project wouldn't begin until the following semester, although I had already committed to joining the team and had registered for the course.

On this specific day, I had arrived early for a class and waited outside, taking a seat on one of the wooden benches lining the main student walkway. The day was pleasant for the first week in November, so I unbuttoned my light jacket and turned my face to the sun, enjoying the warmth. As I closed my eyes, a comforting stupor settled over me as the babble of student's voices receded in the background. I pushed away a nagging feeling that I should review my notes for today's class rather than rest like this. But it felt so good.

My eyes bolted open as someone brushed against me on the bench. Matt smirked. "Odd place to take a nap, isn't it?"

I sat up straight. "Oh, hi. I was early for economics, and well, one thing led to another."

He chuckled. "I get it." He gazed at the passing students, his eyes constantly searching, always alert. Did anything ever go unnoticed by him? "College isn't easy. We have a lot on our shoulders. And soon we'll be taking the toughest course of the program. I'm glad we have you on our team, Phil. I wanted to be sure you understood how I felt."

The compliment felt good. "We'll be spending plenty of time together. We should get along with each other."

"Exactly. But more than that, you have what it takes. I can tell already."

"What, because you found me dozing on a bench before class?"

He laughed again, a throaty sound that gave me the feeling that no matter what, he trusted me. "No, because I consider myself an excellent judge of character. Adding you to our team completed it, rounded out the rough edges."

I wasn't sure what he meant, but he must have given it more thought than I had.

He clapped me on the shoulder as he rose. "You're going places, Phil. I can see it already. I love the intensity you bring to the table; it's what won me over."

I was at a loss for words, but he didn't give me the chance to respond. "How about we all meet for dinner sometime soon? I'll ask the others on the team and text you with the details." A crooked grin creased his face, an expression that would become more familiar in the days to come. "Try to stay awake for your next class." He joined the crush of other students and became lost in the crowd.

Even back then, he was challenging me, urging me to develop into a better person. And as I grew to know him more, I observed how much of a leader he was. Never was I able to understand why the Spirit of Elthea choose me to wield her powers rather than him. And now, because of my actions, he had become a Bot, our most feared nemesis.

Phil, I can never hate you. You did what was necessary to save a defenseless tribe from annihilation. It was brilliant. You eluded death and kept us alive. The Bots were ready to kill us, remember? And you didn't give in to their demands. There's nothing more you could have done.

As always, his message bolstered my emotions, made me believe I could accomplish more than I realized. Despite it all, my self-doubts lay right below the surface once again. How could I do this without my teammates here to help?

Matt, I'm not sure if I can bring you back, and I don't want to risk it. Neither can I destroy the Bots without injuring the Spirit of Elthea. I'm in a bind, and don't know how to get out of it. I need you—all of you—like never before.

He took a moment to respond.

Here's my advice. Now that you better understand who they once were, use that knowledge. They survived annihilation once, but they became something other than the Elite and Reapers. If anyone can figure it out, it's you, Phil.

My heart sank, knowing he had no answer.

I wish I had your confidence, Matt. I wish we were all together again.

Another moment passed before he responded.

We will if you believe it. Be yourself, use your intuition. It has never failed you before, and it won't now.

His voice faded, and I feared his time with me was about to end.

Tell Diane I'm sorry. She must hate me now more than ever. And tell Cass I love her, always will. I promise you, I'll bring you all back, or die trying.

As the stillness stretched out, I wondered if he had already left. When he replied, he was hesitant.

Di doesn't hate you. None of us do, Phil. You're our only hope, and sacrificing yourself will do no good. Live to fight another day, whether or not you can rescue us. Goodbye, for now.

My throat closed, nearly choking me, unable to respond. Would I ever see any of them again?

REALITY CAME RUSHING BACK AS MY EYES FLUTTERED opened. Unable to focus, I blinked, trying to clear them. Still not able to see, I realized my entire body hurt: eyelids were like sandpaper, every inch of my skin was on fire, and my bones felt as if someone had broken each one and forced them together again.

I groaned, struggling to lift my head, searching for the

strand of energy that would allow me to keep fighting the Bot attack. I croaked, "Must continue. Can't stop now."

Hands pushed against me, forcing me down. I struggled to push them aside, the weight of responsibility hanging heavy over me. If I didn't stand against them, who would?

Still blinking, I tried to clear the morass clouding my thoughts and vision. Why was I so exhausted? As my eyesight returned, I saw Tess's daughter Rae standing over me, worry lines etched on her face. I stopped struggling against her, feeble as my attempts were.

"You're awake," she smiled. "We were worried about you."

Her voice sounded like music. I looked at her, seeing a white stucco ceiling above us. Why were we here in my room when we should be in the fields around Haven?

Trying once more to lift myself by putting an elbow under me, I grimaced and fell back. "What happened? How did I get here?"

"Mostly by me carrying you," a deep voice answered.

Turning my head was a mistake as waves of vertigo came over me. Shutting my eyes, I clenched my stomach, hoping to avoid getting sick. This voice belonged to Bryson. The lanky young man of Haven had, unnoticed by me, become an accomplished member of The Guard. "Thanks for not dropping me."

He snickered. "What makes you think I didn't?"

"You stopped the attack," said Rae, ignoring Bryson's remark. "The Bots have not returned."

Keeping my head still while squinting my eyes open to avoid another bout of dizziness, I took in Rae's concerned expression as she looked down at me. "Are all of them gone?"

She hesitated, knowing what I was asking. "Yes. If your friends were among them, they are not here now."

I let out a breath, feeling my strength return. "The Bots will be back. Like me, they needed time to regroup and recover. How long have I been out?"

Bryson moved to the other side of the bed. "Two days." He put a hand on my shoulder. "Everyone was concerned at first because your breathing was so slow."

Rae added, "We all took turns watching over you." She looked at Bryson. "Maybe you should tell Bevon and Ja'Krill. They asked to be notified the moment he awakened. Also, if you don't mind, please bring a bowl of soup from the kitchen; it might help him."

"Of course." He nodded, glancing back before letting himself out.

I grinned. "Still sending him on errands, I see."

She returned the smile. "He'll be a captain one day, which I find difficult to believe. He's no longer the awkward boy, someone I needed to keep out of harm's way."

"Nobody's safe, Rae. They're going to continue lashing out at us until we're all dead, or until I relent and give them what they want."

"Which is?"

I replayed the conversation in my head with the Bot

before they attacked. "They need to use me as their weapon."

The smooth lines of her face blended with the chiseled hardness gained from working as a member of The Guard. In this moment, she looked much like her mother. But unlike Tess's carefree nature, Rae was wary of strangers, as if she always kept one hand on the hilt of a blade, at least mentally.

She furrowed her brow as she considered what I said, giving a slight shake of her head. "That's not who you are, Phil. You would rather die than become a weapon for the Bots."

My heart sank. "And there you have the crux of my problem. Without a suitable alternative, I'm as good as dead. If I can't save my companions, and I won't agree to their demand, they will kill me. How can I sustain another attack?"

"But you beat them back. You did it once, you can do it again. Can't you?"

I shrugged. "The lost race of the Draas helped me. Next time, I might not be so lucky."

"Everyone here would be defenseless against the Bots without you."

"Ah, that sounds familiar, Rae. I'm afraid you're not the first person to use that argument. But with me dead, the Bots would have no reason to attack you. It's me they want, not you or anyone else here. They left you alone for many years before I showed up. Why would they choose to destroy Haven if I were dead?"

She frowned. "And you're so sure about that?"

Something inside me quivered. The Bots had no compunction about killing. They might level this place out of anger or in spite. Who could predict anything about them? Matt's words came to me again. *Live to fight another day.*

I sighed. Like it or not, that was my only recourse.

25

NEVER TO BE MORTAL AGAIN

The morning sunshine washed over me as I stood waiting and watching. After days of anticipation, I could sense the Bots approach once again. They would never relent. We are all products of our past, but now I understood how that was true about the Bots.

I balled my fingers into a fist and relaxed them, only to repeat the motion. When had this become a habit? What would a therapist say about my latest mannerism? The answer was obvious: I put too much on my shoulders. But what choice did I have?

Our enemy would soon appear, and I had to steel myself for another confrontation. Did I have the strength to beat them back once more? The previous battle had taken everything and then some. And now they would use all their might to destroy me, or bend me to their will. The Bots and I are both driven by instincts built into our psyche from long ago. What other recourse did we each have?

The town of Haven stood a hundred yards behind me. Would the people there, humanity's only outpost in this world, survive the coming battle? I owed the townsfolk a great deal. But what if the Bots gave me no option, forcing me to choose between the villagers and my closest friends from Earth? They once threatened to kill my friends if I did not capitulate to their demands. What would I do if they once again provided me no other recourse: watch my friends die or join the Bot's cause? I didn't want to even consider it at this moment.

Around me stood my closest friends from this world. Bevon and Ja'Krill stood on either side of me. I had told them they should stay within the town and what little protection it might offer. Ja'Krill had responded, "Shall we cower as if we were weak and fearful while you have all the fun?"

Bevon was likewise unyielding. "I have kept you out of trouble more times than I can count, and I will probably need to safeguard you for the foreseeable future. Just try not to scorch me with one of your energy bursts."

Regardless of the situation, Ja'Krill and Bevon always made me smile.

Fanning out around them stood my other companions, each one determined to keep me safe. They had already saved my life on multiple occasions, always staying with me despite the risk to their own safety. I was not alone.

The two other Astari, Quintia and Riyaad, remained shoulder to shoulder. They had been at my side, protecting me from the moment I set foot on the Raised Isles of

Loralee as several Bots launched their first assault against me. It was a harrowing experience, a feeling which has not diminished with time.

The Stonewraith, Torermak, a giant of a being, towered above everyone else. What would any of us do without the Stonewraiths? The fortress of Haven would not exist, and the villagers would never have survived all this time. Torermak also guided us through the dead zones as he discovered an underground shelter for us in the abandoned home of the Draas. Maybe the Draas will now make the difference in this conflict, tipping the scales in our favor.

The medallion around my neck, a gift from the Draas, now glowed. The Draas simulation, named Enia, was sending me a sign that the power of her race would funnel into me when the time arrived. But would even that be enough?

Not the least of my companions, Rae and Bryson, held their blades at their sides, ready to raise them at a moment's notice. I felt as close to them as any of the others, more so because we shared the same genetic makeup, as did all humans. Or did I have a fondness for them because of their imperfections? Like me, like all mortals, we were a race living a flawed existence, never perfect. Was that the bane of humanity or something to be cherished?

The most surprising individuals to join me in the field beyond the shattered wall of Haven were its three leaders: Tess Armstrong, Alan Sabrinsky, and Russell Ingram. Each stood, heads held high, proud of being part of this group.

They remained unarmed—fighting was not their skill. The rest of the villagers took comfort from the three because they provided inspiration, guidance, and order to their society. Like all the others standing here, I hadn't asked them to accompany me today. They insisted on it.

The strangest being of those gathered here was the Oakenrill. The pile of sticks, looking more like a dead shrub, was more powerful than all the rest, save me. He had appeared just as we made our way to this field around Haven, somehow recognizing that I needed him in this time of peril. More than anyone, the Oakenrill taught me the skill to draw upon the energies of Elthea. I felt comforted knowing he had returned to my side.

We waited for the inevitable. Nobody spoke, no rousing speech was necessary. Neither did we have a plan for how to defend the town. We came together in our opposition to the Bots. That was enough.

When the onslaught arrived, it took a form none of us could have expected.

MY RESOLVE FALTERED AS SOON AS THE BOT ASSAULT took shape. How could I fight this?

My assumption was that they would use brute force. But they were cunning, always adding a twist to their assaults. In the past, they employed horrific storms with lightning and thunder. They turned the sky black and set it on fire. One of their most devastating forays was when they transformed the ground into water and used a wave of invisible energy to destroy everything in its path. They could inflict death numerous ways beyond their lethal blades.

But this was a thing from my worst nightmares.

I squinted in the sunlight, wondering if I my imagination was getting the best of me. Could this be real? A horde of figures approached, many thousands. They were neither running nor taking their time. They moved forward with an unshakeable determination.

Something inside me quaked as my resolve faltered. The closer they came, the more I was certain of what the Bots had done. I knew now that their plan was cunning beyond all expectations.

Marching forward were the figures of my friends Cassie McKenzie, Diane Collentenio, and Matt Tyler, each one of them duplicated hundreds, maybe thousands, of times. But even that wasn't the worst of it.

As they came closer, I saw more details. Blood oozed from some of their mouths, others had fresh wounds on their faces or bodies. Limbs dangled or were missing altogether.

No two were alike except for one exception: those who could, held the scimitar blades used by the Bots. All of them marched toward me, the most horrible scene I could have imagined, a zombie army intent on killing me.

How could I fight them? These were my friends, even though I tried to tell myself they were not. My legs trembled the closer they came. I couldn't do this, regardless of what my rational brain was telling me.

"Those are Bots, Earthfriend," Bevon hissed. "They are trying to deceive you. Do not fall into their trap."

I could not wrench my eyes away from them. I focused on Cassie. Her features, except for the deformities, were the same as my memory of her. And there were Matt and Diane, alive again. I could almost believe they would smile and crack a joke, as they always had.

But it became even more terrible.

Their lilting voices sounded soft and serene. They approached me as if we had never parted. Their words resonated inside my head. First the voice of Cassie spoke.

—Phil, my dear, I've returned. It was so horrible as a Bot, but now I've returned. They let me go. Please, come to me, wrap your arms around me once again.

Then I heard Diane speak, the pitch of her tone different from that of Cassie. I could always tell them apart just by their voices.

—You put us through hell, Phil, but thank God it's over. I wanted my life back, and now I have it. You freed us.

Matt spoke next, his words as reassuring as ever.

—I'm proud of you, Phil. You did well fighting off the Bots. I don't know if I could have been as brave as you were.

I stumbled back a step, my face contorted, eyes darting from one college companion to another, hoping I would see something to help me comprehend what I was seeing. Yet, each face I saw only deepened my belief that here were my friends, returned from their captivity as Bots.

As they strode forward, some of them raised their arms as if ready to embrace me. That they still held a blade with one hand didn't matter. My companions would never hurt me.

The mob edged closer. Delusional thoughts ran unchecked through my head. How could these not be my friends? Maybe the Bots freed them. What did it matter that there were hundreds of each person? All I saw were the faces of those I had known so well: Cassie, Diane, and Matt. That was enough.

All sense of rational thinking fled as my mind stopped functioning the way it should. I realized someone was shaking me. Tess had a firm grip on my shoulders. I tensed, focusing on her eyes inches in front of my own. "Get away from me," I snarled.

She gripped me even harder. "Phil, remember what you saw in our Farseeing. Think about the Elite and Reapers. You lived with them through me. This is what they are capable of. Don't squander that experience."

I wanted to shove her aside so I could watch the approach of my closest companions. They were all that mattered. I looked past her.

Tess pounded my chest, which only made me angrier. "Can't you see?" I shouted. "My friends, they're back."

Her unblinking eyes opened wide. When she spoke, her voice was gentle. "If you believe that, Phil, you've killed us all. They've won."

～

Someone raised an invisible shield in front of us as my friends came within thirty paces. "Who?" I jerked my head, looking for the source. It had to be the Oakenrill. He was the only one here with that ability. No matter, I could sense the weakness in the barrier; it wouldn't stand for long. My companions could tear it down.

Tess took a step away from me as she saw my expression change. "Phil?" she questioned, unaware of the shield.

I smiled. "The Oakenrill seeks to stop them. His defense is inconsequential. My friends will have no trouble overcoming it." I waited for them to brush it aside.

She raised her voice. "How will they overpower it? Your friends don't have that ability."

The first shred of doubt entered my thoughts. Something didn't add up.

Bevon forced his way in front of Tess. "Earthfriend, I took an oath to protect you and the other Earthfriends, did I not?"

Yes, he was right, but what did it matter?

"I can neither harm you nor Earthfriends Cassie, Diane, and Matt." He pointed to the mass of figures probing the invisible wall. A few of my friends had already torn sections of it away with an energy force of their own. "Watch now, understand who they are." Bevon extended his lance and dashed toward those who had broken through the shield.

My throat constricted. He couldn't be telling the truth, could he? The Astari had always been faithful, especially Bevon, and they were logical. I tensed as he swung his lance at the figure of Cassie, every muscle in my body wanting to prevent him from carrying through with the motion. But I held back, now unsure.

The figure who was Cassie parried his blow and swept her blade around, nearly cleaving him in half. He avoided the deadly stroke by jumping back. How had she learned to fight like that? He had no time to recover as the figure lunged forward, thrusting her blade at his mid-section. Bevon stumbled as he retreated a step, raising his lance to ward against it.

The Astari was off balance as he backed away. Cassie saw her opening and smiled. She sprung toward him, blade swinging, intent on finishing him. I reached for the weave of energy to put an end to it before one killed the other. Just before I could act, an arrow struck Cassie's chest. The look of dismay on her face broke my heart. This was my fault.

But Cassie kept moving. With a superhuman effort, she swung her sword at Bevon. Even though her aim was off the mark, he barely dodged the blow. Before she could bring the blade around again, he jammed his lance into her gut. Green blood spurted from her wounds.

At that moment, sanity flooded back. I understood this wasn't Cassie. Nor were the others Matt and Diane. Like a charm losing its spell, the full knowledge of the Bots' deceit washed over me. Maybe I knew from the beginning, but didn't want to believe it. They recognized my fatal flaw all too well. The people they had mimicked were everything to me.

Before the monsters came any closer, I drew a weave of power and constructed a force around us, extending over Haven, as I had done during the last attack. This barrier was more substantial than the one formed by the Oaken-rill. "Now the hard part," I muttered, watching as the likeness of my friends came to an abrupt stop before the invisible wall. Unlike Cassie, Matt, and Diane, the Bots could sense the use of Elthea's energies and realize I had blocked their way.

Admonishing myself for being duped, I clenched and unclenched my fingers, still unsure about what to do. Alan Sabrinsky sidled up next to me. He rarely spoke to me unless I initiated the conversation, so I glanced sideways at him, waiting to hear what he might say. Tess had explained that he was the most gifted of the three programmers. I had also observed that his advice about the Bots was often astute. "What do you see, Alan?"

He hesitated a moment. "I believe what just happened was a ruse. They knew you would recognize the hoax."

I frowned. "Then why do it?"

He rubbed his chin, eyes never leaving the horde in front of us. "Perhaps they were trying to tell you something without saying it. Or maybe they didn't even understand themselves why they did it."

I grimaced. "This is no time for riddles, Alan. What do you mean?"

"Think about your Farseeing with Tess. You saw what we experienced when living with the Reapers and Elite. Many of them were content during that era, at least as much as possible. But then, when they developed into Bots, they became angry. They were no longer Reapers and Elite. Maybe they want some of that existence back."

"I don't understand. What part of their past life?"

Alan paused, as if he wasn't willing to speak it out loud. "Phil, you gave them a soul, but that's not what they were missing. They once lived in a community, not a perfect society, but one that worked for them. Both the Elite and Reapers always wanted more; it was the nature of who they were. But mostly, they existed within their framework of everyday existence. Maybe you need to restore as much of their original life as you can."

"Their culture self-destructed!" I yelled. "They wouldn't exist now if they had not snuck a seed of their DNA into your minds, giving you the ability to recreate them as computer code." He winced, and I understood he still blamed himself for the survival of the Bots. "They're cunning, Alan. No way you, or Tess, or Russell could ever have known what they were planning. What's done is done, and now we've got to figure out how to stop them and get my friends back. That's my only concern."

"Then give them what they desire."

"They want me. I'm the key for them to rule the universe. They've said it again and again."

Alan shook his head in frustration. "I understand, but we both know that path leads to our annihilation. Offer them an alternative by restoring some of their past life. Hold it out to them in exchange for your companions."

I barked a laugh of disbelief. "Are you kidding me?

What would they possibly agree to? Even after living through the Farseeing, I still have no idea. Besides, I'm not a god, Alan, and we don't have the time to figure out what would satisfy them."

He gazed at me calmly, as if he had made his point. "You gave them a soul without knowing what it would accomplish, an act some might say was god-like."

I exhaled, ready to shout and tell him how much harm came from that choice, how my companions became Bots because of it. But he held out his palms to forestall my outburst. "The Bots took your friends captive, but they didn't kill them, and neither did they execute you. Because of your decision, you saved an innocent race. You may think you made a huge mistake by doing it, but with your back against the wall and no other options, you accomplished the impossible. Now, do it again. Use your intuition. It has served you well in the past."

A voice thumped in my head as those around me jerked with surprise. The Bots were speaking to all of us.

—*Delay no further, Philip Matherson. The human captives will soon become Bots, never to be mortal again. Our offer still stands. We will restore them only if you bind yourself to us. Do it now or live the rest of your life without them.*

Time was up. I had to act.

26

IF YOU EVER LOVED ME

Whatever decisions I made here and now would change the fate of worlds. Countless lives hung in the balance as I considered my next steps, knowing that those of us from the Utopia Project were of scant concern in the larger scheme of events. At this moment, as well as throughout history, powerful forces would always prevail over the weak. Who was right, or who was wrong, mattered little.

The Bots, in the likeness of my companions, had paused before my shield. They were in no hurry, as time was on their side. The longer I delayed, the more my friends turned into one of them.

As I watched, in a blink of an eye, they shed the facade of my friends and changed back to their normal appearance, huge, faceless beings, each one appearing the same as the next. I could never tell one Bot from the other—I doubted anyone could.

I considered Alan's plea, saying that the Bots wanted something from their past. Could I alter them to look the same as the original Elite and Reapers? Did they even want that? I had once believed that giving them a soul would satisfy them. Would this be any better?

The moment had arrived, yet my resolve faltered. I had been desperate when I committed the act of forcing a soul into their psyche. It was a last-gasp effort, and even now I wasn't sure how it had happened. But wasn't this as dire a situation? A female voice sounded in my head, the tone of someone I knew intimately. It was Cassie.

—*Do this for me, Phil. You must kill me, each of us. Taking our life is an act of kindness, not an affront to the spirit of this land. Please, if you ever loved me, you must act while you still can.*

We should be together, her and I. Such was our destiny, but the Bots had intervened. And now, would she die because of me? Was it so bad to end her existence rather than knowing she would continue living in her current form?

There are fates worse than dying. I had never believed that until this moment. If our roles were reversed, wouldn't I expect the same from her? How could I refuse her now? If only we had more time together, how delightful would be a life without Bots. But that would not be the future written in the stars for Cassie and I. Would it?

I willed myself to do what she asked, knowing it was necessary, knowing it would be the most terrible deed I could ever commit.

My eyes watered as a fleeting memory came to me, an image of Cassie during happier times when we were at Woodbery College. We had finished a conversation about how glad we were that the school week was over. She left me with a smile on her face. Watching her move away from me, she suddenly spun her head around to look at me as she continued walking away. Like two young school kids, our eyes locked. The smile on her lips and the shimmer of her face were the stuff of dreams. Her grin broadened, knowing I was still looking at her. The thought of that moment would stay with me forever, warming me even when the coldness of death took me.

The recollection fell away as I steeled myself for what I had to do. Because of my heightened emotions, I could now identify the three I loved. Cassie was everything to me, but I cared for Diane and Matt no less. My task was a simple one; they would feel no pain.

Cassie's words filled me with such deep sorrow. *Please, if you ever loved me, you must act while you still can.*

The moment had arrived, yet my heart ached, my mind awash with emotions. And the strongest of feelings I felt at that moment was love, the elixir of all passions. What could be more powerful?

This will finish with us dead. I would fulfill her last wish, but I would forfeit my life as recompense. How could I continue living knowing I had taken their lives? The four of us would die together. After so much uncertainty, my choice was now crystal clear, with no other options available. This was the end, and I felt little regret or remorse, only resolve.

27

THE WORLD PAUSES

trace of doubt refused to be silenced. Something within me whispered: Do you have nothing else? A recollection came to me from this morning while striding out here. The sight of a little boy in the village had captured my attention. He was only six or seven, and he watched me pass, an expression of awe on his face at seeing me. Stories about me had spread like wildfire through Haven, and this lad, not even in his prime, already considered me a hero.

Would we leave him to die at the hands of the Bots? What about the rest of the humans in the town? Those standing here with me deserved to live.

I reached out to Cassie with my thoughts.

—*We have not lost everything, not yet, Cass. I will give all I have. And in the end, if we fail, we will all perish. But first I must try.*

Not waiting for a response, knowing there was nothing

left to be said, I drew upon the energy of this land. Ambient forces surged inside me. Yet, they were not enough. Far more was needed.

Needing every bit of skill and power for my plan to succeed, I pulled up more energy, more than I had thought possible.

The Oakenrill understood my need as he also gathered the land's magic to himself and added his to mine. He was more talented than me, although not as strong. Yet he bolstered my capacity across the spectrum.

All my willpower remained focused on one aim. Failure meant death. The amount of power required would either kill me or ensure victory. There would be no surrender. My body shook as I struggled to keep it pent up inside me, and for a moment, I feared it would spew out like a blowtorch, obliterating everyone around me.

The Bots understood I was drawing on massive amounts of energy, if not my purpose. They countered by extracting as much magic from the land as they could gather. They drew upon more, preparing to fend off whatever I threw at them.

The ground shuddered and the air crackled from the powerful forces in play, both the light and the dark. This was a battle for life itself, two entities with nothing to lose. The future of mankind, the destiny of the universe, the lives of four beloved friends all hung in the balance. It was both a terrible and wonderful thing to witness.

A huge double-sided hammer materialized over our heads as the Bots went on the offensive. At fifty yards long, it blocked the sun above us. A thunderous blast reverberated from the air, which was displaced by its appearance. The force of the wind, when it hit the ground, knocked everyone off their feet, but somehow, I kept my balance and remained standing. If the hammer dropped, it would smash us to smithereens. The Oakenrill understood this and countered the threat by sending a portion of his energy upward to form another shield.

Our enemy was doing what they always do: attempting to confound others with theatrics. Creating a weapon over our heads was a ploy to divert my attention away from my task. They were drawing upon massive amounts of energy, way more than what I had thought possible. That was the source of our danger, not the hammer.

Ripples of heat and power swirled around me, wavelengths spanning the spectrum of light and beyond. This was one of the few times that others without the ability to wield the powers of Elthea could see what was taking place. The scene was terrifying.

Gritting my teeth, I felt the strength of the Bots continue to increase. What were they planning? My resolve faltered. How could I defeat such a massive force?

This would be a fight to the death. I dissolved my invisible shield put into place to stop the arriving Bots. Its purpose was no longer relevant. No barrier could protect us from this onslaught. We needed all our strength for the clash of forces that was to come.

A moment later, the giant hammer above us vanished

in a swirl of smoke. The Bots also understood they had to focus their attack.

With power churning around me, my thoughts drifted to Eric Webster, the fifth member of our utopia team. He had given his life when we were captured by the Bots to save the rest of us. I would do no less; I owed him that much.

The energy surging through me was enormous, more than I had ever used before, but it wasn't enough. Reaching out with my senses, I grabbed for more magic, anything the Spirit of Elthea could provide. But I was already taking all that I could gather. Nothing remained.

The medallion around my neck blazed, searing my chest. I screeched with both agony and triumph, knowing the Draas were infusing me with their enchantments.

Every fiber within me demanded that I unleash the energy against my enemy before they struck first. I could no longer delay. The world paused, tense with what will come.

The magic flowed out of me as it carried out my wish, engulfing the Bots. They resisted by blasting me with a force intended to rip the skin off my bones.

On this day, they were no match for my strength. With the combined forces of the Draas and the Oakenrill, we would be too much for them. I deflected their onslaught so that it did no harm.

As my magic hit them, they jerked around as if electrocuted. Wave upon wave swept over them, remaking their composition, realigning their DNA.

From this second forward, the Bots would never be the same. What remained uncertain was whether their transformation would spark peace between us or make them more dangerous. That's a chance I needed to take.

Yet, the thought persisted: I had already failed miserably once by giving them something they didn't want. Was I making the same mistake again?

Time for regrets had passed as waves of energy continued to imbue them with my blend of magic. Whether seconds passed, or hours, I would never know. My entire resolve focused on pushing more power through me until I had accomplished my purpose. Right or wrong, the Bots would experience my justice. These monsters once had a purpose in their lives, and maybe—just maybe—this would give them one again.

Before long, the torrent of magic emanating deep within me began slowing to a trickle. Had I succeeded? Was my task finished, or had I accomplish nothing at all? I had only a little energy left.

Not to be deterred, a small stream of energy still flowed out of me. Would it be enough to finish what I had started?

The flow sputtered; it was all I had left. Ending it, I felt as if all my strength had spilled out of me with the magic. My knees gave way, and I would have fallen to the ground if firm hands hadn't supported me. Ja'Krill and Bevon clasped me. Blinking away the black spots swarming across my vision, I looked out at the Bots to see what I had achieved.

My heart sank. How could this fail after all my efforts? The Bots were like they always were. Their hulking bodies and faceless heads appeared to mock me. I expected them to speak in my head at any moment, saying: Is that all you have to give? To what purpose?

"Earthfriend?" Bevon questioned. "What just happened here?"

I didn't have the strength to explain how much of a failure I had been. With watery eyes, I focused on the mass of figures. They hadn't changed at all. My breath came in a ragged pant. "It's over, my friend. I hoped to accomplish something wonderful, but all this was for nothing."

Letting go of Ja'Krill and Bevon, standing on my own with my forehead creased, I stared at the Bots. How could I have been so wrong? Tearing my eyes away from them, I gazed at my two companions. "Now comes the most painful part. My attempt failed, and I must keep a promise to end the lives of my friends. They will not live the rest of their existence as Bots. Neither am I willing to serve those who wish to destroy us all. We are doomed."

Their eyes became wider, understanding my meaning. Ja'Krill was the first to speak. "Earthfriend, because of you, I am alive today. When the Bots had killed everyone I had ever known, including my family, I was about to end my life, having no reason to continue. You gave me a purpose. I beg you now, do not throw it all away. You have so much more to accomplish."

Bevon remained silent. He knew me all too well to change my mind when I was like this. I always marveled at how my Astari friend could understand my feelings so thoroughly. The Oakenrill, however, was not so tactful. He crept behind me. "Do not be a damned fool, not now. I did not spend all my time training you for no reason. If you learned anything from me, it was to use your head. On this occasion, you are doing nothing of the kind. Look around you." He raised one of his branches and waved it toward those standing near me. "Capitulate now, and all of them will suffer." He then added a humph to underscore his sentiment.

My other friends had used this appeal. It had worked before, but this time I had no other choice. Cassie, Diane, and Matt would not continue to exist as Bots, and I could not live knowing I had killed them. Although most of my strength was gone, this would require only a small weave of energy. Better to finish it now than delay.

My eyes lingered on the Oakenrill, realizing he had done all he could to help me survive, all in vain. "You have given me a splendid gift, my friend, by teaching me how to control Elthea's powers." My shoulders slumped. "I tried my best, but it wasn't enough. Perhaps you will find another champion."

Gazing around at the others, seeing their anguished faces, I knew I had let them down. What could I say at the end of it all? No words would come, no grand speeches.

There was nothing, so I nodded, hoping they would understand.

Someone nearby called out. The young lad, Bryson, shouted, "Master Philip. Look!"

A flicker of annoyance crossed my face. Why did that fellow always prattle about something inconsequential at the worst possible moment? I tilted my head to peer in his direction. He pointed toward the Bots.

My eyes shifted to what he was looking at. Pinpricks of swirling lights clustered around several Bots. In the space of a heartbeat, gleaming specks circled a dozen others. I drew a shuddered breath as the miracle cascaded to all the remaining Bots. After so much misery and self-doubt, my efforts had succeeded.

The Directive, essential to the Reapers and Elite, was once again fused into the essence of the Bots.

HOPE DASHED

"My God," Tess gasped. Only she, Alan, and Russell—the three who had once lived amongst the Reapers and Elite—realized what had taken place. She turned and gazed at me with raised eyebrows. "How did you do it? We never understood their Directives, but somehow you've restored them."

My gaze remained fixed on the multicolored symbols and grids floating around each Bot. Already, the images were pulsing and oscillating, much as they had with the Reapers and Elite. A grim smile came to me, knowing I had succeeded. But how would the Bots react?

Still studying our enemy, I answered Tess. "Nobody understands how to create a soul, but somehow I gave them one." Gazing at her, her eyes were bright with fascination. She deserved a fuller explanation. "The magic of Elthea doesn't require me to comprehend it fully. My intent is sufficient."

Despite the achievement, a doubt in my heart lingered. Would the Bots accept this as a wonderful gift? For them, a Directive was more tangible than a soul. Would it be enough for them to free my companions? Otherwise, all this was for naught.

She shook her head, mystified. "I'll give you this. Your solutions to fend off the Bots are... let's just say they're unique. Who would have thought this was even possible?"

"It wasn't simple, and others helped me, but now comes the hard part. My friends are still Bots. That hasn't changed, and only our enemy can bring them back."

The other allies assembled around us displayed a mix of emotions, ranging from bewilderment to astonishment. Few of them knew what a Directive was, or who the Reapers and Elite were. But they understood that something monumental had just occurred. Here again was a feat they would marvel at for years to come. Although not my intent, it further cemented their connection to me.

Without realizing it, my achievement accomplished what I never wanted: they considered me their leader.

Taking a deep breath, my sense of relief dimmed. What would happen if the Bots still refused to return my friends? Pushing these thoughts aside, I motioned to the others that they should remain where they were as I stepped toward the Bots. Bevon and Ja'Krill ignored my hand signal as they walked with me.

At ten paces away, I stopped. No Bot came forward to acknowledge my presence. Were they too absorbed using their Directives to even notice me?

Using a clear, loud voice rather than convey my message with thoughts, I said, "What you once lost, I have now restored. The Directive is once again a part of you. What you've always wanted is yours. But you must restore the three humans you have taken."

No response. The unintelligible symbols and lines continued to circle each of them, but nobody moved or otherwise paid me any attention. They reminded me of my young nephew back on Earth when he was playing a video game, lost to everything except the game. These Bots were reacquainting themselves with their Directive. Nothing else mattered to them right now.

I flexed my fingers, clenching and then and releasing them. How long should I wait? The seconds tore at me, each more painful than the last. It took all my willpower to stop myself from going over to one of them and pounding my fist against its chest.

Finally, a Bot stepped closer.

—*I have considered your request. The humans are more valuable to us as they are. With them, we can hold you in check and bend you to our will. I will not release them.*

My heart fluttered, but my face remained placid. No reason to let them know the level of my desperation. Why had this Bot spoken in the first person rather than the plural "we," as they had in the past? Had the Directive already changed them? Not knowing if this was a positive step or not, I dismissed it for the moment. The freedom of my companions outweighed all else.

"If you don't return them right now, we will remove

your Directives. You decide." I lied, hoping they didn't realize how weak I was. No way would I be able to wield that much magic soon, maybe ever. "You have everything you want with your Directives returned. The future is yours once again. Are you willing to give that up? When my companions are no longer human, they will have no value to me. You will hold no sway over me and you will not have your Directives."

The Bot lapsed into silence, considering my appeal. Everything now hinged on them cherishing their Directives above all else. All I had learned about the Reapers and Elite through my Farseeing episodes with Tess came down to this moment. Did I understand the aspirations of the Bots better than they did, or was I deluding myself?

The Bot in front of me hesitated, again something unusual for them.

Speaking with all the authority I could summon, I warned them. "This is your last chance. Live with your prisoners or live with your Directive. Which will it be? You cannot have both."

The next moments were the longest in my life. The words, when they came, reverberated in my head, causing me to flinch.

—*I have misjudged you, Philip Matherson. None of us will make that mistake again. Your cherished friends mean nothing to us now.*

My body tensed, not quite understanding what it meant. Was it freeing them, or did it imply something more sinister? I tempered my emotions, fearful that success was at the doorstep, yet still out of reach. As I waited, the Bots drew on a ribbon of power. Unable to discern its purpose, my hope was they were restoring my friends. After only a short time, they let the energy fall away, finished with their task.

What had they done?

My eyes raked the columns of Bots standing before me. All of them were the same faceless monsters. No familiar faces stood among them. A chill swept through me. Had they once again deceived me, knowing I did not have the strength to remove their Directives? They were devious beyond all reason, and it would be just like them to turn this to their advantage.

And then the voice came.

—*I am not finished with you, human. My Directive already tells me we will clash against each other again. I see a final catastrophic battle looming in our future. And when that day arrives, you will be unable to stop us. Our cunning and brute strength will win out. I look forward to that time.*

Had they released my companions? If so, why didn't the Bot say so? Had my ploy failed?

The single Bot before me moved away to stand with the crush of other Bots. And then, one after another, they each flicked out of sight, traveling to wherever they now called home. Within moments, they were all gone—every one of them. Nobody remained, dashing my last shred of hope.

29

TO HELL AND BACK

At that moment, the brightness of the sun dimmed as a cloud cast a shadow around us. What had been a dazzling land full of beauty and wonder now appeared dim and forlorn. The Bots had lied. How could I have been such a fool to trust them? To hell with any integrity they might have had as Reapers and Elite. They were nothing but demons.

Bowing my head, I was too stunned to even cry. They had toyed with my heart, pretending to give back my most treasured companions.

Failure can take many forms. Of all my downfalls, this was the worst.

The world around me fell from my senses as I remained motionless. The songs of birds, the breeze in my hair, the smell of pine no longer affected me. My awareness retreated to a solitary place where there was no pain or troubles. It was too difficult to do anything more. Here I would remain.

Someone tugged at me, intruding on my peaceful domain.

I ignored it. Let them deal with their own problems. My interest in this world had ended.

The pressure on my arm intensified. Opening my eyes, I realized Bevon had grabbed my wrist. "They have not yet won, Earthfriend. This struggle must continue."

I looked at him with dull, uncaring eyes, having no desire to respond.

He frowned. "Please, I beg you. Remain here in the land of the living. You have so much more to accomplish with your life."

Bevon had been with me since the moment I had set foot in this land. He could be almost whimsical at times, like when he took me for my first sail around the raised islands of Loralee. I had been so afraid of falling that he devised a silly story about how he could tie a rope to my chest and have others pull me to the other island.

Now, his face was full of concern, his face pleading with me. If anyone could prevent me from plunging into an abyss, it was Bevon. My stomach unclenched, a modicum of sensation returning.

"It is clear you want to help, my friend." Blinking away tears, I continued, "But how can I heal from this? It's too much for me to accept. Again and again, I stand against them. Each time I lose a little of myself when I fail. And what do I have to show for all my efforts? They have taken those I love most. And it's all my fault."

The tears flowed down my cheeks. "I'm not meant for this; I've never been strong enough. For all my good intentions, I have failed again and again. Everyone I've ever loved is gone, and now I'm left with nothing. You need another hero, someone better at this."

Bevon and the others surrounding us heard my plea, yet responded with silence. The emptiness inundated me, a hollow feeling in my heart. Some wounds are too deep to heal.

Bevon spoke again, his words soft. "Earthfriend, you have it all wrong. Look at the faces of those assembled here." He spread his arms to take in the host who had stayed with me outside the village to face the Bots. They remained there, unwavering. "They will follow you to hell and back. You have gained their respect because you fight for what you believe. Never, ever, think you are alone in this world."

He reached up to grasp my shoulder, urging me toward the others. "Come now, take time to heal." I complied, too bereft of emotions to protest. On my other side, Ja'Krill had remained silent during our exchange. Glancing at him now, I realized he hadn't joined us. He stared at the trees lining the broad fields where we stood.

I followed his gaze, seeing only the grassland and line of trees. Ja'Krill wasn't someone distracted for no reason. "What's wrong?"

He continued to stare off into the distance. Valnorians

had excellent eyesight, better than humans. I squinted at the woods, hoping the Bots hadn't returned. I couldn't deal with them now.

"It is nothing, Earthfriend. But I want to investigate what is out there." He tried to plaster an imitation of a smile on his face. "Bevon is correct. You should go with him now. Stay with the others. I will return soon and report if I find anything."

An edge in his tone pulled me from my despondency. He saw something out there that eluded my vision. "To hell you are. Is this about the Bots?" I didn't wait for an answer. "Whatever it is, I'm coming with you." I wanted nothing to do with those monsters, but I still couldn't help myself.

He looked as if he wanted to argue with me. But a moment later, he relented. "As you wish."

He set off at a rapid pace. Despite my exhaustion, I trotted after him, Bevon at my side. Nothing appeared out of the ordinary, even after scanning the area ahead of us with my enhanced senses. Ja'Krill came to a sudden stop before the edge of the trees. I tried to puzzle out his odd behavior, searching the shadows of the woods for signs of the Bots.

Then I saw it.

Several bodies were on the ground, just inside the covering of trees. He bolted toward them, and Bevon and I followed. At this distance, I could see they were not Bots.

My heart raced as I scanned the forms, faces against the moss-covered terrain, as if someone had struck them where they had stood. No discernible wounds or blood were visible as Ja'Krill went down to his knees next to the closest body, turning it over.

I let out a gasp as I looked at Cassie MacKenzie.

Bevon didn't hesitate as he moved to the others, gently rolling them face up to reveal Diane and Matt.

Without realizing it, I had dropped to the ground next to Cassie and cradled her head. A cold numbness spread through me as I saw her blue lips. Was she alive? Dead? Had the Bots killed them as they once threatened?

Ja'Krill continued with practiced calm, first feeling her neck for a pulse. He pursed his lips, and my heart sank. He released a small stream of power into her. Valnorians did not possess remarkable abilities weaving the magic of the land, except for nurturing life.

Without waiting to see if Cassie responded to his supernatural energy, Ja'Krill moved over to Diane and then Matt, casting a bit of his magic into each of them.

My eyes darted from one to the other of my friends. Their faces were pallid, eyes closed. Would their lives end this way, so close to freedom?

With all my powers, why couldn't I help? But all my positive intentions had already gone awry, and I didn't know how to use my skills to restore life. Her face, more beautiful than I had imagined, remained ashen as my hope waned.

And then a hint of color returned to Cassie. A twitch at the corner of her eye sent a jolt of anticipation coursing through me. I gulped for air, realizing I had been holding my breath. Diane and Matt also stirred.

They were alive. Relief, pent up for so long, washed over me. Still, I tempered my elation, not knowing if they would ever be *normal* again. Would their memories remain intact?

Cassie's eyes flickered open. Her gaze remained unfocused, with no sign of awareness. My life stood still, watching her.

"Cass, it's me. Phil. Can you speak?"

Ever so slowly, her lips turned up in a smile. Her mouth worked as if she was trying to say something. I leaned closer. "It's okay," I murmured. "You're back."

Her lips moved again. "It took you long enough."

Those were the sweetest words I had ever heard. Tears flowed down my face. Diane and Matt were now awake as well. The three of them had been to hell and back, but were safe.

Never again would they leave my side.

CASSIE, MATT, AND DIANE SLOWLY ACCLIMATED TO their original human bodies. Unlike waking from a sleep, they needed time to adjust, and I gave them as much as they required. The others from Haven who had stood around me during the Bot attack had made their way to us —Quintia, Riyaad, Torermak, Rae, Bryson, Tess, Alan,

Russell, and the Oakenrill—each one now dear friends. They cried with happiness at seeing them safe and alive.

Once Cassie was strong enough to stand, I hugged her so tightly she gasped at the force. When we kissed, I wanted it to last forever. All my pent-up worries evaporated as I realized this ordeal was over. It had been so long a time since I felt at peace with myself. She was back.

After we broke our kiss, Matt staggered toward me, his legs still unsteady. "Once again, you saved us. How many times does this make?"

I shook my head. "You were the one who gave me the idea about restoring the Bots to a semblance of their former lives. Your good sense helped me more than anything."

He grabbed me in a bear hug, pounding me on the back. "The best decision I ever made was asking you to join our team on the Utopia Project. Those days seem so long ago." He held me at arm's length. "You've never disappointed me since."

"I'm not sure that's true, but I'll accept your compliment."

Diane strode forward, her face unreadable. I braced myself, not knowing what to expect from her. She was always the most vocal of the group, and often the most critical. Her eyes were unblinking. "You realize I'm going to hate you for the rest of my life."

Had she had spoken with anger, I would have understood. But her voice was placid, catching me off guard. Clearing my throat, I said, "You have every right to feel that way, but I hope you won't. Believe me, I never expected this to happen."

She glared at me, but then her face softened. "If I had thought, even for a second, that you mishandled things, or worse, that you deliberately forced the Bots to do that to us, well, let's just say you wouldn't be alive right now." A hint of a smile came to her lips for the first time. "You can also be thankful that I've mellowed through the years."

She was correct. The younger Diane would not have let me off so easily. My shoulders dropped as the tension flowed out of me. "An apology is little consolation, but I am sorry."

Her smile became more pronounced as she stepped forward and gripped me in a hug. "Just never do it again," she whispered, "or I *will* have to kill you."

I smiled, returning the hug while reaching with my other arm for Matt and Cassie to join in. The four of us remained huddled together that way for a long time, heedless of everyone else.

After giving us time, Russell cleared his throat. He spoke loud enough for all to hear. "This is a day for everybody in the village to celebrate. We haven't had a festival in far too long. I hereby order a feast for all of Haven." He turned toward Bryson. "Soldier, please inform the chiefs and the rest of the villagers that sundown will be a time for all of us to honor Master Philip and his friends."

Bryson grinned and scampered back to the village. The surrounding crowd surged forward to hug Cassie, Matt, and Diane. A warmth filled my heart. All the stress I had experienced for so long was gone.

Cassie smirked as she caught my eye. She lifted her eyebrows as if to tell me she had no choice but to accept their good wishes.

Everyone wanted to share in this victory. Who could blame them?

30

AS FOR TOMORROW

The streets of Haven were lit by more torches and lamps than I had ever seen, driving away the darkness and casting a surreal glow around the village. A bonfire burned in the middle of the town square, where a crowd had gathered to hear the music of blacksmiths and bakers, who, at least for this evening, had become entertainers. The ruined wall existed as a stark reminder that dangers still existed. But that mattered little at the moment, as an exuberant energy hummed amongst the villagers.

I remained next to Cassie, as I had since finding her alive. We stood hand in hand as a trio of residents filled the air with melodies from a stringed instrument, a flute, and drums. Before the song ended, gentle words from another dear friend surfaced in my awareness: *It is time. We should say our goodbyes.*

I scanned the piles of boulders where the main gate

had once stood. There along the edges of the square was the Oakenrill, visible as a small clump of branches in front of the rocks.

Gently squeezing Cassie's hand, I motioned with my head toward that spot. "Come with me. I want you to meet someone." During the hubbub of everyone greeting my friends, he had held back, preferring instead to observe our happiness.

She frowned as I stopped before him, gazing left, and then right. "Um, there's nobody here, Phil. Are you seeing things now?"

Smiling, I gestured to the pile of twigs four feet away. "Cass, this is my good friend, the Oakenrill."

As the sticks moved, the Oakenrill's sign of a greeting, Cassie drew back. The Oakenrill chuckled. "Most humans have a similar reaction. A pleasure to meet you, my dear. This student of mine has long had a soft spot in his heart for you, and I am joyful to see you reunited."

A smile came to me, recalling the time I had spent with this pile of sticks. "We were together for months as he taught me about using the powers of this land." I glanced at Cassie. "If it weren't for him, well, not sure this would be a night of celebration. Nearly all my abilities are because of him."

He moved several of his branches. "Humph. It should have taken half the time, but he spent most of his waking moments yearning for you. His mind was a blob of mush, unable to focus on the simplest of tasks."

I laughed. "You have it all wrong, my friend. The only

reason I agreed to all your crazy training was because of her. Without Cassie to motivate me, I would have left you long ago."

Cassie smiled as she looked back and forth between me and the Oakenrill. "So much has happened in your life, Phil. We have a lot of catching up to do."

"And all the time we need." Looking at the Oakenrill, I said, "Come join us at the festival. You have as much right as anyone to celebrate."

He moved in a way I knew was a shake of his head. "What, and have one of you blundering humans step on me? Or worse, take me for kindling and feed me to a fire. No, thank you. Your race is not the smartest species I have ever met."

I laughed more heartily. "Maybe you could fool me once with your gruff attitude, but no longer. Admit it, you're softhearted to the core."

He made a sound of disgust. "You believe you have mastered the use of Elthea's powers, Philip Matherson. But understand this: you know only a small fragment of the big picture. Do not become overconfident. One day I may need to teach you properly, doubtless from the very beginning, since you have forgotten most of it by now."

My smile faded. "So you're leaving? Right now?"

The branch that was his head nodded. "It is time. My work is done, at least for the present."

"A danger still exists out there. When will I see you again?"

He made the motion of a shrug. "Only the Spirit of

Elthea knows the answer. Goodbye, my friend, at least until fate brings us together once more."

In another heartbeat, he was gone, and my good spirits dimmed. Cassie brushed my cheek with her fingertips. "I can see we have a lot of catching up to do. You'll have to tell me all about your time with him."

I pulled her closer, our bodies squeezing against each other. "Yes, we have to catch up. Why don't we snatch of bottle of wine, go to my room, and get away from these festivities?"

She smiled coyly. "And have everyone in Haven know what we're doing? I think they'll notice you missing. After all, you're the guest of honor." She took my hand and pulled me away from the remains of the wall. "Come on, let's find Matt and Diane. After what we've been through, we should be together again as humans rather than monsters."

I groaned. "The two of them probably snuck off by now."

She stopped tugging on my arm and kissed me. Her breath was warm against my lips. "Don't worry, I'll make it worth the wait."

She led me toward the others, a smile on my face.

WE SEARCHED THE COURTYARD FOR MATT AND DIANE. The musical performances still continued, attracting many people, each wanting to congratulate us, or at the least, pat me on the shoulder as we passed. "I told you, they snuck off together," I said to Cassie when it was clear they were not here.

She elbowed me in the ribs. "Let's look in the main dining hall. The villagers are serving food there."

On this night, workers had moved tables outside the hall to provide service in the warm evening. How the village had organized this activity in such a short time was beyond me. Did Russell think all along that I would succeed and plan this behind my back?

"Nah," I mumbled in response to my unspoken question, earning me a confused glance from Cassie.

Rae and Bryson joined us as we stood at the edge of the crowd. The responsibility of protecting the village against the Bots had been a burden on Rae these last weeks, but this evening she beamed as if she had shed her burdens. Her smile reminded me of the girl I had met so long ago. It looked good on her.

Rae pointed to a spot behind her. "Your other friends are at that end. So are my mom and the commander. You should join them." Her gaze shifted to Cassie. "Phil hasn't properly introduced us. I'm Rae. My primary job has been to keep him out of trouble."

"A task you've failed miserably at," I responded dryly.

She chuckled. "That's because you're so good at getting into it."

Cassie held my arm tighter during the banter while gazing at the assortment of knives Rae always wore. "We don't know each other, but I must admit, you scare me just a little."

Bryson nodded. "Don't worry, she scares all of us." Rae rewarded him with a backhanded slap against his chest.

Cassie continued. "But thank you for keeping him safe."

Diane waved to us from a dozen tables away. Nudging Cassie, I said, "Let's see how Matt and Diane are holding up with all the attention."

Rae and Bryson left us, moving off shoulder to shoulder.

"Are they a couple?" Cassie asked.

Furrowing my brow, I watched them walk away. "If they are, I never realized it."

She smiled as she pulled me toward Diane. "You miss a lot of things."

Our friends sat at one of the large rectangular tables taken from inside the dining hall. Matt and Russell were together at one end, engaged in a spirited conversation, while Diane sat with Bevon, Quintia, and Riyaad.

"Greetings, Earthfriend," said Bevon. He was in a cheerful mood this evening, as was everyone else. "You must try to achieve more victories like today so the commander can proclaim another festival such as this." He glanced at the area where food was being served. "Have you tasted the fare tonight? It rivals that of the Astari Midsummer Celebration on the Floating Isles."

The thought of that festivity made me smile. It seemed ages ago when I first glimpsed the magic and beauty of

Elthea. Since then, our lives had changed in more ways than I could ever have imagined.

"We were just going to help ourselves to a second helping," he continued.

"Third," Quintia interrupted.

He didn't acknowledge her correction. "Can we bring you anything?"

I shook my head. "Enjoy yourself. We're fine for now."

The Astari departed as Diane smiled and rolled her eyes in Matt's direction. "He's back to his old ways, trying to run another organization. Russell and him are plotting something about boosting productivity in the town." She gazed at the surrounding buildings and shrugged. "He thinks we've returned to Earth. Someone should tell my better half we're in a different world."

I chuckled as we took a seat across from her. "You may be stuck with him the way he is. Once an executive, always one. He may never change."

Diane sighed. "Just my luck."

Glimpsing those at a nearby table, I said, "Give me a second while I have a word with Tess Armstrong."

Tess smiled a warm greeting at my approach. "I'm glad everything worked out for you, Phil," she said as I took a seat across from her. "Your friends are back, and everyone is still alive." She shook her head. "I marvel at how you pulled it off. When the odds are against you, somehow you find the one thing that saves the day."

My face flushed at her praise. Since our Farseeing episodes, I felt an affinity toward her unlike anyone else.

"You showed me the way, Tess. Without knowing about the Reapers and Elite, I never would have considered giving the Bots a Directive. That was something they valued enough to end the attack and free my friends. Now, maybe they won't be as hostile."

Her mouth tightened, and she remained silent.

"What's wrong?"

She looked at me without blinking, hesitating for a moment. "A few hours ago, I didn't think we would be alive right now. You pulled off an unbelievable victory from the jaws of defeat. Everyone is proud of what you accomplished."

"But?"

She hesitated. "Phil, I'm the last person to judge another's actions. I made such a mess of everything during my time with the Reapers and Elite."

Tess wanted to say more, but held back. I waited her out.

She let out a breath. "It's just that, well, I can't help but wonder. You gave them more strength because of the Directive. What will they do now that you have restored that power?"

The sound of laughter drifted over from one of the other tables. On this night, people were smiling and everyone was in good spirits. I nodded at a knot of people nearby. "Look at them, Tess. They're happy, at least for now. They deserve as much after all the danger they faced. We gave them hope, and that's something that will stay with them for a long time. I understand what you're saying.

I had considered it, but saw no other recourse. As for tomorrow..." I sighed. "When trouble comes again, I'll handle it the same way I always have: by the seat of my pants."

She smiled. "We then, let us hope you never fall flat on your face."

I laughed, and we hugged each other. An uncertain peace had come to Haven. And regardless of the future, I was forever tethered to this world.

AUTHOR'S NOTE

Thank you for reading my work.

If you enjoyed this book, please take a moment now to write a brief review. Leaving a review on the site where you purchased the book is a great way to thank an author and help others decide the book is right for them. Your rating and comments make a tremendous difference. Please spread the word.

You can subscribe to my newsletter at https://johnmurzy cki.com/newsletter-sign-up-2/. I will never share your email address, and you can unsubscribe at any time.

I also appreciate hearing from you. Use the contact form on my website at https://johnmurzycki.com, or email me at john@johnmurzycki.com.

ABOUT THE AUTHOR

Not long ago, I spent my days as a marketing and sales manager, crafting messages for corporations, primarily tech companies. What I really wanted to do was write fiction—the magical kind that would take readers to imaginary worlds.

So I left corporate life behind and never looked back. Now I mull over enchanted realms and unlikely heroes who defend others against malevolent beings. I wrestle with words and fret about phrases, rewriting them until they evoke just the right emotion. "What if..." is always on my mind as I develop twists and turns in a storyline.

This is the stuff of dreams, a life I always desired.

I make my home in the charming state of Massachusetts. To learn more about me, visit my website at johnmurzyck i.com and subscribe to my newsletter, where I will periodically ramble about bookish topics.

Connect with John:

Website: https://johnmurzycki.com
Email: john@johnmurzycki.com

Follow me on Social:

facebook.com/author.johnmurzycki

linkedin.com/in/johnmurzycki

bookbub.com/profile/john-murzycki

amazon.com/gp/product/B08PZ7LG95

goodreads.com/johnmurz

ACKNOWLEDGMENTS

A huge thank you to the following individuals.

My editor, Marjorie Turner Hollman, for her revisions as developmental editor and copyeditor. She identified plot holes and suggested ways to improve the clarity of my writing. Marjorie is the author of *Easy Walks in Massachusetts* series of books and her latest *novel, My Liturgy of Easy Walks.* You can discover more about Marjorie, her books, and her editing services at https://marjorieturner.com.

Audra Cohen Murzycki for her edits and copywriting assistance. A cousin through marriage, her expertise as an editor originates from her occupation at a trade magazine. She always provides outstanding critiques.

Carol, my wife, for proofreading the final manuscript before publication. She does a great job catching those pesky typos before the book makes its way to final publication.

Paul Silva of Paul Silva Design developed the cover art and

layout. He consistently provides fantastic covers. You can find information about his design services at http://paulsil vadesign.com.